# THE HIDDEN PERSUADERS

# THE HIDDEN PERSUADERS

## A DAN KOTLER ARCHAEOLOGICAL THRILLER

J. KEVIN TUMLINSON

# PROLOGUE

**FIVE DAYS AGO**

"Is everything in place?"

The men and women around the table looked first to each other, nodding each in turn before turning back to face him.

The Chairman watched the wave of affirmation that was making its way around the oval table. All in agreement. All in accord.

The weight of this decision, however, was heavier than usual. It was rare that the Chairman felt such personal hesitation over something so unanimous. In all the years since he'd taken this role, he'd never felt so out of sync with the Board. Not this board, at any rate. The second board. The *secret* board. The hidden organization within a hidden organization.

Secrets within lies within riddles. It had been a way of life for the Chairman for as long as he could remember.

With these few, the secret board, there had always been

some sense of unity, as if these men and women were just an extension of his own personality, his own power and influence.

They were unified by purpose. They wanted to change the Jani from within.

Not a simple task, considering the Knights of Jani were a two-thousand-year-old secret order with tendrils of power and influence woven through just about everything—from governments to corporations to amusement parks. Changing something so vast, so entwined with reality, so rich in history—it was far from an easy task. It was as close to impossible as anything could be.

They were doing it, though. Slowly, over centuries, but it was happening. And the people in this room were unified in their goals, always on the same page.

But now ...

He nodded as well. The vote was cast. The decision was made.

"We begin in one week."

"A week?"

The voice was younger. Male. The *new* one. The one the Chairman had opposed, but the rest of the Board had voted in almost unanimously. The impatient, impulsive go-getter.

The *Influencer*.

Among the Jani it was customary to use call signs. For some, these came from military careers. Others chose their own names. And some, like the Influencer, were named by their peers. His reach, his fame, his personal power and charisma, and above all his audience—or his *platform*, as he called it— these had been the drivers behind his christening as the Influencer.

"In a week we will have already lost all momentum," the younger man said. He stood, moving so that he was silhouetted by the large windows displaying the night skyline of D.C. The

Capitol glowed in the distance. The Washington Monument towered and radiated, like a solid beam of light pointing mankind to the gods above, the heavens and the stars, as if it were humanity's destiny to ascend. America's destiny. The Influencer stood before the view as if he had created it all by the wave of his hand.

"No," he said, shaking his head. "We should act now. Tonight. We should give the call."

"You're being impatient and imprudent," the Chairman said calmly, his voice quiet but firm. "This Board never acts in haste. Every move is calculated. Every action is measured and ..."

"And delayed," the younger man interrupted. He, too, spoke calmly, quietly, firmly. But somehow his voice carried more youthful energy, more vibrancy, more charisma. "We have already calculated. We have already measured. And we have already decided."

The lights in the room were low, casting a cool, wintry glow onto everyone present, allowing for deep, saturated shadows to fill the corners and undulate across the polished oak of the conference table. The things decided here were best considered in those shadows. The work that came from this Board was best done under cover of darkness, with discretion.

But the Influencer wasn't accustomed to being unseen, unrecognized. He had a following. A *platform*. He was given to deciding and acting quickly, and changing his mind slowly. To the world out there, the crowds of admirers and followers who clung to the Influencer's every word, he was a charismatic *wunderkind*. To the Chairman, he was merely impulsive.

There was no room for impulsiveness here. That was what the Chairman knew. What he had always known. Planning, patience, and cunning were how the order had risen in power. And it was how the Chairman had risen to power within the organization. Prudence, wisdom, and patience were the Chairman's tools, and he was a master craftsman.

But the age had turned, and now men like this—*influencers* who had no patience and saw impatience and impetuousness as virtues—were starting to redefine wisdom. They were beginning to replace prudence with decisive, immediate action, under the auspice of a new aphorism: "We can pivot if we need to."

The arrogance. The unearned confidence. The gall. It made the Chairman's stomach churn.

But he had been outvoted by the Board, and the Influencer had taken a prominent role with the board. He had influence, even here. The Chairman would abide by the traditions and rules, even though it galled him for this young man to have unearned power.

There was another difference between the Influencer and the Chairman, and it was a difference that the Chairman thought of as foolish, even dangerous.

The Influencer wanted them to step out of the shadows and into the light. He'd made this known from the start. His was the way of *reach*, of *followers*, of having all eyes, ears, and minds tracking him as he moved, hanging on—depending on—his every word and his every thought. The Influencer wanted to redefine the Order, to ... to run some sort of *PR campaign* and introduce the world to who and what the Order was. No more operating behind the scenes. No more operating in the shadows. This would be a new day, a new light, and they'd walk out into it, in full view of the world, and *pivot* if they made a mistake.

It was absurd. It flew in the face of *millennia* of wisdom and experience. It seemed typical, to the Chairman, that this generation thought they were somehow mentally superior to every generation that came before them—that they alone knew the truth of the world, and knew how to usher in a new age. It was the way of the young. It always had been.

*Children*, the Chairman had thought. Every generation assumed it knew better than the last, taking the lessons that were hard-earned by one generation as if they were common sense. As if everyone who came before should have simply known better, seen clearer, thought with more perspective.

Unearned confidence and unwarranted disdain were the earmarks of every new generation. Today, however, it seemed that anyone with a YouTube account had the power to build or destroy lives. Allowing that to infect the Order could be disastrous, in the Chairman's opinion. Revealing their existence to the world was a mistake. The Chairman knew it straight to his marrow.

For now, at least, they remained clandestine in all of their operations. For now, they were sticking to the shadows, where they were most comfortable and most effective. The Board was intrigued by the Influencer, but they weren't yet ready to give up the safety of darkness.

But a move like this—an impulsive, hurried move to take action before giving it time, before taking a moment to study and consider all the potential outcomes—this would move them closer to the Influencer's vision. And, the Chairman feared, closer to the fall of the Order.

The Influencer's voice had been heard, and to the Chairman's dismay, there had been a wave of nods and agreement, though no official vote had been called. It may as well have been.

"Act now," the younger man said. "Make the call now. We'll take them by surprise. We'll make progress while they sleep."

Nods again. An ocean of agreement that the Chairman couldn't ignore.

He cleared his throat, and leaned forward, his left hand a fist, his right hand clasping it, his elbows on the table.

The Chairman looked over his hands at the men and women gathered in shadow.

Did they even realize what the Influencer was committing them to?

Not this decision. Not the push to start now, to refuse to delay for only one week. That was just one small sign.

What the Influencer was proposing was a sweeping change to the way the Order operated. He was pushing them toward evolution. And in every leap of evolution, the old world died while the new world arose.

The Old Gods would be replaced by the New Gods. And the New Gods would shed the skin of the old Order like a snake slithering its way into the open, baring its fangs, threatening to strike down its enemies.

The trouble with a snake in the open, the Chairman mused, is that sooner or later someone comes along to chop its head off.

"Shall we vote?" the Chairman asked, though he knew full well what the result would be. They had already voted, even if unofficially.

Once more the wave of nods swept around the oval of the table, coming at last to the Chairman, who hesitated only an instant before he shook his head in objection.

It wasn't unanimous then. For once they were not all in agreement. But the die was certainly cast, all the same.

He sighed. "We have a majority consensus," the Chairman conceded. "We act tonight."

The Influencer, still standing with his back to the D.C. skyline, turned now to look out over that glittering horizon. He had his back to the others as if he was leaving them behind, here in the shadows and darkness of the boardroom, so that he could go out and join the array of manmade stars and monuments of power that spread like jewels over the landscape.

The Chairman wasn't sure, but he thought he caught the faintest reflection of the younger man's face in the glass pane of the window.

He thought he saw the Influencer smile.

It sent chills through him—a ripple of dread that rolled through him, from his throat to his guts, to his very bowels. He wasn't sure if he wanted to shiver or to gag. He suppressed both.

He rose, along with the rest of the Board, and they all left the Influencer to gaze out upon the worlds he was set to conquer.

# CHAPTER ONE

Kotler clung to the rock face, his hands chalked for grip, his arms and legs trembling slightly from the effort. He tried not to think about the burning in his arms and shoulders, in his side, in his legs. He tried not to think of the sheer drop below him.

He glanced down and saw the vertical horizon of rough stone, tufts of green growing from some of the crags. Beyond that, in every direction, was a landscape of colorful New Hampshire trees, an inferno of oranges and yellows and greens, painted over the terrain like a secret work of art. Artwork that you could only see if you were insane enough to grip and hoist your way up the side of a rock, hand-over-hand, inch-by-inch, without so much as a man with a gun chasing you.

Still, it was breathtaking.

As long as he wasn't plummeting toward it.

"Catch up!" Liz yelled down to him.

He looked up, seeing her move like she was born on the mountainside. Her dark skin contrasted pleasingly against the lighter slate grey of Cathedral Ledge. A goddess held to the mountainside by her own power and strength. Kotler never stopped being impressed by her.

Without pausing she turned her attention back to the rest of her climb, tugging at the line, making sure it was secure, and scaling the stone with speed and grace that Kotler envied.

She was leaving him further and further behind, and Kotler knew it was time to get moving.

His arms and legs burned from the exertion, his fingers ached from the pressure of supporting his weight, but he pulled, he pushed, he gripped. Sometime later he finally reached the summit, and pulled himself over, rising to stand beside Liz as she stood near the edge, smiling out over the pastoral New Hampshire scene before them.

She laughed. "Took you long enough. Didn't you just do a climb like this, a few weeks ago? In Mesa?"

Mesa. The mountains of the Sonoran Desert, where a network of tunnels and caves had been the site of intense conflict, and where dozens of SWAT officers had been injured or killed, caught between two clandestine forces as they battled for control of a vault of ancient secrets.

The Jani—ostensibly the good guys, though the verdict was still out in Kotler's estimate—and the New Gods. Or whatever name they were calling themselves, at any given moment. They were an offshoot of the Jani, and a rogue faction bent on using ancient knowledge and items of power to give them control over world governments, and thus over the world itself.

The bad guys, and Kotler was very comfortable in calling them that.

The circumstances surrounding his time in Mesa had done a lot to make him rethink his relationship with Dr. Liz Ludlum. He had realized that he couldn't allow himself to fall back on old patterns and habits if there was going to be any hope of happiness with her. He couldn't treat her as secondary to his pursuit of knowledge, his search for meaning in history and the universe. He couldn't keep secrets from her if he honestly wanted this to work.

Which was why Kotler had felt guilty since Granger—one of the Jani—had made him an offer to join their ranks, to be part of the organization. It would mean leaving behind everything Kotler knew. His consulting work with the FBI. His career, writing and speaking about history and anthropology.

Even his relationship with Liz.

All of these things were very important to Kotler, though not precisely in that order. And this was a terrible deal. Yet, he hadn't said "no."

What bothered him was that even now, as he stood with Liz and looked over the idyllic New Hampshire landscape, as he looked into her glowing and inquisitive eyes, he still couldn't determine why he hadn't just said no.

Kotler shook his head, smiling and laughing lightly. "We were up against the clock at the time," he said. "There's something to be said for the motivation of not wanting to be shot."

"I can relate," Liz smiled, nodding.

That was true, Kotler knew. Liz had been kidnapped a few months ago, held hostage by two former Soviet operatives who'd gotten into the mercenary business. She'd been tied up and threatened, used as leverage in an elaborate plot to push Kotler to do as he was told.

She had also fought her way out of captivity and proven herself more than capable of not only taking care of herself but of taking care of the bad guys. Liz had been instrumental in taking both out, and saving Kotler's life in the process.

She was, as Kotler had always suspected, incredibly formidable.

Kotler studied her face for a moment, as she looked out over the horizon. His heart was pounding, and only partly due to the climb. Liz could get his heart racing with just a glance.

He put his hands on his hips and turned his gaze to look at the scene, feeling the calm of it wash over him. It was peaceful here. He was with someone he loved and respected and admired. He had a life anyone would envy.

The niggling feeling in his gut, however, still asked:

*Why didn't you say no?*


AFTER RETURNING to their campsite Kotler got a fire started and got to work preparing a meal for the two of them while Liz used the little camp shower to clean up. Kotler kept his eyes and his mind on the food, struggling to stop himself from dwelling on Liz being stark naked only a few feet away.

They'd been taking things slow.

Too slow, if Kotler was reading Liz right. She'd hinted, indicating that she was ready to take things to the next level any time he was. And Kotler, for his part, was more than willing.

But he hesitated here, too.

In his life, Kotler had been with a lot of women. He had, for a time, been something of a womanizer, he was willing to admit. His wealth and lifestyle had made him a bit of a celebrity. And this had only been exacerbated after his appearances in a few History Channel and Discovery Channel programs. Following the events in Pueblo, Colorado, after the theft of the Coelho medallion, Kotler had enjoyed a great deal more notoriety. It was as if the media was intrigued by the angle of a wealthy, independent anthropologist who was beholden to no university or other organization. "A real-world, modern-day Indiana Jones," some called him. He wasn't entirely opposed to the comparison.

His consulting role with the FBI's new Historic Crimes

Division had also given him a popularity boost. It had leaked out gradually, as Kotler was spotted at several high-profile crime scenes alongside his partner, Agent Roland Denzel. It hadn't taken long for someone to put the pieces together.

All of that had added to the air of mystery and intrigue surrounding Kotler, and there were certain women—and even a few men—who wasted no time letting him know that the intrigue was working for them. Kotler had enjoyed a few relationships with beautiful women, some of whom were celebrities themselves, but he hadn't had any serious connections with them. They were flings. Indulgences. He took them for what they really were—temporary spoils from a life that the public found unusual and intriguing enough to reward. Ephemeral pleasures. It wouldn't last.

His serious relationships had all ended in disaster. Some even in death. Evelyn Horelica had been one of those, and in his most honest moments, he could acknowledge that the two of them had been doomed well before she'd been abducted and used as a bargaining chip against him.

Gail McCarthy had been a completely different story. She had dogged him for nearly two years, manipulating him to help her further her agenda and rise to power within an organization she'd inherited from her grandfather and his business partner. For a time she'd been in control of the most powerful smuggling network on the planet.

She had died at Kotler's hands—the only way he could see, at the time, to stop her from acquiring a power that would let her rule the world.

That action, the decisions that had driven it, the consequences of it—it all still haunted him.

So yes, he'd decided to take things slow, both to protect himself and Liz from any unnecessary pain, and also for the simple reason that he wanted this to work, and he knew it was worth it.

This decision, to take his time, had led him somewhere he never expected—a life of celibacy, but also a relationship that might just be the best thing to come into his life in years. With someone—it could not be understated—that did not want to kidnap, torture, or murder him.

So far.

The only trouble was that now that he was considering a future with Liz, the devil had sidled up to ask if he'd rather have the world instead.

And he hadn't said no.

Liz unzipped the flap of the little shower stall they'd set up. She was wearing a T-shirt and a pair of khaki hiking shorts, both of which did little to hide her form and mostly served to accentuate it. She was toweling her face and neck, patting herself dry, and she slipped her feet into a pair of sandals so she could walk over to join him.

Kotler smiled up at her as she took a seat in one of the folding camp chairs.

"He climbs. He cooks. He solves ancient mysteries. My man," she smiled.

"Wait until you eat this before complimenting me on the cooking," Kotler replied. "There's a reason that most of my meals come from restaurants."

"Are you saying there's something the multi-hyphenate, multi-talented Dr. Dan Kotler, man of adventure and climber of mountains, can't do?" Her eyes were wide in mock surprise.

"Do, yes. Do well, maybe not so much," he laughed. "But I've managed to live through my own cooking, so you might, too."

He used a small hand towel to take the frying pan off of the folding grate that spanned the fire. The contents were sizzling and aromatic, and as Liz held a plate out Kotler spooned a small pile of chopped potatoes, onions, and ground beef for her.

"So it's hash?" Liz asked, smiling.

"Only the finest," Kotler grinned.

She laughed lightly and used a fork to take a bite. After a moment, she nodded. "It's good," she pronounced, dabbing at her lips with a paper napkin.

Kotler let out a breath. "Chalk up one more skill for the amazing Dr. Kotler," he smiled and spooned a portion for himself. "Rudimentary cooking skills."

He took a seat beside her, and the two of them stared out over the fire, into the rolling distance of the New Hampshire wilderness. The sun had just started to set, and the light of the sky was a brilliant array of reds and purples and deep blues, almost a counterpoint to the Fall-like hues of the valley stretching before them. The shadows started to grow deeper in the forest, saturating the ocean of color until it was washed over and homogenized by the impending night.

"It's beautiful here," Liz sighed. "I'm glad you invited me."

"I'm glad you agreed to come. I felt like we could both use a break."

"Amen," she said. "Oh! Wait, I have something!" She stood and rushed into the tent.

The tent they would share.

Tonight.

Kotler felt his heart pounding again, and this time he couldn't blame it on the climb.

A moment later, Liz came out of the tent with two plastic wine glasses, filled with red liquid and capped with foil flaps and plastic tops. "I didn't want to bring glass," she said. "I hope this is ok?"

"Perfect," Kotler said.

Liz smiled and opened a glass for each of them, then

rejoined him next to the fire. They sat, sipping wine and savoring both the meal and the surroundings.

It was a perfect evening.

They chatted about the scenery, about the climb, about the wine and the food. The conversation turned then to things back home, books they were reading, documentaries and other programs they'd watched.

"I felt just sick to my stomach," Liz said. "I mean, I cried!"

"Cried!" Kotler laughed. "But it isn't even real!"

"Listen," Liz said, leaning forward and giving him a critical look, the plastic cup of wine tilted perilously in her hand. "When that dragon died and hit the water, I felt it! That was Dani's baby! Mother of dragons!"

Kotler laughed again and shook his head. "I've never seen it."

Liz bolted back as if she'd just been slapped, her eyes wide and her mouth hanging open. "Oh my God, what did you just say?"

Kotler shrugged. "I've been busy! I don't really watch a lot of fictional TV these days."

"You should! Dan! This is history!"

Kotler laughed. "Fake history!"

Liz laughed as well, then nodded. "True. But you're the one who is always looking for some kind of unifying theory of human meaning. Don't discount fiction. There can be a lot of truth in the stories we tell ourselves. I think you told me that once." She smiled coyly, teasingly, proud of the point she'd just made.

Kotler wasn't quite listening, however.

He was studying Liz. Her face. Her mocha skin. Her bright eyes. Her lips.

She noticed.

His heart pounded again, and he leaned forward, hoping.

She met him halfway.

The kiss was sweet. It lingered. They had kissed before, and he knew they would kiss again. And again. But this time felt special. This moment felt unique.

"I think ..." Liz said quietly, her forehead pressed against his, "... it's time to go to bed."

"I think you're right," Kotler said, just as quietly.

They arose and walked hand in hand to the tent. They each kicked off their shoes, and Liz stepped inside first. Seconds later, Kotler stepped in, and without even zipping the flap closed the two of them attacked each other.

Clothes flew to the corners of the tent. There were giggles. There were quiet mutterings. There were fumblings and caresses.

A phone rang.

There was cursing.

"I'm sorry," Liz said. "That's ... it's the special ringtone. The one I have set for Dani."

"Agent Brown?" Kotler asked.

"It means there's an emergency," Liz said.

Kotler nodded. He understood.

Liz bent and picked up the phone, answered. Kotler tried not to listen to the conversation but caught snatches of it. To keep from prying, to distract himself, he picked up his own phone.

It had been set to vibrate, and there were half a dozen calls and messages from Agent Denzel.

Kotler read through the texts and listened to a voicemail. He looked up as Liz stood before him, phone dangling to her side.

In unison—in twinned regret—they spoke at the same time

...

"We have to go."

# CHAPTER TWO

THE FBI OFFICES were a rush of measured chaos as both Kotler and Liz stepped out onto the dedicated floor of Historic Crimes Division. They parted out of the elevator, a quick peck on the lips as Liz rushed to the forensics lab. Kotler made his way up the rising curve of stairs to the second level and along the catwalk overseeing the bullpen of agents below. He rapped on the glass door to Agent Denzel's office.

Denzel was on the phone, standing and staring out of his window at the Manhattan skyline. He turned and waved Kotler in.

Kotler took a seat, conscious of the fact that for the second time in 24 hours, he was trying not to listen in on someone else's phone conversation. This time, at least, he wasn't feeling regret over any what-might-have-beens. He and Liz had promised they would make up the time lost, once the current crisis was dealt with.

Kotler had to admit he was secretly relieved for the pause.

He was frustrated, in all the usual ways, for sure. But the brief interlude also gave him a moment to think it all through, to consider his relationship with Liz in light of the offer from Granger, to join the Knights of Jani. And a moment to consider his *consideration*—to ask himself why he was even entertaining such an offer, knowing what it would cost him.

Because it would cost him everything he thought of as himself and his life.

For now, he'd keep his focus on current events, helping in any way he could.

Kotler was fiddling with his phone, reviewing emails, doing some spot research on what little he knew, when Denzel ended the call and hung up, leaning forward and pressing both hands onto the surface of his desk. His expression was grim.

"Fourteen," Denzel said.

Kotler blinked at the news. "Fourteen ..." So many people, it seemed impossible. It hinted at something well-organized. "What do we know so far?"

Denzel shook his head and sighed, exhaling in a long breath. He looked like he hadn't slept much in the past 24 hours, which seemed about right. Judging from the state of the offices, no one in the FBI was getting much sleep right now.

"So far we know that these guys burst into a Senate hearing and made off with ten members of Congress and four of their aides. The whole thing was broadcast live on C-SPAN, so there's no keeping it out of the media. Every news station on the planet has been running it on repeat for the past day. Speculation is all over the place."

"Do we know anything beyond the speculation?" Kotler asked.

"Not yet. No word from the people who did it. The video is being scanned and scrutinized pixel by pixel, but if they've found anything, it hasn't trickled down to me yet. The witnesses and the remaining Congress members have all been sequestered for the moment. There are security details on their families, but word is all of them will be rounded up and put in a secure location together, to minimize the number of personnel needed."

Kotler considered this. "Ok. So what's our role in this, exactly? I imagine Secret Service and the NSA are involved, as well as the FBI. How does Historic Crimes factor into this?"

"It's an all-hands scenario, for a start," Denzel said. "But that call you walked in on was the fifth one I've gotten from my superiors this morning, from all the way up the food chain. They've given me some specific directives. Which is why I called you and Ludlum in. You've been requested."

"Requested?" Kotler asked, surprised. "By who?"

"By people high enough in the pecking order that they aren't bothering talking to me directly or explaining their reasons," Denzel replied. "I don't know why. Not yet. But they just requested that you and I be at a meeting in DC in two hours. We board a helicopter in twenty minutes."

Kotler glanced down at his attire—jeans and a plaid button-up over a black T-shirt. Clothes meant for camping and hiking, not meeting with high-powered government officials and God knew who else. "I don't suppose we have time to swing by my apartment for a change of clothes?"

"You heard the twenty minutes part, right? You'll be fine." Denzel stepped away from his desk and grabbed his suit jacket from the hanger by the door. He pulled it on as he moved out onto the catwalk, motioning for Kotler to follow him.

"I have got to start keeping a change of clothes here," Kotler muttered as he rose from his chair and trailed after the agent.

THIS WAS a war room if Kotler had ever seen one.

He and Denzel were seated alongside a dozen other people, around a large, rectangular conference table. The table was oriented so that everyone in the room could turn to face the bank of flat-panel monitors that dominated one entire wall, from floor to ceiling. At the moment, however, everyone, including Kotler, was facing the opposite direction, where a four-star General—General George Pershing—was briefing them on what he'd just learned from the President.

Of the United States.

It was surreal, just being here.

Kotler kept quiet during all of the discussions and planning and strategizing, and he was grateful that he'd been handed a legal pad and a pen as he'd entered. He was making a note of key facts as they arose, but that was mostly a way to keep himself alert and attentive, to start piecing details together in a way that made sense to him. He wasn't having much luck with that, but the exercise kept him present in the conversation.

The real trouble was that he couldn't fathom why he was here.

He wasn't a strategist, and he had practically no background in negotiating with terrorists—beyond some personal experiences that were really more about maintaining his survival, and that of the people he cared about, than any negotiation "best practices." So far, no one had asked his perspective or opinion on any of the details of the abduction, on the nature of the operation, or on the demands of the terrorists—or lack thereof. And as far as he could tell, there was nothing of historical or archaeological significance associated with the event, beyond the fact that it was going to be one hell of an addition to the history books going forward.

Kotler just couldn't understand why he was here. Nothing in his skillset would make him more valuable than any of thousands of experts, negotiators, and profilers.

Why had his presence been requested?

The conversation was tense, but without any direct

engagement or a personal stake beyond concern for the congresspeople and their aides, Kotler's attention threatened to drift. He fought this by noting details, jotting speculations, even calling to mind historical precedents that might be relevant or might offer some strategic direction. He was absolutely certain that the men and women in this room did not need his perspective on the Alexandrian wars or the Battle of Waterloo to piece together a strategy, but it was an engaging enough exercise that it helped him to feel relevant and useful.

He'd become particularly involved in outlining the abductions in light of Sun Tzu's *The Art of War* when he suddenly realized that the four-star General had said his name.

Twice.

He looked up from his notes to realize that everyone in the room was fixed on him. "My ... apologies," Kotler said, feeling his face go flush and sweat start rolling down his sides. "I was ... making some notes."

"Dr. Kotler, I had a note myself," the General said, his voice a low and gravelly growl. "From the President. He requested that you be included in these discussions, as recommended by one of his trusted advisors."

Kotler felt his pulse quicken, and his eyebrows went up. The *President* had requested him? "I ... I'm flattered. But to be honest, General, I can't quite see why. So far, nothing about this seems to be in my wheelhouse. I'll help in every way I can, of course, but at the moment, I'm not sure how."

General Pershing nodded to the wall of screens at the opposite end of the room, and Kotler hesitantly turned, along with the others, to see the displays come to life. A series of images appeared, including still frames from C-SPAN, video of black-garbed military SWAT sweeping a remote location, and what seemed to be a live stream of a man garbed in a tan prison jumpsuit, sitting on a bunk with his arms wrapped around his knees.

Kotler stared at the man and felt the heated flush of his skin drain away, the sweat running down his side dried instantly into rivulets of ice.

There before him was a face Kotler had not seen in four years and had never expected to see again.

The face of Anwar Adham.

Kotler's jaw had dropped, but he recovered control of himself, glancing across the table to Denzel. The agent looked as shocked as he did, staring at Adham with at first surprise and then a set grimness.

Anwar Adham was, in many ways, the reason Kotler and Denzel even knew each other. Four years earlier Adham and his men had attempted to detonate a home-brewed nuclear bomb under Cheyenne Mountain, in an attempt to destroy NORAD and cast the United States into a panic-fueled war. They had used an underground river that had once been sailed by the Vikings, as a means of traveling from the Northern Territories to the far Southern region of North America, emerging in Pueblo, Colorado, of all places.

Kotler and Denzel had both become involved in the events in Pueblo after the Coelho Medallion had been stolen—an artifact discovered by and named for Dr. Eloi Coelho, a friend and compatriot of Kotler's. Coelho had eventually died after being injured in a gunfight with Adham's men, and Kotler had nearly joined him after being kidnapped and tortured in a network of smuggler caves, forced to aid Adham in solving the mystery of the Coelho Medallion, to give the terrorists access to the underground river.

"How can he still be alive?" Kotler asked General Pershing. "He ... he died, on that river. I shot him myself—saw the blood. His ... his body was never recovered."

"He was found clinging to a rock downriver," Pershing said. "He'd been treading water for two days. The cold water had helped staunch the bleeding, is our best guess. Either way, he was damn near dead when we found him. Our people pulled him out, patched up his wounds, and buried him someplace where even he can't find himself. He's been in that cell ever since."

Kotler shook his head and turned back to the image of Adham. He studied the man. He was slimmer, more gaunt than the last time Kotler had seen him, though he'd been a fit and trim man even then. This was the thinness of captivity, Kotler knew. The frame of a man who'd had a regimented three prison meals per day.

Likewise, Adham's hair and beard were unkempt and long, untouched by either trimmers or oils in years. When Kotler had last seen him, the man had a glow of wealth and power about him, a look of refinement and impeccable grooming habits. Now, he looked clean enough, but he seemed pale and disheveled. It was clear he hadn't seen daylight in some time.

"Where is he?" Kotler asked, a harder edge to his voice than he had intended.

"That's classified," Pershing said, watching Kotler closely, measuring his reaction. "But you'll be taken to him this afternoon."

"Taken to ..." Again, Kotler looked around the room, at the gathering of far more qualified and far more powerful people, then turned back to the General. "Why?"

"We believe his organization has ties to the abduction," Pershing responded. "We want you to question him. You know him. You were instrumental in identifying him, last time. And we've heard about your ... facility ... with reading body language. You were the top choice for interrogating him about this."

"What do you expect him to know, after four years in a cell?" Kotler asked.

"Right now," Pershing replied, "we're looking for anything and everything we can get. You're our best bet for that, so it's going to be on you. And on Agent Denzel, of course."

This last was said with a finality that told Kotler there would be no point in questioning it further. It had become a fact of life now. Kotler looked again to Denzel and saw the resolution in his partner's eyes. Denzel would do his duty, Kotler knew. Which meant Kotler would help, in every way he could. For Denzel's sake, and for the sake of those members of Congress.

Still, there were things Kotler needed to know.

"What was it that made you think Adham had ties to these abductions?" Kotler asked.

Pershing again motioned to the screens at the end of the room. A grainy photograph appeared—an enlarged and enhanced image featuring a partially obscured tattoo on the neck of one of the abductors. It was obscured by the man's collar and the chin-strap of a helmet, and it was only visible thanks to digital enhancement. But Kotler knew instantly how it was connected to Adham.

Kotler had seen this symbol before—a Viking rune that meant "gateway." It had been one of the runes engraved on the Coelho Medallion, and on a totem that Adham and his men had stolen and forced Kotler to translate. Kotler had detailed this in his debriefing, complete with accurate sketches and scans of the rune. Its appearance must have triggered the Adham connection.

But it wasn't the rune alone that made Kotler feel a slight queasiness in his stomach.

He stood and moved to the screen, peering closer at the enhanced image. The rune was encircled by a pattern reminiscent of certain Mayan designs, which served to cement the connection to the Coelho Medallion further. But arcing along the interior of the circle was a series of Latin characters—and in fact, there were enough of them that Kotler recognized a Latin phrase, despite the overall tattoo being obscured. A single Latin phrase that translated to something that sent dread pounding in waves into Kotler's stomach.

"*Novensiles,*" Kotler said. He looked up and saw that everyone in the room was watching him closely.

"What does it mean?" Pershing asked. "We saw the characters, but I was told it wasn't a complete phrase."

Kotler shook his head. "It's not. And ... it could be a bit of cognitive bias on my part." He looked at Denzel, who was staring at him just like the others.

"Cognitive bias," General Pershing said quietly. "Why is that, Dr. Kotler? What does it mean?"

Kotler looked from Denzel to the General. "Novensiles," he said again, his voice firm. "It's Latin."

He glanced at Denzel, who had a perplexed expression and was shaking his head, telling Kotler he didn't know what it meant, or why it was relevant.

But he would, Kotler knew. He of all the people in the room would understand why it was relevant.

Kotler turned back to the General, huffed a breath. "It's Latin," he said again, steeling himself against the twist in his guts. "It translates to 'New Gods.'"

# CHAPTER THREE

SENATOR ARANIA ACOSTA was new to Congress, but even she could tell that this was something far from ordinary.

When the men had burst into the Senate hearing, she'd been the one with the floor, questioning one of the three Silicon Valley founders who had been asked to talk about online privacy and data breaches.

This wasn't really her area of expertise.

Less than a year earlier she'd been a barista, slinging coffee for the masses of New York City, barely scraping by on a salary that was just above minimum wage. Plus tips.

Between double-hot-no-foam-low-fat-lattes she'd heard plenty of conversations about the tech industry, passionate arguments over online security, even dramatic-sounding stories of identities stolen and lives ruined. But that was as far as she'd ever looked into it. That, and making sure her Instagram privacy settings were on point.

Her platform had been less about social media and more about social reform. She was fighting for the everyday New Yorker, who slaved under an unfair and unjust system where the rich made all the rules, and people starved because their minimum-wage jobs weren't enough to pay for food, let alone rent and other expenses. Living in New York City wasn't cheap.

Neither was living in other cities across the country, for that matter. She assumed. She really hadn't been to many other cities, but her team told her things were just as awful. Her team told her a lot of things.

They had recruited her for all of this, hiring her out of a casting call, and then prepping her with a sort of crash-course in politics and history and economics. They had groomed her to be a shining representation of Socialism. They had told her that as a Socialist, she was at the forefront of a new era of equality and the redistribution of wealth. It would be a new era of social consciousness for the United States, where education and healthcare and housing and food and pretty much everything would be free.

It all sounded so good, even if she didn't quite understand how all of it could work.

Acosta hadn't known she was a Socialist—or even what a Socialist was—until her team had told her what it meant. But the idea of redistributing wealth, giving people free healthcare and a free place to live, using all that money being hoarded by the rich to raise everyone else up—she'd never even imagined that such a thing could be possible. She was all in. And before she knew it she was handing over her apron and taking over an office, with a staff and a very large salary, and a whole new set of responsibilities.

So this hearing hadn't been entirely in her wheelhouse, but it was part of the job. Her team had briefed her on what questions to ask and what statements to pounce on, if the Silicon Valley people said this or that, or didn't answer a question with a yes or no, or tried to insert more information than she was looking for.

The yes or no questions, those were her favorite. Acosta memorized dozens of them, and she liked that no matter how anyone answered, her team had written a response that made those guys the bad guys and made Acosta the hero. She barely knew what was going on, half the time, but she felt absolutely brilliant after these hearings. She felt like she'd just defeated someone smart by being smarter. It was a rush.

When the men in black burst in, shouting and pointing guns, Acosta wasn't entirely sure what was happening. She'd been in the middle of asking a question and thought maybe some Republicans in the audience were getting rowdy. That happened sometimes. Neo-Nazis and fascists and white supremacists would come to these things and make a scene. She'd almost gotten used to it, and she knew that if she just waited, just kept her eyes on the person she was questioning, not only would the ruckus pass but it would mean a great photo op. The media loved her, and they loved showing her being strong.

But it took only an instant to realize this time was different.

One of the men approached her from behind, grabbed her and yanked her to her feet. She'd barely managed to stand and walk before she found herself shoved through one of the doors and pushed along down a corridor.

The men had grabbed other Senators, too, as well as practically all of Acosta's team members, who were in the room, gathered close to her during the hearing. They were always close enough to signal or whisper or mouth something she needed to know.

She had come in with six aides, and four of them were herded out along with her and the others.

All of them were pushed, threatened if they stumbled or

lagged or talked, and ultimately forced into a couple of large SUVs. Their doors locked from the outside, and a metal plate divided the back from the front. The windows were blacked out, throwing everyone into deep darkness as the doors closed. Acosta found herself crammed into the SUV with five other people, blind and squished uncomfortably against the car door.

They talked frantically as the SUV started moving, and they tried to assess who was in the vehicle, what everyone thought might be happening, and who might be responsible. "Terrorists" was the consensus, but no one could get more specific than that.

The conversations eventually died out as the SUV rolled on relentlessly, carrying them further from the Senate floor, deeper into the unknown.

Acosta was afraid. She was crying. She took deep, trembling breaths, trying to get herself under control. More importantly, she was trying to get *mad*.

She'd had a lot of success with being mad. It got her results. It got her press coverage.

The tours she did along the border, inspecting the camps where families were detained as they tried to cross into the United States—those were almost always fruitless. But finding a way to be publicly outraged about something, *anything*, consistently got her the kind of press coverage her team required. Being angry and disgusted when touring corporate offices or city government buildings always yielded sound bites and photo ops that her team applauded. They still lectured her and tutored her when she slipped and said something without thinking, or when she went offscript. But over time she was getting better at all of this. Being publicly angry was becoming a weapon she could use to get whatever she wanted.

If she could get mad, she could claim some authority. She

could have some control. It was all she had. The only weapon in her arsenal.

The SUV stopped, and the doors were flung open. More armed men yelled and pointed guns and ordered them out, then shoved them ahead, corralling them into a large room with no windows and only two doors, one on either end of the room. Both doors were slammed and locked as the Congress members were pushed inside.

Gathered in the harsh fluorescent light of the large room, Acosta and the others stood, blinking and trying to get their bearings. The men left them, without a word, with no instructions, and without much in the way of creature comforts.

In the middle of the room were stacks of rations, along with a pile of folded blankets. In one corner of the room was a stainless steel toilet with a water fountain mounted on top. From the looks of things, it would be the only source of both relief and water—and for how long was anyone's guess.

Acosta shivered with revulsion, though she wasn't sure if it was from the idea of having to use the toilet in front of a room full of people, or from the notion of drinking toilet water from that fountain. Both were repugnant and humiliating. Total human rights violations, which probably meant their kidnappers were Nazis. Or worse ... *Republicans.*

Things settled after a while. The frantic worrying and questioning and shouting and pounding at the doors started to die down. Eventually, everyone retrieved a blanket and huddled in any spot they could find along the walls.

There were fourteen of them in all: Ten Senators, mostly Democrat, and Acosta's four aides.

There was some question about that, from the three Republican Senators in the room. Why had the men grabbed Acosta's people, and no one else's? Wasn't it strange, they wondered aloud, that Acosta was the only one who'd been grabbed with a team? Wasn't Acosta the one speaking when all of this went down? Was this another dramatic ploy for press coverage? Another wailing attempt to get attention and leverage it to push her Socialist agenda?

There had been some bitter bickering back and forth over that, and Acosta had managed to get mad and stay mad, to be outraged, to accuse the Republicans and even some of the more moderate Democrats of having orchestrated all of this themselves, to derail her social reform efforts.

She threatened. She demanded. And ultimately she was told to can it by one of her own team.

"We're here. We're stuck here," Cameron Michaels said, squaring off with her at the pique of her tirade.

Cameron had been one of the originals—one of the group who had cast her and tutored her into all of this. He was the one who came down on her hardest when she slipped up in a press interview, or when she flubbed a question or statement in the Senate. He was the one who reprimanded her like she was a child when she screwed up.

He was also her lover, which made all of this so much more difficult.

"What do they want?" Acosta asked again, leaning in and whispering in an angry, clipped hiss. She wasn't expecting an answer but she was so frustrated with all of this that she wasn't sure what else to do or to say. She wasn't sure who to trust, either.

But Cameron—she might love Cameron. It was hard to say. He made her feel simultaneously strong and afraid. Right now, she needed him to tell her this was going to be alright.

"Again, we don't know," Cameron said. "But we will. We just have to wait."

She couldn't believe how calm he was. This didn't freak him out? This didn't worry him? This didn't make him angry?

Cameron was always the one with the plan, with the rebuke, with the guidance, and now he was just keeping quiet and ... what ... *waiting?*

There were a lot of questions, and no answers in sight. No one came in to check on them or talk to them. They were just here, stuck in this room together, with no way of knowing what was happening out in the world.

Eventually, Acosta joined the rest of the Senators and aides, draping a blanket around her shoulders and hunching against the wall, sliding to the floor as she glanced over at the stainless steel toilet-fountain.

She tried not to think about her increasing need to pee.


Liz had been asked to coordinate with the rest of the FBI's Forensic specialists on examining evidence from the scene, but there wasn't much to work with. The most useful information was coming in from deep analysis of the C-SPAN video, as well as footage from a handful of other cameras from the scene. The team that had infiltrated the Senate had been fast, efficient, and clean, leaving behind only scant physical traces that had proven all but useless.

Eventually, she found herself returning to the rest of her caseload, and recommending that her team do the same. They would get an alert if they were needed. But for the moment they had other cases that needed their attention, and couldn't be ignored.

Dani was out of the office, working as part of the manpower assigned to protect the families of the congresspeople who had been abducted. It was busywork, for the most part. Important, but still busy work. Agent Brown and hundreds of other agents were pulled from their regular duties to babysit people spread all over the area, with no real indication of an actual impending threat. It was all precautionary, and it was taxing the resources of virtually every government agency and department.

Liz stood from her desk and stretched, feeling the creak of muscles that were tight from stress and frustration and worry. She considered taking the elevator down to the gym and getting in a workout, to blow off steam. Or maybe going for a run, though she was reluctant to be too far away from the office right now. There could be new information at any moment, and delays could mean the difference between life or death.

She settled for taking a small break, going down to street level and walking the block to a local coffee shop. An espresso and the short walk would do her some good, and she could be back in her office in minutes if something came up. She made sure her phone was with her, and the ringer was on.

The little shop was as busy as always, filled with office-dwellers venturing out for a quick jolt of caffeine. Liz fell into line and eventually reached the service counter. She placed her order and then waited among a small cluster of other patrons, each keeping to themselves, not even making eye contact.

Despite being about as busy as she'd expected, the coffee shop had a strange energy. She realized why, after hearing a few snatches of conversation.

Everyone who actually was talking was talking only about the C-SPAN footage.

They were all wondering and worrying about what it meant. Were these foreign terrorists? Or a local terrorist group? Were they aligned with this or that political party or movement? What did they want?

That question weighed on everyone the most.

Since the abduction, there had been no word from the group that had done this. No one was stepping up to claim responsibility. There had been no demands made and no threats given. These armed men had absconded with fourteen men and women, straight from the Senate floor, and simply disappeared without a word or a trace. And they were entirely off the radar of every law enforcement agency in the country— which meant they had resources. And power.

Liz had been working alongside thousands of other forensic investigators to milk any physical evidence they could find for anything it could tell them, but she'd forgotten that the forensic evidence wasn't the only thing remaining silent.

The lack of demands or public statements was causing everyone to jump to conclusions, and that was creating an atmosphere of terror and fear on a level higher than any bomb or mass shooting could have done. Not since 9/11 had the city seemed so tense, so ready to become unhinged. Tensions were rising.

Liz found herself wondering if maybe that was the idea.

"Pardon me," a man's voice said from behind her. "But I believe that is your coffee on the counter."

Liz looked up, spotted a cup with her name on it, and grabbed it. She turned to the man, smiling, intending to thank him.

She froze.

The older man standing before her was DB—the contact who had been feeding Liz and Dani information related to their investigation into the origins of the FBI's Historic Crimes Division.

He was watching her face, and then motioned for her to follow and join him at the lacquered wooden bar stretched along the shop's front window. Liz glanced around and then walked to the spot beside him.

"Things are quite hectic today," DB said. "There is a lot for everyone to focus on."

"Yes, there is," Liz said, placing her cup on the bar. "What ...

what are you doing here? Do you have more information? This isn't really the best time."

"No, I suspect that's true. But some things choose their own timing." He reached into his pocket and took out a small, plastic case, about the size of Liz's thumbnail. He placed it on the bar and slid it across to her.

She picked it up, pinching it between her thumb and fore-finger, examining the semi-transparent plastic. Inside she could just make out the outline of a smaller object.

"This is a SIM card," Liz said. "Like what you find in a mobile phone."

DB nodded. "Yes. You'll want to put that in a phone later this evening, approximately 8 PM."

Liz looked at him. "What happens at 8 PM?"

"You'll get a call," DB said. "With information you'll want to follow up on. That chip will allow for just one call, incoming only, for a duration of three minutes. After that, it will burn out." He turned away from the bar then, brushing at his coat, and looked at her over his shoulder. "I recommend using a disposable phone. I'd hate for your regular phone to be damaged."

"DB," Liz said, her voice holding a stern edge of impa-tience, "with everything that's happening ..."

"It's related, Dr. Ludlum," DB said, an edge to his own tone that was unusual for him, in Liz's experience.

The older man's eyes were hard, and Liz could see a hint of something there. Not for the first time she wished she had Kotler's ability to read people. But it was evident that DB was deeply concerned about something. It was also apparent that if Liz wanted answers, she would have to do as he said.

DB left her at the bar and made his way out into the busy Manhattan street. In seconds he was engulfed by a wave of humanity, completely obscured from Liz's view. Gone.

She glanced at the SIM card again and slipped it into her pocket. She would do exactly what DB had told her to do, when the time came. He hadn't steered her wrong so far, even if he was a bit cryptic about everything he shared.

If this was somehow connected to the abductions, she couldn't afford to ignore it. Evidence was too scarce, and any opportunity to open this up and solve it would be welcome.

She thought of Dan, somewhere in DC, and felt a sudden worry for him. He could take care of himself, she knew.

The problem was, he was always in some situation where he was *forced* to take care of himself. He was a magnet for trouble—everything from shootouts to abductions to torture. In just the short time that she'd known him, he'd been in all these things and more. It was a worrying habit, in a man that she loved.

Liz picked up her coffee and hurried back to Historic Crimes. When 8 PM came, she'd be ready.

It was going to be a long day until then.

# CHAPTER FOUR

THEY HAD no idea where they were.

Kotler and Denzel were first transported on a plane with no windows. When that landed, they were shuffled and transferred into so many vehicles at so many different blacked-out locations that Kotler was beginning to feel like the Queen in a game of three-card monte.

To make things all the more disorienting, their phones were confiscated before boarding the plane. Kotler's smartphone—his tool of choice for just about everything, these days—was currently in a box somewhere back in DC.

He felt a little naked without it.

Here, though, in this dark facility deep underground in God-knew-where-USA, his phone wouldn't do him much good anyway. There'd be no signal, in or out. No access to Google or any other resources, and for certain no calls or texts. Government dark sites were funny that way.

Kotler and Denzel were led through a maze of corridors lined with heavy metal doors, escorted by two men who looked as if they could bend steel with their bare hands. They had the air of men who might apply their steel-bending to the arms and necks of anyone who got out of line, though Kotler was unwilling to test that theory.

No one spoke. No instructions were given. Kotler and Denzel knew instinctively what was expected of them, and they followed without question.

Eventually, they arrived at a door that the first guard opened by placing a finger on a scanner. As the door clicked open, he held it with one hand, then turned to the two of them and spoke his first words since they'd met. "Everything in this room is monitored from multiple angles. Everything you say and do is recorded and analyzed. Video, audio, and body scanning are in effect at all times." He tilted his head towards the door in his thick hand. "This door locks from the outside, and we will open it to bring the prisoner in, then open it again when it's time for him and the two of you to leave. After the prisoner is removed, you'll wait, seated, until the door opens for you."

And with that, Kotler and Denzel were ushered to their seats on one side of a rectangular metal table and left alone in the windowless room.

"No pressure," Kotler muttered.

"I think pressure is exactly what they're going for," Denzel replied.

They sat in silence for a few minutes until the door opened again, and two new guards brought in a chained and shuffling Anwar Adham.

Kotler was watching the man's face as he entered, and saw the flash of recognition, followed quickly by rage. And then, to Kotler's surprise, the micro-expressions ceased, replaced by signs of serenity and calm. It was as if a switch had flipped in Adham's head, turning on a sense of inner peace and tranquillity. Complete zen, even here in prison.

It was a show, Kotler realized.

Adham had put his time here to good use, at least as far as he could. He'd spent the past four years thinking about the events in Pueblo and Cheyenne Mountain and had done the one thing he could do that no one here could prevent—he'd learned to master his body language.

*He knew,* Kotler thought. *He knew he'd have to face me again one day. He's prepared.*

This wasn't good. General Pershing had made it clear that one of the reasons they considered Kotler an asset was his ability to read body language, coupled with his personal knowledge of Adham. Now, in seconds, that advantage had been taken away. Kotler would be just as blind to what Adham was thinking as anyone else in this facility.

For a brief moment, Kotler felt a twinge of despair. None of this was what he'd signed up for. He was an archaeologist, specializing in *cultural anthropology*. He maybe happened to have a few unique skills that made him somewhat useful in his consulting with the FBI. He knew people and knew how to read them.

But he wasn't a trained interrogator. Lives were depending on this, and he was an amateur who had no idea what to do.

Except ...

Kotler had learned to read body language as part of a bigger picture. It was a habit of his, to cultivate new skills that might further his quest—to find the underlying meaning of what it meant to be human. He was trying to solve the greatest riddle of creation, to find the purpose for humanity in the vastness of the universe. The answer to the question: "What does it mean to be human?"

And for that, he had studied a broad range of disciplines. Body language was one. But he also studied how humans think, both as a group and as individuals. He made a personal and obsessive study of how individual psychology fit into the psychology of groups and cultures so that he could have a deeper understanding of the motives of others, their self-concepts. He wanted—needed—to know how individual psychology could influence cultural identity. Or vice-versa.

He was good at understanding the motives and intentions of people. Body language was only one tool in his arsenal.

"Dr. Kotler," Adham said, allowing a smirk to cross his lips. His British accent gave him an instant air of refinement, and Kotler knew that he had indeed studied in some of the top schools in the UK.

Adham glanced to Kotler's side, flicking his eyes in Denzel's direction without turning his head. "And Agent ... Denzel, correct?"

"It's been a few years, Anwar," Kotler said. He was watching Adham's eyes, looking for leaks of micro-expressions, traces of a break in his discipline. He remained unreadable.

"It has," Adham said, nodding. "Four years, held prisoner by your government, allowed not so much as a window to see the world."

"You seemed pretty ready to be buried under Cheyenne Mountain, last time we saw you," Denzel said. "You're definitely a lot more alive than we had assumed."

Adham turned then and studied Denzel, his eyes flicking up and down, taking measure. Ultimately he returned his gaze to Kotler without reply.

A signal, Kotler knew. Contempt not only for Denzel but for the government and authority the agent represented. But also a message: Anwar Adham considered no one to be worthy of his attention.

No one, that was, except Kotler.

"I had planned to survive as a symbol of your country's power collapsed in upon itself. I succeeded in surviving, even with multiple gunshot wounds. In my back."

Kotler gave him a tight smile. "You were running away at the time. The bullets didn't know. But I think you've fared better here than I did when I was in your custody."

Adham nodded several times. "Regrettable. But you proved to be a worthy opponent. So how may I serve you, Dr. Kotler?"

Kotler inhaled and exhaled slowly, then leaned forward slightly. He was watching Adham closely. If the terrorist was going to break discipline over his body language, this was the most likely time. "Tell me what you know about the Novensiles?"

Adham's body language remained steady and inscrutable, but ... *there*. Kotler saw it, the tiniest flash, the slightest widening of his eyes. So subtle, so subdued, Kotler couldn't even be certain that he'd seen it. He would watch the footage from this conversation—there would be close-ups of Adham's features. But for now, Kotler believed he could trust his intuition. The sign had been there.

Adham *knew*.

The man recovered quickly, instantly, and settled back in his chair as if pondering. He frowned and shrugged. "Latin," he said, casually. "It means 'New Gods.' Usually a reference to the gods who rose to replace ancient deities in the pantheon of the Romans and other cultures. I believe that in some mythologies, they were numbered as nine deities, associated with the muses."

Kotler nodded. "Thanks for the refresher, but I know the history of Roman theology. Just as I know that you're fully aware of the more modern-day iteration of the Novensiles. The New Gods that are an offshoot of the Knights of Jani."

Again Adham shrugged. "I'm afraid they do not let me have access to media here. I only know what I read in what few books I am allowed to have. And, of course, what I brought with me." He slowly tapped his temple with the middle- and forefinger of his left hand, staring into Kotler's eyes as he did so.

Adham might be masking his body language, but he was making no attempt to hide his anger with Kotler. He blamed Kotler for his current circumstances. He may have considered Kotler a *worthy* enemy, but he was still an enemy.

"They've made their move," Kotler said. "Their endgame has begun."

He was bluffing. Gambling. This was, at best, an educated guess about the plans of the New Gods—the Novensiles—based on everything Kotler had learned since first encountering the Jani. The Novensiles had spent the past few years raiding Jani vaults, taking whatever resources they could find and consolidating power to make some final play. World domination, according to Granger—the Jani who had made Kotler an offer to join them in the fight.

That invitation, too, was part of what made Kotler think this approach might work with Adham. If Adham was one of the Novensiles, if he'd once been a Knight of Jani, then it was possible that he'd been privy to their long-term plans to some degree. Enough, Kotler hoped, to give them something to go by.

"I know nothing of this," Adham replied. "As far as I am aware, *Novensiles* is simply a Latin term with perhaps some historical significance. Surely you do not mean to say that the gods are real and planning some sort of war?"

Kotler was watching him, and to his credit, Adham maintained an iron control over his micro-expressions. But there was something there. Some hint that Kotler was picking up on that might tell more of the story than Adham had intended.

*Planning some sort of war.*

"Maybe," Kotler said, leaning back slightly. "That does seem to be their M-O. It's certainly how they chose to use you, as an asset." Kotler laughed, a slight bark as he shook his head. "You know, call it cognitive or cultural bias—and I'm almost ashamed to admit this—but I and everyone else assumed you were just some sort of Middle-Eastern terrorist cell, trying to stir the pot and create more conflict. It hasn't been until recently that I've learned the truth."

"And what truth is that?" Adham asked. His voice was measured and disciplined, but Kotler caught the hint of something in it. An inflection that wasn't quite as controlled as his body language. Adham hadn't been allowed to speak much in the past four years. He hadn't had as much practice at controlling his vocal patterns. He had control over his body, but control of his voice was less refined. And now he had slipped.

"That you are an operative of the Novensiles," Kotler replied. "Or the *Diathan Ùra*. Or the *Alihat Iadida*. Or one of the hundreds of other names the New Gods use to try to throw us all off. You were a tool of the Novensiles, and you still are. You're only alive now, in fact, because they want you to be. That's right, isn't it?"

Adham said nothing.

But his control was slipping.

Kotler was catching tiny flickers. A tightness across his brow. A set of his jaw. The slight pulse in his throat, accentuated by his gauntness after years in captivity. And there was a flush to his skin and ears, made noticeable by the fact that he was so pale from four years away from the sun.

Adham's captivity was working against him, and though the information he was leaking was scant at best, Kotler's intuition and skill were picking up on it. He was getting a read.

Which meant he could make some progress.

Kotler glanced at Denzel, who had agreed to be there as a silent, intimidating presence. Denzel was staring at Adham, almost unblinking, his arms crossed over his chest and his expression neutral but firm.

Kotler leaned in closer to Adham. "I've been in contact with the Jani. They've invited me to be one of them."

He was taking a risk, revealing this here, in a room where not only Denzel could hear this news but where the hundreds of people sure to be monitoring and reviewing this conversation could hear it as well. He hoped he could play it off as a ruse, but he needed Adham to believe it. And so Kotler let his own discipline crack, allowing his own body language to tell the story. To scream the story, he hoped. This was the truth. This was real. He wanted Adham to know that.

He watched Adham's features and saw the flicker he'd hoped for.

"They want me to join them, and to help them in this fight ... this war, with the Novensiles."

Adham was quiet for a long moment, and then Kotler saw the flicker of curiosity play across his eyes and his lips. A small smirk. Adham leaned forward slightly and asked in a whisper, "And what was your response, Dr. Kotler?"

Kotler smiled and shrugged. "I told him I'd think about it."

There was a beat, and then suddenly Adham laughed, loud and sharp enough that it made Denzel tense and jerk, as if he were ready to take Adham down.

Adham shook his head and leaned back in his chair, holding his hands up, palms out. A sign of surrender.

Kotler was watching, and he saw the instant that Adham had decided that there was no sense in hiding any longer.

Adham was still smiling when he said, "You did not say no. That is as good as saying yes. I am impressed, Dr. Kotler. There have been few outsiders invited into the order over the past two thousand years. It is a legacy organization."

Kotler almost let his reaction to this statement slip but held it in check. Adham had just openly admitted to his knowledge of the Jani. He'd just essentially confirmed that he was one of them. Or had been at one time. He had confirmed quite a bit with his casual statement, and it was the opening Kotler had been hoping for.

"We've been authorized to make you an offer," Kotler said, looking again at Denzel.

His partner remained stoic, arms crossed and expression hard. But Kotler could see a bit of surprise registering there. Or was it concern? He'd clicked to Kotler's confession, about the offer from Granger and the Jani, at any rate. There would be questions. Questions Kotler wasn't comfortable answering just yet.

That would come later.

For now, Denzel lowered his arms and leaned forward, resting his elbows on the metal table spanning between them and Adham.

"If you cooperate, and it leads us to the Novelties ..."

"*Novensiles,*" Kotler corrected, shaking his head.

"... we've been authorized to move you to a less restrictive facility. You'll still be a prisoner. You'll still have no contact with the outside world. But you'll have a window that lets you look outside any time you want."

Adham's eyebrows went up, and he looked from Denzel to Kotler and back again. "A window ...," he said. "That is all?"

"A few other perks," Kotler said. "Better meals. Yard time. Television. Books."

"A softer sentence, in other words," Denzel said. "But not by much."

Adham studied both of them, then laughed. "A death sentence," he said.

Denzel blinked and shook his head slightly. "How so?"

"The people you are up against ... do you think they are unaware of this deal? Do you think they could not reach me, even here?"

Kotler had been prepared for this. "Anwar ... you know as well as I do, you were sentenced to death the minute I was told you were here. I know that the Jani and the Novensiles have people in positions of power in pretty much every world government, including the United States. They know we're here, and they know that we're going to be able to use this conversation to gain some leverage. Whether you talk or not, they're going to eliminate you, eventually. If you tell us what we need to know, right here and now, then you can live the rest of your days with sunlight, good food, and reruns of *House*. Otherwise, they'll eventually find you dead in your bunk, in this underground tomb."

Adham wasn't looking at either Kotler or Denzel as Kotler spoke. He stared instead at the steel table, its cold, hard surface dimly reflecting the track lighting above them.

Kotler knew, just from the man's posture, that Adham believed him.

Kotler felt sick inside, just saying the words. They were really a bluff—or had started that way. But as he'd spoken, he realized they were true after all. General Pershing had essentially sentenced Adham to death just by showing Kotler and the rest of the people in that briefing room that the man was still alive and in captivity.

This really was the only chance Adham had for a moment of peace and joy before leaving this world. This deal was all Adham had, in terms of hope.

Adham looked up then, locking eyes with Kotler. "Alright," he said. "I will tell you all I know."

## CHAPTER FIVE

It was 7:58 PM.

*Close enough,* Liz thought.

Earlier she had stopped by a bodega in a neighborhood about twelve blocks from her own and bought a phone, plucking it from one of the spinners by the counter. The clerk offered to sell her a pre-paid card for minutes, but she passed.

"I'm replacing a broken phone," she said, though she wasn't sure why she felt she had to explain anything. In fact, it was probably best if she kept all conversation to a minimum—to keep herself from being memorable.

It was paranoid, but it felt necessary. Extra layers of precaution, to keep things from being easily traced back to her. Just in case things went really bad.

Back at her apartment, she unboxed the phone and pried off the back, removing the battery and exposing the SIM card slot. She set the phone, battery, and back cover aside, and placed the SIM in its plastic case next to it. And she waited.

She had made a salad for dinner but had left it untouched on the counter. She tried watching something on Hulu, but couldn't focus on it, and the noise started to bother her. She played some music but ended up turning it down low, so that it was just a hint of audible texture in the room.

Every sound, every movement, was a distraction, but not the sort of distraction she needed most. Her attention was laser-focused on the phone and the tiny SIM on the kitchen counter.

Time crept by, and now, finally, it was two minutes until 8 PM.

She took the SIM card out of its plastic case and inserted it into the phone. Once the battery was in, and the back of the phone was clicked into place, she powered it up and glanced over to see the time.

7:59 PM. Better.

She placed the powered-up phone on the counter and watched it like it was a bomb. The final minute crept by. She sipped from a cup of coffee. And then, with a suddenness that startled her, the phone rang.

She glanced at the clock before picking it up. 8 PM on the dot. Punctual spies were the best spies.

She answered the phone.

"Hello?"

"Dr. Ludlum," a voice said from the other end. It was distorted, deeper than natural. *Masked*, she thought. "We don't have much time. Dr. Kotler and Agent Denzel are interviewing a prisoner in a secret facility. They'll be off-grid for several hours. The Congresspeople are in danger. You'll need to go to the address that will appear as a text on your phone."

From beside her, Liz's regular phone alerted her to a new message. She glanced at it. A blocked number, but the contents were indeed an address.

"What do I do at this location?" Liz asked.

"You'll know when you get there. Take your bag."

"My ... wait, my forensics bag?"

"Have Agent Brown meet you there. You'll find evidence that will help in tracking down the abductees. You'll also find evidence that will help in your investigation into Historic Crimes."

"My ..." she started, then shook her head. "Who is this? Is Historic Crimes tied to whatever is happening here?"

"It is," the voice said. "Though indirectly. The answers you're after are coming, Dr. Ludlum. First, the Congresspeople and their aides need to be rescued, and you can help with that."

"Who are you?" Liz asked again. "What's your stake in this?"

"I'm ... someone who cares what happens to Dr. Kotler," the voice said. "That's all I can tell you. That, and one final thing—tell him no matter what he chooses, there's something to lose and something to gain. He'll have to decide which he wants more."

"What does *that* mean?" Liz asked.

But time was up. She heard a crackling sound and felt a growing warmth in her hand. Then she smelled the acrid, metallic scent of smoke from burning electronics and melting plastic.

She dropped the phone onto the counter just as tendrils of blue smoke wafted from it in tiny billows. She looked around and spotted an oven mitt hanging from its hook by the stove, and pulled this on. She picked up the phone and dropped it in the sink, then ran water over it until the smoke died away.

She'd dismantle it and finish destroying it before disposing of it in pieces all around the city. There'd be no way to trace it back to her or to whoever had called.

But there was time for that later.

For now, she looked at the address on her phone, and forwarded it to Dani, along with a text.

*Meet me here in half an hour*, she wrote. *It's related to the abductions. Come alone.*

She thought for a moment, then added, *Bring your badge and your gun.*

ACOSTA HAD MANAGED to overcome her revulsion and humiliation and to use the facilities. Several people, even including a couple of the Republicans, were kind enough to stand with their backs to her, holding their blankets to provide some privacy. They were doing this for everyone, but she really did appreciate it personally.

All of this—the holding room, the toilet, the fountain, the people huddled on the floor and against the walls—it all made her think of the crisis at the border.

She had toured the border a couple of times now, homing in on immigration holding facilities and bringing along a photographer and videographer to document everything. To her surprise—and her annoyance—Cameron had called off the video and photo tour of the secure facilities. Acosta had been livid when she'd found out, but once she got inside, she suddenly agreed with him.

Inside, things were not what she had expected.

There was overcrowding, for sure. Too many people in too small of a space. People had to sit cross-legged in the middle of the floor or lean against each other.

They looked uncomfortable.

But they did not look *miserable*.

No one looked as if they'd been beaten or raped or tortured, which was what she'd been told to expect. No one looked like they'd gone without food for weeks, or hadn't been treated for injuries or illness. No one looked as if they were on the verge of death. They just looked ...

Bored.

Some even stood and leaned against the bars of the room, talking to her in Spanish, but oddly smiling at her, almost leering, trying to convince her to get them out, to let them go free. She answered in Spanish, said she understood them, understood what they were going through. But their responses weren't about their misery—they were about jobs, about cousins living in various parts of the country, about spending their life savings to have a Coyote run them across the border. They weren't begging for food or water, weren't begging for medical care. Only a small handful even asked about children or other family members who were being detained elsewhere in the facility. Most seemed focused only on escape. *Let us free so we can run.*

Acosta had expected moans of pain and anguish, looks of fear, dirty faces, haggard expressions. She had hoped to capture forlorn looks and auras of destitution. But all she could find as damning evidence of a Republican-generated crisis on the border was that the facilities weren't large enough to handle the flood of people attempting to cross the border from Mexico and into the United States.

That was kind of appalling, but it wasn't the smoking gun that Cameron had told her to be on the lookout for.

Photos and videos of this would not help her case—that US immigration policies were racist and inhuman, and that thousands of people were being treated like animals instead of like people. Any photos of this place would just remind the American public of an overcrowded jail, and would further cast these people as criminals. It would make it even harder for her to argue for reform since most Americans thought of border crossers as "illegal" anyway. As if any human being could be "illegal." No person was illegal! But this ... this wasn't going to convince anyone.

Cameron had been right to keep the cameras out. Seeing these people in a cell would only set their cause back.

Since she couldn't bring her photographer and videographer into the facility, Cameron had told her, she could control the narrative in other ways.

"We announce that you weren't allowed to document conditions there," Cameron said.

"But they were willing to let us take cameras in there," Acosta replied, nodding to the facility she had just toured. "We cleared it with them days ago."

"It was verbal," Cameron said. "Nothing in writing. All done over the phone, instead of email."

Acosta thought about this. "That seems weird."

Cameron didn't acknowledge the statement but carried on.

"Our move is to play up the overcrowding," he said. "We tell the world that there isn't enough space, no privacy, not enough healthcare. We have people currently digging up every case of every person who has gotten sick here. Or who came in sick. There have been some deaths, too, which we were counting on."

"Counting on?" Acosta asked.

"We knew there had to be some. It's exactly what we want to call out."

Acosta had registered this, though slowly. She thought she knew what Cameron meant. They'd known that conditions were bad. There had to be some deaths, considering the number of people who were trying to cross over, and the dangers they were facing. Some had arrived at the border on the verge of death anyway.

Acosta's team was going to publicize those deaths, and use them as proof that conditions here were horrible.

It was just ... conditions *hadn't* been all that horrible. That had shaken Acosta's faith in Cameron's plan a bit. He tried to comfort her, to assure her that they were bending the truth to help shed light on the real problems here—the issues that were being hidden from them.

"This is just what they wanted us to see. We know it's worse at other locations. Those are the places they won't show us."

She knew what he meant. And she suspected he was right. Still ...

Everyone here was fed and had access to drinking water. The overcrowding was pretty bad, but she'd seen worse during hurricane evacuations and emergencies. And there was another small problem—she had been one of the people who had voted "no" on a funding initiative that might have helped to build more facilities and provide more resources. She was, in part, responsible for there being limited resources here.

It wasn't that simple, of course. There'd been more riding on that vote than funding for immigration services and border patrol. The initiative would have broadened the powers of US Immigration, practically making them a military force with nearly unchecked authority. She couldn't allow that. So she'd done what her team—what Cameron—had advised her to do. She voted against the initiative, and let the funding die on the vine.

Now she was once again doing what she had to do. After leaving the holding facility, she stood in front of the cameras and took to Instagram and Twitter. She started berating the President and the Republicans for their lack of sympathy and empathy for thousands of men, women, and children on the border.

In her tirade she mentioned that the photographer hadn't been allowed inside—the public didn't need to know who had told them not to enter—but he had been allowed to take photos of the perimeter of one of the facility's buildings, surrounded by a hurricane fence topped with razor wire. Acosta had posed, had played things up, had made a show of being in grief over the people suffering on the other side of that fence and that cinderblock wall. She couldn't see them—no one could see them—but she worked to give the impression that she knew they were there, and knew they were suffering. She let the emotion flow.

The videographer had captured as much as he could, too, getting menacing shots of razor-wire and fences, imposing slate-grey buildings, armed guards on the ground and in watchtowers. He captured footage of long stretches of the border wall with dozens of people attempting to make their way into the United States, only to be met by men aiming intimidating and scary-looking weapons. That footage managed to make a fairly quiet scene feel like a military war zone. Cameron had beamed over it. Acosta had smiled, nodded, agreed that it sent a message.

It was all very melodramatic, and in some ways completely overblown. But Cameron assured her that the point was to tell a story that could motivate Americans to make a change.

"We give them some fiction to help expose the truth," Cameron said.

"Isn't that lying?" Acosta asked.

"Yes," he said, smiling "We're lying about something small so we can reveal the truth about something big and ugly and awful. But it's not really a lie, is it? We know things are horrible here, and all along the border. They won't let us see the real stuff, so we have to make a show. We have to use the story so that people vote the right way."

It made sense to her. She'd slowly come to accept it. Cameron and the others were so smart, knew so much about how this game was played. She'd never studied anything like this in college. She'd mostly played volleyball and went clubbing. When they'd put out the casting call for this, it was her roommate who had signed her up. She'd never even thought about going into politics.

But here she was. And people needed her. Lots of people. Sick people all over the country. Poor people all over the country. These people, held at the border and told they don't matter. That they were *illegal*.

She could live with the lies and the stories, now that she was thinking the right way. It was better to be on the side of morality, to do what was right, than to be strictly honest. Lies were tools, just like anything else.

The goal was to get to the truth by any means necessary, and to force the United States to enter a new era—the Socialist era. Everyone would have everything they needed or wanted when that became the new reality. The lies would be proven to be true—or would be decided to be true.

Borders would be dissolved. Medical care would be given to everyone. Wealth would be redistributed. Shame would be felt by everyone, reparations would be made, and the country could finally get better.

It would be a brand new age, and she would go into the history books as the woman who saved the world from capitalism and cronyism and greed.

All she had to do was keep lying.

But right now, in this moment, as she tried to forget having to pee in front of a bunch of people and how scared she was, the lie was feeling a little more like her own personal truth. Here in this room, with thirteen other people all around her, all trying to get comfortable and all afraid of what was coming next, it was easy for her to work up a rage over how she was being treated.

She just needed some place to point that rage.

# CHAPTER SIX

THEY WATCHED as Adham moved out into the prison yard, wary of deception, blinking in the sunlight before sneezing. He raised his chained hands and shaded his eyes.

"It hurts," he said quietly. He turned to them, smiling. "I thought I'd never see it again."

"You have twenty minutes," the guard said to them before stepping away.

"Start talking," Denzel said. He waved to the prison yard as well as the blue skies above and the thick, wooded landscape beyond. "Or this goes away for good."

Adham nodded, then glanced around. The yard was fenced in on all sides, with rolls of razor wire crowning the top of each segment. A guard tower rose into the sky in one corner, and Kotler noted that not only were there guards present, but they were actively scanning the grounds around the prison, the skies above, and of course, the prison yard itself.

It made Kotler feel both safer and more paranoid, knowing that if anything so much as a drone approached from any direction, it would be met with deadly force.

Adham walked to a spot of shade created by the imposing concrete walls of the prison facility. Kotler and Denzel joined him.

"My father was a member of the Knights of Jani, as was his father before him. For as many generations as we can remember, there has been a member of our family in the Order. Though we did not particularly share the Christian views espoused by the others, we were dedicated to the vision and mission of the Order. The preservation of history's most powerful artifacts, in the service of humanity. It was a noble cause. But ultimately, doomed to failure."

"Doomed," Kotler said, shaking his head. "The Order has managed to not only stay active but to stay hidden for two thousand years. What could possibly doom it at this point?"

"It is doomed by its own avarice," Adham said, sneering. "Its own arrogance. For two thousand years, the Jani served as guardians of humanity and world order. And then, just over two hundred years ago, things changed."

"Two hundred ..." Kotler said, then shook his head. "Are you talking about the founding of the United States?"

Adham said nothing but gave the briefest of nods.

"What does the US have to do with a two-thousand-year-old secret order? Wait ... I hear it now," Kotler said, shaking his head.

Adham smiled.

Denzel turned to look at Kotler. "What is it?"

"This sort of thing," Kotler said, waving generally at Adham. "It's been a part of our nation's DNA since the country was founded. The Founding Fathers, themselves, were all Freemasons. Or reputed to be. There's strong evidence for it, at least. Extend that only a tiny bit, and there's a connection to the Knights Templar—or, if we go by its full name, The United

Religious, Military and Masonic Orders of the Temple and of St John of Jerusalem, Palestine, Rhodes, and Malta. Kind of a mouthful, but it was a way to identify them as a military order, and to establish their jurisdiction and mission. The Knights of Jani ..." Kotler looked to Adham, who nodded his confirmation, "... were an offshoot of the Templars."

"Why does everything come back to the Templars?" Denzel said, shaking his head. "Or Nazis. Wait ... the Nazis weren't Templars, were they?"

Kotler cringed. "No. But there were German Templars. I'll tell you later."

"The Jani," Adham interjected, "were established with a broader perspective than that of the Templars. They realized that just as the preservation of the relics and history of Christ could be used to amass power—that governments rose and fell on such things—the same could be true for any relic of history. Art, historical documents, treasures of all kinds. While most simply thought of these things as wealth, the Jani knew them for what they were."

"And what was that?" Denzel asked.

Adham made a sour expression, as if he were weary of speaking to someone of inferior intellect. Which, Kotler realized, was likely how Adham thought of it.

"Power," Adham said. "If you control history, you control the world. If you control wealth, you control the world. If you control the symbols a culture identifies with, you control the world."

There was a sobering moment as both Denzel and Kotler silently absorbed this.

"The Jani realized all of this and determined they would be the keepers of history, as it were. And they went wherever they felt they could best accomplish their mission. They were always very active in roles of government, and they used those roles to deepen and broaden their influence. Then It became obvious that the Templars were pushing for a new and self-sustaining government. One with no history of its own, and so it represented a new opportunity. They could *invent* a nation's history and further their agenda. That new government became the United States. And it was not just any new government."

"The New World Order," Kotler said.

Adham nodded. "For a century, the Freemasons and Templars both worked toward a grand plan, to create a new world order that would sweep the old away. The Jani opposed this, at first. But gradually they began to see it as an opportunity. If they controlled a powerful new and emerging government, they could use it to influence the rest of the world. The objectives of the Order could be extended. Now they could not only preserve these items of power, keeping them from falling into the wrong hands, but they could take measures to ensure that the Order had the influence to shift the tide of history in favor of anything they wished."

"That sounds familiar," Kotler said. "It's exactly what the Novensiles are trying to do."

Adham laughed lightly and shook his head. "No, it isn't. The New Gods have a better plan. We are tired of hiding. And we are tired of watching the world become more corrupt, watching the evils of Capitalism and unchecked wealth and political power make this world a hell for everyone who is not one of the elite. We can no longer watch as the Jani hide in plain sight, pulling the strings of power so that they are forever in control. We will, instead, use the resources of the Jani to reshape the world into something better. We will use the resources and lost technologies of history, along with the power of modern science and technology, to make ourselves an unstoppable force, sweeping away the old to establish the new. We will rule the world, but our rule will be benevolent. And we will be worshiped as gods by a unified and grateful population."

Adham said this last with such zeal that it put both Kotler and Denzel on alert. As it faded, however, Kotler shook his head, smiled, even laughed a little.

"You keep saying 'we,'" Kotler said. "But you won't be a part of that, will you? Not anymore. Not much of a reward for someone who risked his life trying to blow up NORAD."

Adham shook his head. "The New Gods are bigger than one man. I knew this, going in. I would do it again. All of it."

"But you're going to tell us what we came here for," Denzel said.

Adham looked at him, his expression haughty. He nodded. "Yes," he said.

"Why?" Kotler asked.

The sad expression shifted, and Kotler saw hatred boil in Adham's eyes. "Because you cannot stop it, and I want you to see that as close up as possible. Because you are planning to join the Jani, and I want you to see that you have chosen the wrong side. And because, frankly, I believe this will lead to your torture and eventual death. Making you a threat to others in the Order will expedite your demise."

"Comforting," Kotler said with a tight smile.

"Enough," Denzel grated through a tight jaw. "What can you tell us?"

"I have names," Adham replied. "Officials in your government. I was not privy to much. I was not part of the upper echelons of the Order, and as you can imagine, information was kept well-siloed. But I do know a few names. It should help to move you in the right direction."

Denzel patted his pocket and frowned. He looked at Kotler. "They took my notepad and my pen," he said.

Kotler shook his head. He pointed to the guard tower, then to the cluster of cameras over the door leading back into the prison. "Don't worry. They're recording every word of this." He looked at Adham. "Start talking."

# CHAPTER SEVEN

Hours later, as darkness was spreading its way across the landscape, Kotler and Denzel found themselves back on the plane with no windows. It had been a long day, they were both dazed and exhausted after a couple of hours of debriefing. They were relieved, however, to finally have a moment to chat.

It was a sure bet they were still being monitored and recorded. It made Kotler a little paranoid, and he caught himself frequently guarding what he said. Denzel seemed unconcerned about any of it.

He was more distracted by the tight quarters.

"Claustrophobia kicking in?" Kotler asked.

Denzel let a deep breath out. "Started in the prison. Kicks up a notch when I'm tired. If this thing had any windows, it might help."

"Feel like talking?"

"Please," Denzel said, nodding.

"Did you recognize any of the names on that list?" Kotler asked.

Denzel shrugged. "A few. A couple were surprising. I'm pretty sure they're all being rounded up already. There isn't much time to waste, and there's really no need to wait for us to get back before sweeping in."

"What will our next move be?" Kotler asked. "Once we're back on the ground, I mean."

Denzel shook his head. "No idea. I think our part in this may be done. Or ... well, they'll probably still want me helping to find the congress members or to protect their families. They might want me to be part of the investigation into some of these names, but I doubt it. They're going to want to act on that list as quickly as possible."

Kotler nodded at this. "What about me? I mean, I doubt they need an Anthropologist at this point."

Denzel shook his head. "You're a consultant. Your skills aren't really needed right now, so you're free to do whatever you want. Though you might have to do another long debriefing when we land. After that, go on vacation for all I care. I'm just sorry you can't take Liz away right now."

"Liz," Kotler said, shaking his head. "I wish I had my phone. I'd love to talk to her, see how it's going. Mostly just talk to her, though."

Denzel smiled. "In a couple of hours," he said. He paused a moment, and his demeanor suddenly turned serious. He leaned forward slightly, his expression stern but curious. "Back there, in Adham's cell ... you said Granger made you an offer." He was studying Kotler carefully. "Was that true?"

Kotler hesitated, looking at his partner for a moment. He opened his mouth to speak, then closed it. He nodded.

Denzel leaned back, and Kotler could see the surprise mixed with concern on his friend's face. Denzel looked off briefly as if staring through the side of the aircraft. He shook his head. "Why didn't you tell me?"

Kotler sighed and leaned back. He also shook his head and gave a small shrug. "Honestly, Roland, I'm not really sure. I haven't told anyone. Not even Liz. Though I planned to. I just ... I wanted to think about it."

"What's to think about?" Denzel asked. "I'm pretty sure it's a yes or no question. And I'm also pretty sure that saying yes means ... well, means saying no to everything else, right?"

Kotler looked away. "Yeah," he said quietly. "That's exactly what it would mean. Joining the Jani would mean walking away from everything in my life."

"And yet you didn't just say no," Denzel said. "Which means what exactly?"

Kotler shook his head again. "It means nothing yet," he said. "Other than I'm considering it. Or I was. I think ... I think I've decided to say no."

"And what made you decide that?" Denzel asked.

Kotler was about to answer, about to explain, when suddenly there was a jolt from the aircraft. Objects went flying around the cabin, and Denzel and Kotler were jostled in place. Kotler's head smacked painfully against the side of the aircraft.

"Prepare for impact!" a voice said over the speaker above Kotler's head. "Brace yourselves, we're going down!"

Kotler felt a sick sensation rise in him even as the plane spiraled downward. Their descent was steep enough and rapid enough that it created a sort of anti-gravity, and loose objects floated all around them. Kotler felt himself rise in his seat and quickly clicked and tightened his seatbelt.

He looked to Denzel, who was gripping the arms of his seat, wide-eyed, his own belt firmly in place.

Masks fell from the ceiling, and both Kotler and Denzel struggled to pull them on.

Kotler had only just managed it, snapping the strap over the back of his head, when he was once again slammed against the side of the aircraft, shaken and jarred, and suddenly surrounded by the screech of metal and the wailing and raging roar of an airplane crashing.

It was the last sound Kotler heard before unending darkness enveloped him.

# CHAPTER EIGHT

LIZ STOOD across the street from the address she'd been given, keeping to the shadows, waiting. She watched the front entrance of the building, which turned out to be an old red-bricked tenement house, divided into twelve apartments on three floors. The address she had was for one of the ground-level units.

It was obvious that people were living in the tenement, but what wasn't so clear was whether any of them had anything at all to do with the abducted members of Congress. Anything was possible, of course. But as Liz watched, all she could see were people going about their lives—returning home from work or shopping, bags of groceries or other items in their arms, fumbling with keys, chatting with people on the street. A younger woman came bounding out of the front door of the building, dressed in tight-fitting workout clothes and taking the steps two at a time before sprinting along the sidewalk and disappearing around the block. She showed no sign of worry or apprehension, even though it was night out.

This was a good neighborhood, with well-lit streets and

everything in good repair. It wasn't so different from Liz's own community, in fact. So if there was anything dark and sinister in that building, it was going to come as a shock to everyone. It was going to cast a shadow on this place. Liz found that unsettling.

A black sedan pulled into a space just down the street, and Agent Danielle Brown stepped out, looking around as if she expected to start taking fire at any moment. She spotted Liz and looked both ways as she crossed over to meet with her.

"Liz," Dani said, glancing back over her shoulder at the address they'd come to investigate. She looked weary. She was put together, as always, but she had dark circles under her eyes, and her hair and skin had a light sheen of oil, as if showers were quick if they happened at all. "What the hell is going on?"

Liz shook her head. "That's ... to be determined. But this is a tip from our friend DB."

Dani blinked. "DB told you to come here?"

"Well, not him exactly." Liz sighed and told Dani the story from beginning to end. "I stopped at three different places to dump the phone and the SIM card. I had to use a pair of surgical pliers to pry the thing out. It was melted pretty good."

"Liz," Dani said, shaking her head. "That's ... you destroyed evidence."

"No, I haven't," Liz said. "So far, there hasn't been any crime, so there's nothing to cover up. At worst I've disposed of some damaged personal property."

Dani sighed. "Ok, I get it. I think we're getting onto some pretty thin ice at this point, though."

"The thinnest," Liz agreed. "But we knew this was going to shake out this way. For now, I feel pretty alright about the fuzzy lines, as long as we're making progress, and no one dies. But I feel like ..." She shook her head. She nodded to the building across the street. "This feels different."

"Did the voice on the phone give you any idea of what we'll find in there?" Dani asked.

"They said to bring my bag," Liz said, hefting her grandfather's vintage doctor's bag by the handles, showing it to Dani. "That sort of makes me feel a little nervous."

"Me, too," Dani said. She reached under her coat and unsnapped the restraint for her weapon, and then produced the leather wallet that held her FBI badge and identification.

Liz had her own ID on a lanyard, which was currently tucked into the pocket of the jacket she was wearing. She took it out now and laced it around her neck but zipped her coat enough to conceal it. If she needed it, she could pull it out. No sense causing a stir without cause.

"Let's go see what this is about," Dani said.

They crossed the street and walked up the short set of stairs to stand in front of the building's front door. It was locked, and beside it was a call box with buttons for each unit.

"No Super listed," Dani said, inspecting the name tags on the box. She looked up. "What unit did your address point to?"

"1-D," Liz replied.

Dani peered again at the call box. "No name on that one."

Just then the door to the building opened and a young man, maybe in his mid-twenties, came out with a large, red-furred retriever. He smiled and nodded at Liz as he passed.

Dani reached out and grabbed the door and looked back at Liz before the two of them entered.

Inside, the entry hallway was a little on the narrow side—with signs that the interior had been renovated and updated at some point in the recent past, maybe within the past five years.

It appeared that the building's owners had remodeled it so that each unit had a bit more floor space, with the halls being just wide enough to meet ADA compliance, allowing a wheelchair to have space to maneuver. Still, the hall was narrow enough that under her heightened anxiety, Liz felt like the walls might be closing in. She took a few deep breaths, in through her nose and out through her mouth, until the feeling passed.

Dani was obviously on full alert as well. Though she didn't draw her weapon, her hand hovered close to her jacket as they approached 1-D, and when they stood in front of the door, she reached into her coat and kept her hand on the butt of the weapon. She looked to Liz, who nodded.

With her free hand, Dani rapped on the door and waited.

No response.

"Try the handle," Liz urged.

Dani reached out and gingerly touched the doorknob, then gave it a turn.

The door wasn't locked.

Glancing once more back at Liz, Dani pulled her weapon now before gently pushing the door open.

"This is Agent Danielle Brown with the FBI," she said into the darkened interior. "We're responding to a tip. If anyone is inside, please make yourself known."

Again there was no response.

Dani pushed the door the rest of the way open, letting light fall in a rectangle onto the floor of the apartment. She entered, her weapon leading the way, and Liz followed after a beat.

Inside, Dani reached and flipped the light switch by the door, turning on the dim overhead light. They stood, inspecting their surroundings.

There was nothing here. Not a stick of furniture, not so much as a nail in the wall. The place was empty.

It was a small space, and Liz figured that at one time it had been a single-room efficiency. With the remodel, a tiny bedroom had been built by putting up a dividing wall in the living room. The wall bisected a large window at the back of the unit, with square glass bricks stacked from floor to ceiling, with a slight gap between the bricks and the glass of the window. Liz could see the brick of the building across the way and glanced up to see a rolled shade that could be pulled down to provide privacy for both the living room and the bedroom at once.

It was the clever sort of compromise that came with neighborhood gentrification—building owners improvising to accommodate an incoming clientele of young professionals who wanted a place in the city, without compromising on living conditions.

The sort of place Liz herself lived in, now that she thought about it.

Beyond the bedroom was a tiny bathroom with an old claw tub and a toilet, and not much else. There was a kitchen at one end of the main living space—a countertop along the wall with a small oven and three-burner stove, a tiny sink, and a narrow refrigerator.

Not a lot of space. No place for a single individual to hide, much less ten members of Congress and four of their staff.

This looked like a dead end.

"You're sure this is the right address?" Dani asked.

Liz shook her head. "It's the address they sent me. I just don't know what we're supposed to find here."

Dani considered this. "They told you to bring your bag," she said, nodding to it in Liz's hand.

Liz lifted the bag in answer.

"So there's evidence here. Something only a forensic specialist could find."

Liz inhaled and exhaled, then nodded. "Ok, then. Let's treat it like a crime scene."

# CHAPTER NINE

THE CHAIRMAN WAS uneasy with how things were going, but he kept it to himself. He tried to convince himself that he was just falling back on the old ways, back into old patterns—back to his upbringing as a Jani. He was just feeling what his father and his grandfather and even his great-great-great-grandfather might have felt.

Guilt. Anxiety over these decisions. A sense of having betrayed the Knights of Jani and everything the Order had stood for over the past two millennia.

But this was what the Chairman had wanted and worked for since he was a young man. This release, this shift and turn from the old ways and toward embracing a new idea about what role the Jani could play in the world.

The Novensiles—the New Gods—were inevitable.

After centuries of standing by, watching the world devolve into the wretched state in which it currently existed, it was time for a change. The Jani were too passive. Their influence was becoming weaker as time passed. Having Jani operatives embedded in the highest stations of the world was worthless and meaningless if the Order did nothing with that power, if they made no effort to actually *influence* history, rather than simply preserve it.

That was how the Chairman had felt as a young man, and it had caused him to be on the outs with his father and his grandfather for most of his life. Thankfully his father had kept his son's inclinations toward rebellion as quiet as he could manage, even to the point of paying others to cover up the messes.

The Chairman watched this, studied it. He saw the great lengths his father went to, to protect his son but also to protect the Order. But more than that, the Chairman saw how power and wealth could be used to change perceptions and to rewrite history.

He had, eventually, learned that he could have more influence and control over his own destiny if he stopped openly fighting his father and the Order, and instead went along with the game, gaining his own influence, wealth, and power, and using each to subtly nudge the world into an outline of what he really wanted. "If you can't beat 'em, join 'em."

And then make them serve you.

All his machinations had led him here, to this place and time, to this level of power within the Order. He was the Chairman—he knew secrets. He had influence. He saw the bigger picture and had the power to issue commands.

The trouble was, with more insight into "the big picture" came more understanding of what it was his father and forefathers had been dedicated to. The Chairman hadn't quite changed his resolve over the years. But he had changed his perspective.

And he had suffered losses. Terrible losses that made him question his role, made him wonder if the Order demanded too much. In the midst of his loss and suffering, however, it was the

Order that had provided him with purpose, with shelter from the storm. The experience had softened his view, if not his resolve.

He still believed that change was necessary and that it was inevitable. But he also saw that some of what he had envisioned, some of the plans he had helped the Novensiles to formulate and put into action, were less about invoking positive change and putting the power of the Jani to better use, and more about grabbing as much power as possible and becoming conquerors.

Or gods.

*Novensiles* was more than just a name—it was a bid for destiny. Especially with the current plans.

This avarice and power lust had always made him uneasy. But now, with the latest bid for an unnatural power, the unease had become a knot of anxiety and dread. The Chairman soon found himself facing a question that robbed him of both sleep and appetite:

*What have we become?*

His role in all of this was still secret. He still operated as part of an order within the Order—a cadre of Novensiles embedded within the Jani, who were in turn embedded in the halls of every great world power.

The Chairman still had a chance to turn this around, if he wanted. It would cost him, he knew, just as it had cost him nearly three decades earlier. But he had survived that, had thrived despite the cost, and he would survive this as well.

He might lose his position, but he could keep his life, and not an inconsiderable amount of his power and influence.

And perhaps the Jani could start to repair the damage that the Chairman and the Novensiles had done.

The change that the Chairman had wanted could still come from this. He would be the one to step up and make it happen. His line, as well, would play a part. That line that had nearly come to an end, as a warning, as retaliation.

The Chairman's next move could make up for all that he'd done.

It was a good decision — the right choice. But the Chairman was finding it hard to take action. After a lifetime of quietly and secretly rebelling against the Jani, of working with a growing cell of rebels within the Order, he now found that he was reluctant to let it all go. It would be like turning his back on his own identity. Even though he knew that the Novensiles were set to destroy the Jani and claim dominion over the Earth, to unleash a power that had been buried in history with the hope that it would never return, his pride—and his fear—prevented him from making the decision he knew he would have to make.

There was a knock on the door. It was loud and insistent, startling. And without even turning away from the window, the Chairman knew that the Influencer was standing in his doorway.

"Got a minute?" the Influencer asked, his tone bright and charming.

The Chairman paused a moment and then finally turned slowly, nodding for the younger man to enter.

The Influencer was maybe a third of the Chairman's age. Younger, even, than the Chairman's grandsons. He was trim and lithe, well-muscled from hours in the gym.

He had a name, but the Chairman never used it. Never out loud. That was the rule here, in these halls. All names were left on the street. Within these walls, the secrecy of the Order required that names be forgotten, that codenames and callsigns would be used. That was the way of the Jani.

But the Influencer was not Jani.

He was an outsider, with a wealth of resources. He had

learned of the Jani, and of the Novensiles, just by being connected to the right people, being in the right places at the right time. Once the Influencer had caught the scent of a secret organization with tendrils penetrating the great powers of the world, he had used his own power to angle his way into the Order.

It had been easier than the Chairman would ever have imagined, and that was frightening all on its own.

The Influencer had arrived by vote—something that hadn't been done often over the centuries but wasn't entirely unheard of. Being invited to become a Knight of Jani was a rare honor, and it meant that one had achieved a level of respect and value that made them a powerful resource.

No one turned down an invitation to the Order. No one who lived.

But the Influencer would never have turned that offer down. He'd fought for it. Sought it out. He had arranged for it, by pushing and nudging and setting up meetings with the right people, saying the right things, making the right gestures.

The Influencer was, as far as the Chairman could determine, the perfect embodiment of the newest iteration of the Order. He was a Novensile, through and through.

"Everything is going to plan," the Influencer said, smiling with perfect teeth framed by his tanned, blemish-free cheeks. "The congresspeople are tucked away, for now. There's been a hiccup, with a list of some of our people being leaked."

"Anwar Adham," the Chairman nodded. "I'm aware."

"I've already arranged for him to be repaid for his role in that," the Influencer smiled.

"Why bother? His knowledge is mostly out of date, and he wasn't privy to all that much to begin with. He and his line were always something of a necessary discomfort among the

Jani anyway. Anwar was one of us, but his goals were far more petty and self-serving. Let him rot in prison."

The Influencer shook his head. "That's not how we do things. He betrayed us, so he ..."

"You're telling *me* how we do things?" the Chairman asked. His voice stayed low, but he couldn't help letting a bit of irritation into his tone. "You've been one of us for less than two years. I am a lifelong, multi-generational legacy in this Order."

The Influencer never lost the smirk on his face but nodded. "You're right. I only meant that we can't allow betrayal. That's the way you legacies have always worked, isn't it? It's why we have this place," he looked around, motioning toward the walls of the Chairman's office.

It was a secret facility operated solely by the Novensiles, embedded right in Washington D.C. and kept secret even from the Jani. The Chairman and the others had cloned the structure and resources of the Jani, including their tendency to operate right under the noses of power. Hiding in plain sight was their way, and it had worked for two-thousand years. It worked now, as the Novensiles grew in power and influence within the Order.

The facility was a safeguard against discovery by the Jani. It was a hiding place, a safe space where the Novensiles could work and plot and plan without being discovered. Discovery would lead to all of their deaths.

Or worse.

The Chairman knew all of this. It weighed on him.

There were many things worse than death, for those who betrayed the Order.

The Influencer was right. Their way was to strike down those who betrayed them. The Chairman was fooling himself to think otherwise. There would be no real mercy.

"The damage has been done," the Chairman said grimly. "What are we doing to mitigate it?"

"Well, there isn't much we can do to protect the names Anwar gave them, but they're inconsequential to us anyway. Most were dedicated Jani. There were two Novensiles on that list, but they aren't part of our current operation, and they know nothing of importance. We've decided to let them have this win, to rout the evil and insidious infiltration and feel good about themselves."

The Chairman nodded. He knew that the "we" in that scenario was actually the Influencer himself. The decision should have been brought to the Board, and by extension, the Chairman, but time was of the essence, after all. That would be the excuse the Influencer would use, and it was impossible for the Chairman to argue against it. So he wouldn't bother.

"What about the FBI agent? And ... the anthropologist? Why did Pershing send an anthropologist to meet with Anwar?"

The Influencer actually laughed out loud. "You don't know? Dr. Dan Kotler. He was a big part of taking Anwar down, during that thing in Pueblo. He's kind of turned into a nuisance all around. He's even gotten an invitation to join the Jani. I couldn't believe it."

"An ... invitation?" the Chairman asked. His heart suddenly started pounding.

The Influencer was not oblivious or obtuse. For all of his arrogance, he was actually a quick study and could read people very well. It was part of why he had reached the level of success he had obtained. It was also what made him most dangerous, in the Chairman's eyes.

"What's wrong?" the Influencer asked.

The Chairman stepped to his desk and opened the laptop there. He entered a series of commands and accessed a database that few people on the planet even knew existed. "I was never told about an invitation," the Chairman said.

The Influencer frowned and shook his head. "Alright. So you're... a little out of the loop. I mean, I get it. I get pissed when my people don't brief me on something, but this isn't really all that important ..."

"No one gets invited to join the Jani without my knowledge," the Chairman said, looking up from the laptop and staring down the younger man.

The Chairman didn't add anything further. There was more to be concerned over than this invitation. But the invitation alone was enough.

For once, the Influencer seemed at a loss. He stared back and gave a quick shake of his head. "I don't..."

"If he's received an invitation, it came from someone outside of my circle of influence. For this board, among the Novensiles, I am the Chairman. Among the Jani, I go by a different name. I am Scout. I vet all incoming Jani—all decisions regarding new members for the Order come to me. Just as yours did. Just as all of them have since I inherited the role."

"All of them except this one," the Influencer said quietly. "Which means ..."

"Which means I've been purposefully looped out. Which means someone, somewhere, knows something or suspects something."

"It means you've been compromised," the Influencer said, frowning for perhaps the first time since the Chairman had met him.

The Chairman said nothing but suddenly regretted having this particular conversation with this particular man.

"I'll look into this," the Chairman said, trying to recover. He needed to change the subject, to shift the Influencer's thinking so there would be time to regroup, to determine the path going forward. "You said you're taking care of Adham?"

The Influencer inhaled and shook his head. "Yes, absolutely. He's being dealt with." He looked past the Chairman, to the D.C. skyline. "The others, too. Their plane ..."

The Chairman's head ached from the pounding in his veins. "What about their plane?"

The Influencer looked back to the Chairman, then shook his head and smiled, as if shaking off whatever brooding thought had preoccupied him. "They've met with a little accident in the air. It's all cleared up."

The Chairman felt sick, and was nearly blind from the spike in blood pressure, but he nodded, then indicated the laptop in front of him. "I have work to do."

The Influencer also nodded. "Of course," he said. "I have work of my own. A business to run, plots to seed, worlds to conquer. You know the drill."

He turned and left, and the Chairman followed to the doorway. He watched the Influencer walk through the ornate outer office, past the receptionist's desk to the elevator. As the doors opened and the Influencer stepped inside he turned, his eyes meeting with the Chairman's one last time.

A small smile played on his lips, and the Chairman felt an icy chill stab him in the gut.

He closed and locked the door to his office and immediately raced back to his desk. He sat before his laptop and began frantically moving and copying files, sending private messages, making arrangements. Mostly, he was securing a cache of information.

If he survived this, information would be his shield.

And he was making arrangements while praying fervently. The last hope might be gone. That was what pressed against the insides of the Chairman's skull, threatening to burst out.

His next move was risky, but he was beyond caring now. All his previous plans were officially unraveled, and this play was his last. His best chance at restoring hope. He made the arrangements.

This plane was going down. It was time for him to bail out and hope he had enough influence of his own to survive the crash.

# CHAPTER TEN

THERE WAS nothing but blackness and disorientation and pain.

So much pain. In his head, in his shoulder, in his side.

Kotler stirred, opened his eyes wider, and still saw nothing.

His last memory was of a rage of noise, so loud and frightening that it was all he could do to think and to act, to tighten his seatbelt, to lean forward and cover his head.

*Roland*, he thought.

He coughed, which hurt in more ways and in more places than he was comfortable with. He struggled to move, to push whatever debris lay on top of him and to shove it off to one side. Whatever it was, it was heavy and bulky—one of the overhead bins, perhaps? It made a metallic wrenching sound as he pushed it up and away, as far as he was able.

He still couldn't see, and for a moment he felt his heart pound and his head pulsing. A sickening question boiled up from his guts—what if he had been struck blind? He felt panic clench his stomach, quicken his breathing, threatening to make gorge rise in his throat.

He forced himself to get a grip, to slow his breathing. He

used the exercises taught to him by his instructors and his Yogi
—the failed, miserable exercises he had endured in an attempt
to reach enlightenment, but which had only helped him be
maybe a little more centered, and to achieve a bit more calm in
the face of stress. Enlightenment was a lifelong pursuit anyway,
he'd long ago decided. Or perhaps that was just an excuse to
cover how miserably he kept failing at it. But in moments such
as these, he needed the strategic benefits of remaining steady,
and his training was at least good for that.

Rational thought returned, slowly, reluctantly, like
molasses sifting through a strainer, oozing until it covered his
mind.

His heart rate slowed, and his thinking cleared. The panic
over, rationality began to inform him. He knew the odds of
being struck blind by a blow to the head were pretty slim. A
blow significant enough to cause cortical blindness would have
to result from a severe concussion. His balance would be off,
he'd be nauseated, he'd have a severe headache. He did have a
headache, he realized, but it was starting to fade, and was more
of a bruised feeling on the back of his head. The nausea he'd
felt subsided as the calm rose and he regained control of
himself.

He could think now. He could reason. He knew the odds
and the realities, and knew that he did not seem to have a
concussion.

He wasn't blind. He could be sure of that. The cause of his
inability to see was simply darkness.

That tracked. As his awareness sharpened, he remembered
they were in the fuselage of a windowless aircraft. And that
aircraft had gone down. Power—even emergency power—must
have been disrupted. That meant heavy damage.

What could bring an aircraft down and disrupt even the
redundant electrical system?

He had a hunch, and the implications of it weren't good.

"Roland?" Kotler croaked, then cleared his throat and said again, louder, "Roland?"

"Kah-."

It was a weak syllable, and to Kotler, it sounded almost panicked.

Roland. His claustrophobia. It was post-traumatic stress from his Special Forces days, from when he had been trapped underground in a desert tunnel for days, as his squad died all around him. Roland had suffered from claustrophobia ever since, and though he'd managed to overcome it on more than one occasion, Kotler knew a situation like this would make that next to impossible.

"I'm coming, Roland! Just hold on! I'll find you!"

Kotler would have given his left arm for a flashlight—or even better, his mobile phone. But he had to settle for groping in the dark.

It wasn't easy. There was unseen debris all around him, including a few ragged blades of torn metal. He had to move carefully, and his movement was hampered by his injuries. Everything Kotler did brought him pain.

He first worked at the buckle of his seatbelt, managing to click it open. The fuselage was at a steep tilt, and when Kotler tried to stand, he had to reach back and steady himself quickly. He grabbed the headrest of his seat, which had apparently been jostled loose from its upright and locked position. It moved, sliding back as Kotler grasped the headrest, causing him to stumble and bump his injured side on the arm of the seat.

He cried out, winced, raised one hand to his side, and steadied himself.

The pounding in his head intensified, but it was manageable. He reached up, felt his face and head for any sign of wetness or tenderness. He did come away with blood, mostly from a stinging cut over his eyebrows. But otherwise nothing. No major head injuries, at least.

Managing to stand upright, but still, with no visible light, Kotler imagined the layout of the fuselage as he'd last seen it. Roland had been sitting across from him, and there had been a small table between them. But Roland's muffled voice had come from further away.

Kotler passed a hand through the space where Denzel's seat should have been and found nothing but open air. He touched the floor, and his fingers met with jagged metal, puckered upward. There was buckling in the floor here, as if the plane's fuselage had bent at this spot.

Denzel's seat had been torn away in the crash. He could be anywhere within the plane. There was no way Kotler could find him just by groping about blindly.

"Roland, can you make some noise? I'll find you!"

"Kah-Kotler," the agent said. His voice was quiet, strained. "Here ... I'm over here."

Kotler oriented himself on the voice. "Are you hurt?"

There was a series of coughs. "I think so," Denzel said. "I'm in pain. But I ... I can't move."

Kotler heard the note of panic and moved quickly toward his friend. The floor was a wobbly series of peaks and valleys, and there was debris everywhere. Progress was slow and painful, and Kotler found himself blindly scaling unseen mountains of jagged metal and disheveled seats.

Denzel coughed again, and to Kotler's relief, it was close by.

He felt around, and eventually his hand touched Denzel's shoe. "I'm here," Kotler said. "I'm going to get you out of this."

He felt around some more, following Denzel's foot to his leg, then on to a jumble of debris that felt like metal cases. They must have been in one of the overhead bins.

Kotler began moving these, tossing them aside, feeling his way along.

After a moment, a hand gripped his forearm.

"Kotler, help me stand up."

"Are you sure that's a good idea?"

"I'm wedged between these seats," Denzel said. "I'm hurt, but I can feel everything. I may have some broken ribs. I think I have some internal injuries. I'm not sure. Pull me up."

Kotler felt around until he had a hand on the armrest of another seat. He gripped Denzel's arm with his other hand. "Ok, on three," Kotler said.

"One ... two ... *three!*"

He pulled, feeling his own injuries scream in protest. He felt something tear in his side but decided the damage was done. He'd worry about it later.

Denzel moved up and toward him. He and Kotler both moaned and groaned with the effort and the injuries, but after an agonizing moment, Denzel managed to get his feet under him and to hold himself up, leaning against some of the debris. Kotler let go, gasping, and dropped to his knees, leaning against the angled row of seats.

"You ... ok?" Denzel asked, huffing from the darkness.

Kotler huffed a few times himself. "I think maybe you aren't the only one with some broken ribs," he said. "Or worse."

"Ok," Denzel said, shifting around, making noise in the dark. "We need to find a way out of here." There was a pause. "Why aren't there any lights?"

Kotler took a few breaths, as deep as he could manage, and replied, "Something fried the electrical system. Emergency lights should be on if nothing else."

"They should be on their own power supply," Denzel agreed. "Unless someone hit the battery disconnect?"

"I ... I think we were hit by an electromagnetic pulse," Kotler said, struggling to his feet.

"An EMP?" Denzel asked, his voice perplexed.

"It makes sense," Kotler replied. "Someone brought this plane down. An EMP would leave the plane itself intact, but it would shut down anything electrical. The fact that we have no emergency lights ..."

"Got it," Denzel said. He coughed and groaned.

Kotler felt around until his hand rested on Denzel's shoulder. "Behind me is the front of the plane," Kotler said. "I think."

"And ... an exit," Denzel gasped.

"Let's see if we can find it."

They moved slowly, groping in the darkness, feeling their way along and navigating an invisible trail of fallen items and obstacles. It was a hard, excruciating trek over an unseen terrain of jagged metal and unidentifiable obstacles. Eventually, however, they reached the space just outside of the cockpit.

"The emergency release should be on the door," Kotler said.

He heard some tapping, followed soon by a wrenching noise and a shaft of dim light falling in on them, bright enough, at least, to dispel their immediate darkness.

Moonlight, Kotler realized. It was nighttime.

"Can we get into the cockpit?" Denzel asked.

Kotler turned and examined the door. In this post-9 1 1 culture, there was simply no way to open the cockpit door from this side without a key or special tools. They might be able to get in, given time. But something told Kotler it would be a waste of effort.

Denzel banged on the cockpit door, calling out for the pilot. They listened, waiting. Denzel banged again, though it was weaker, and the pain of it was clear on his face.

Still, they heard nothing.

"I smell smoke," Kotler said. "And fuel."

"I smell it, too," Denzel replied, his voice a hoarse rasp. "We'd better get out of here, assess our situation from the outside."

Kotler couldn't agree more, and the two of them spent the next several minutes boosting and helping each other climb up and out of the fuselage, each wincing and grunting as they went.

Outside, standing on the side of the plane in the night air, they surveyed the Armageddon before them.

The plane had held up rather well, considering. It was built to be more or less an armored transport, to move high-level officials from place to place and provide a modicum of protection against attack. The hull of the plane contained armored plating —a sacrifice of fuel efficiency and range in exchange for the slim chance of surviving a missile strike.

A good thing, considering their current predicament. The armor plating may have saved the two of them. And, Kotler hoped, the limited range might mean they were close to civilization.

The aircraft was far from intact—the wings, the tail section, and a considerable amount of the outer skin of the craft were all strewn in a fiery tear across the wooded landscape behind them. The night was lit by hundreds of small fires—and one big one.

"That's one of the engines," Denzel said, pointing. "And the jet fuel ... I think a tank has ruptured."

"We need to move as far from here as we can get," Kotler said, looking around. Over the mangled nose of the cockpit, he could just make out a stretch of rocky terrain. "We're in the mountains," he said. "Though I don't really know which mountains."

"We'll work that out later," Denzel said. "Let's move."

They moved, crawling forward in an attempt to skirt a line

of fire below them. They crawled along the outer skin of the plane, and out over the mangled remains of the cockpit.

Kotler saw, now, that even if they'd managed to open the door between the cockpit and the fuselage, it wouldn't have done any good. The nose of the craft had been caved-in to the point of being nearly inverted, and all that seemed to remain of most of the cockpit was a mangled twist of metal and some dangling shards of glass. Kotler and Denzel had been in the most heavily armored section of the plane, and it had been a miracle that they'd survived.

Kotler suspected, however, that if they didn't manage to get to the ground and far away from here, their miracles might just run out.

They climbed down from the cockpit, dropping the final few feet to the rocky soil. Kotler landed on a wobbly stone, and lost his balance, dropping back against the side of the plane. He put his hand out, steadying himself, and now saw for the first time something they'd both overlooked before.

The plane was balanced precariously on the very edge of a precipice, which dropped hundreds of feet into the darkness below.

"The pilot ..." Denzel started, then huffed. He reached out a hand to help Kotler stand upright and steady. "He saved us," Denzel finished. "Look."

Kotler looked to where Denzel was pointing. Trailing behind them was a twisted wreck of landscape, with felled trees and a blazing track of ruined airplane parts. Fires lit the trail like watchtowers, and it ran like a serpent for miles.

"He brought this thing in on its belly, sliding through the terrain. Couldn't have been easy. Without power, a plane this size is basically a brick with wings. He had to have had a hell of a time getting it to the ground like this, instead of plunging into the mountain nose-first."

"And he had a sudden stop," Kotler said, pointing to the wall of rock in front of them. It showed signs of impact as if the plane had rammed into it and bounced back a few feet. And now, as they stood back from it, they could see the yawn of a valley beyond, cast in darkness broken only by shifting patches of moonlight as the clouds passed overhead.

"Let's move," Denzel said. "I'm not real sure about the fuel and fire situation here, but I think we should ..."

Before he could finish the sentence, there was a roar and whine from somewhere behind them, and the engine they'd seen lying on the ground suddenly exploded, throwing debris in all directions.

They took cover, ducking under the wreckage of the plane, but Kotler saw right away that they needed to move again, and *right now*.

The plane shook, and tilted, and Kotler dove and pushed Denzel to the ground just before a jagged spike of twisted metal passed directly through where the agent's head had been, seconds earlier.

The plane's wreckage continued to groan and shift, and Kotler and Denzel watched in horror as it first rose high into the air, then tilted sharply, falling in a cacophony of screeching and banging metal, tumbling down the side of the mountain until it crashed for the second time at the base of the cliff, far below.

Kotler and Denzel both huffed and stared, crawling forward the few scant feet to the edge, realizing for the first time just how close they'd come to being in that fiery wreckage, hundreds of feet down.

It took a long moment for both men to pull themselves together, huffing and groaning, feeling their injuries and the weariness of the night. Kotler's strength was all but spent. He wasn't sure how either of them could move from this spot, but he knew they had to. The fire ...

He froze as he saw the look on Denzel's face.

"What is it?" he asked.

"Listen," Denzel said. Then he pointed. "There!"

On the horizon, rising over the distant ridges of the mountains, a cluster of military helicopters appeared and moved toward them.

"Rescue?" Kotler asked.

Denzel shook his head. "I don't think so. Run!"

They ran, as best they could, limping quickly away from the fiery crash site and into the darkened forest that was the only cover they had here.

Denzel was right, Kotler realized. They'd acted too quickly, gotten here too fast. As if they'd known the plane would be here.

This wasn't a rescue. It was a cleanup.

The pain pulsed within him to the point of making him want to throw up or pass out or both, but he pushed, he raced along. Kotler and Denzel leaned on and supported each other as they moved into the darkened mountainside forest that was their only source of cover.

The enemy was coming.

# CHAPTER ELEVEN

LIZ HAD GONE over the entirety of the apartment, painstakingly collecting even the smallest samples. With Dani's help—and thanks to the fact that the apartment was completely empty and very small—it had taken a little over an hour. Record time, and Liz and Dani had both been glad of it. They would be hard-pressed to explain why they were there, if someone asked.

After the search, they'd come away with a few fingerprints, some hair samples, and one scrap of paper that looked to be torn from an envelope flap. It had a bit of glue residue, and Liz figured that, along with the hair samples, might be a good bit of DNA to work with.

Now, back in her lab in the FBI's Historic Crimes division, she was running all of the tests and preparing the samples herself. She couldn't ask anyone else to help—it would open the door for questions she wasn't yet prepared to answer. Better to keep this off the radar as much as possible, for now.

Dani was back on babysitting duty, seeing to the families of the abducted congresspeople. She couldn't have been any help with this part anyway, but it would have been nice to have her around to talk to and swap theories. All of this—the secrecy, the sneaking around, the work to hide things—it was long, lonely work. And if Liz was honest with herself, it was all starting to stress her out.

Some of that may have been due to the current climate, however.

Tensions were high in the offices, and in the building as a whole. Resources were stretched thin, and nerves were frayed. The buzz and speculation on the street were running like wildfire, with near-paranoid theories about what this was, and why it had happened.

Most of the rumors leaned toward terrorism—but the lack of any public statement or demands from the abductors was making speculation run to extremes. It was also amping up tension across the nation, even around the world.

No news. No word. Silence was breeding fear and anxiety.

Liz concentrated on seeing if she could discover anything from the materials she'd found in the apartment. The contact on the phone—the one DB had put her in touch with—had implied that this would have some connection with the abductions. That was a wispy sort of motivation and justification, but it was enough. Anything that might provide a lead to both the origins of Historic Crimes and to the abductions of the congresspeople was worth pursuing.

But she was at a bit of a dead-end, at the moment.

Liz had reached a point where she could go no further on her own, and though she wasn't keen to enlist the resources of the FBI in something she was trying to keep off the books, there were some things she simply couldn't do without a little help.

DNA analysis was not a strictly solo pursuit.

She had been able to isolate traces of DNA from the samples, particularly from the scrap of envelope. But to sequence them properly and find any possible matches would require sending them to the central lab and waiting weeks or even months to get the results. Liz figured she could expedite that if she indicated that this was part of the investigation into the abductions. The danger there was that someone higher up in the chain of command was sure to notice a new thread of evidence, and would start asking her where these samples came from and how she'd come to be in possession of them.

Questions she wasn't quite ready to answer.

Though maybe it wouldn't be such a bad thing, in the end. If it helped to find the abductees faster, to get people back to their families and to end the wave of paranoia and fear sweeping the nation. It might be worth any heat she'd take for operating outside of protocol and chain of command.

But it would effectively end the investigation into the origins of Historic Crimes, and it could put both Liz and Dani in a boiling pot of trouble—scrutiny of their actions, certainly, but more dangerous was the prospect of some high-up, shadowy figure deciding they were a liability worth eliminating.

It was worth remembering that this could be a deadly game.

This was a constant, nagging worry at the back of her mind. She felt a growing sense of anxiety, the deeper she and Dani looked into all of this.

The work, the details and minutia, were an escape, and she kept her focus on solving the problems associated with their search. This problem—how to get the DNA sequenced without raising suspicion—was tricky, which made it perfect.

What Liz needed was a way to get these tests expedited without bringing unwanted attention into the mix.

The central lab worked on a priority basis, and that meant that some cases got bumped to the head of the line automatically. The abductions of the congresspeople would certainly fit that bill. But there were other cases already in progress, and just as pressing. Liz had been part of sifting through forensic evidence for most of these in one capacity or another. It was possible that she could slip her tests into a less scrutinized, lower priority case. Maybe she could put some pressure on it, see the results faster. Maybe ...

It was no good. She couldn't insert this evidence into any of these cases without causing a lot of trouble. For a start, it might derail a legitimate investigation, throwing everyone into a wild goose chase that could result in the bad guys going free. Or worse.

Morally, ethically, Liz couldn't stomach that. She was already walking a fine enough line as it was.

What she needed, after considering the problem for most of a day, was an independent, third-party lab.

She had spent years working for the NYPD and knew all of the labs that were in use around the country. Some were better than others. And as a matter of course, she tended to rely on the labs that were the highest rated. Maybe she should consider one of the labs that wasn't as impeccable?

What about one of the labs that was on the "naughty list?" This was the list of labs and other resources that were no longer utilized by law enforcement because they, themselves, were under investigation for issues such as mistakes that led to false arrests, or worse ... flat out manipulating results to influence a legal case. Some of these labs were still in operation, squeaking by as test labs for ancestry services and employment drug screenings and the like. Low-rent establishments with shady reputations, making their living by scraping the bottom of the barrel of bio work.

Maybe she could trust them enough to analyze these samples, and to expedite them as part of "getting back in good graces."

She shivered at the idea.

Most of the services were repugnant—having violated both written and unwritten codes of conduct for facilities such as these. They were the equivalent of ambulance-chasing lawyers. Their services might serve some purpose in the world, but the aura of distrust surrounding them made them unpalatable.

Liz wasn't sure she could stomach working with any of them.

It wouldn't work anyway. These services would actually be *more* prone to play everything by the book, to document everything officially, and to tie their results to an open case number. If their goal was to restore their reputation and reclaim government contracts, they'd be diligent in their record keeping. They'd make it even more likely that someone in the FBI or elsewhere would discover what she was up to.

Using any lab that routinely worked with law enforcement was going to be too risky. That was just a fact.

But what about labs that *didn't* routinely work with law enforcement?

As she thought about it, and about what she really needed, she realized there were alternatives out there. Labs that rarely if ever worked directly with law enforcement.

There was a small lab, in fact, right here in New York, that occasionally took on overflow from the NYPD, though it wasn't strictly geared toward law enforcement. In fact, its principal purpose was to look at DNA that was typically a lot older than the standard New York crime scene.

Sometimes thousands of years older.

The genome sequencing and research labs at SUNY—the State University of New York.

While the SUNY lab wouldn't have the resources to match their results against the national database, Liz was confident that she could do that part herself. It would be a lot easier to mask a database query than to try to keep the whole lab process under wraps. A query from her would also garner far less scrutiny than a query from an outside lab. She could easily pass it off as eliminating known figures from the scene, or something similar. No one would be all that interested in results that eliminated suspects.

All she really needed was enough identifying markers to run through the database and allow her to find a match. If anyone happened to notice her query, she could easily point to any number of cases in her backlog. She could even tie it to the weed-out for the abductions, if necessary. There were so many profiles being run in conjunction with that case, at present, that no one could possibly notice two or three more.

Unless one of those results happened to be a good fit as a suspect or other lead. At that point, hiding the results was out of the question. She'd just have to risk it and work out answers to any hard questions that might follow. And live with the results.

That was later. Right now, she finally had a way to move forward, and she was going to take it.

She reached out to the SUNY lab, sending an email from her official FBI address, though there was some risk involved with this, too. If anyone decided to look closely, they could puzzle out precisely what she was doing, and she'd be right back to answering uncomfortable questions. But she figured she could make more progress, faster, if she could flash some official FBI cred.

She kept it pretty straightforward—things were hectic because of recent events, FBI resources were stretched thin, she needed a hand with some casework, she would appreciate the professional courtesy, and so forth. All true things, and she felt no guilt over mentioning them if it would help grease the wheels.

For good measure, though, she mentioned Dan.

It was kind of a sneaky move, she knew. But dating Dr. Dan Kotler, famous anthropologist and "modern-day Indiana Jones," did occasionally have its perks. Beyond the obvious ones, of course.

For a start, he was wildly popular on the SUNY campus, giving regular lectures to standing-room-only venues. And though he often claimed he lacked respect among his peers, from Liz's perspective, this did little to dampen the buzz when it was announced he'd be making an appearance at a conference or event or lecture.

So name dropping her boyfriend ... it couldn't hurt.

It only took an hour to get a response. As she'd hoped, she got an enthusiastic reply from SUNY. They'd be happy to help out, and please tell Dan he was welcome to come back any time.

She thanked them via email, then packaged her samples to be transported to their facilities. She'd deliver them herself— the easiest way to enforce a chain of custody, but also the best way to keep them under the radar. She could swing by as she left the office.

That was a load off. For now.

It would still take time to get the results, but she hoped she'd see something much faster than usual. The implication that they might be helping to save the abdicated congresspeople might be enough to put a spin on things.

It felt good to have the DNA sorted. That just left the fingerprints.

She and Dani had managed to lift three viable prints from the scene. From her cursory examination, Liz could see they were distinct, which was good. They might all belong to the same person, for all she knew. But she had a left thumb, a left forefinger, and a right middle finger, all nearly complete, and definitely intact enough to provide a match if one existed.

Three chances.

Getting results for these was a lot simpler and faster than DNA sequencing. She could simply run them through the FBI database. She wouldn't even have to worry much about covering her tracks—she ran prints routinely and had more or less unfettered access to the database, as needed. Plus, she and her team were currently running prints to eliminate anyone from the investigation who was already vetted and cleared. Thousands of prints were going through the database throughout the day, from agents and specialists all over the country. No one was going to notice three more. Unless, of course, they resulted in a hit that got the attention of someone higher up.

She had already scanned and digitized the prints and was running them against the federal database. The results would take about 24 hours. She'd get an alert on her mobile phone when they came back.

She leaned away from her computer, stretching, feeling her muscles loosen. It had been a tense few days, and she wished Kotler were here. She knew he was busy with some other aspect of the investigation—she wasn't cleared for some of the details. But from what he had been able to tell her, he was making something of a milk run, interviewing a prisoner some-where. It required going dark for a while—leaving his mobile phone behind.

She smiled at the thought of Dan Kotler without his phone. It was almost absurd.

Wherever he was, she was glad he was far from the chaos here. She'd love to see him, would love to go to dinner and talk about literally anything but the abductions or Historic Crimes or anything related to their work at all. Right about now she'd kill to hear him lecture her about cultural psychology in ancient Mesopotamia or the economic advancements of the Phoenicians or the knot writing of the Inca. Anything at all, really. She didn't mind his enthusiasm for the minutia of ancient civilizations, but right now she actually *longed* for it. At the very least, it would mean he was here, and safe.

Kotler's tendency to find himself in the middle of all the shooting was a bit alarming. Somehow, he managed to turn academia into a combat zone. It was troubling.

But she was content knowing that, for once, he was safe and out of the line of fire. Right about now he was most likely snoozing on a flight back to New York. Maybe he'd arrive in time for the two of them to take a little break, get out and get some fresh air.

It'd be good to take a walk in the park.

# CHAPTER TWELVE

THIS WAS no walk in the park.

Kotler and Denzel were both injured, barely managing to stay upright as they raced through the darkened wilderness. The trees here were evergreens—some variety of pine, Kotler figured—and there was no underbrush to impede their progress.

Or to hide them.

They managed to hobble away from the flaming wreckage of the crash site before the helicopters made it to the ridge, but God only knew how far ahead they might be. Those birds could have hovered and dropped troops without bothering to land. There could be people hot on Kotler and Denzel's trail right at this moment.

Their only choice was to keep pushing ahead.

They'd been running at the top speed they could manage for perhaps an hour when Kotler pulled up, gripping his side and gasping.

"Can ... barely breathe ..." Kotler said. He leaned against a tree, huffing and panting, feeling like his lungs were constricted. He felt like he was going to die. Which might have been true in more ways than one.

Denzel leaned forward, resting a hand on the tree trunk that was currently propping up Kotler's raised and pain-riddled frame. Denzel winced as he put weight on his arms, then straightened and lowered himself to the ground, panting and sweating.

"We're not going to last like this," Denzel said in huffs. "We're in bad shape. We have no provisions, no tools. We're stranded God knows where. And I'm pretty sure the bad guys are closing in."

"Seen any signs?" Kotler asked, warily.

Denzel shook his head. "All gut instinct." He winced and coughed. "Of course, my guts aren't in the best shape at the moment."

Kotler looked at his friend. Denzel looked pale. He'd been pretty steady, moving without hesitation. But it was clear his injuries were worse than Kotler's own. His military training and discipline were keeping him moving, but that wouldn't hold out forever.

They needed rest and medical attention.

They needed a miracle.

There was a sound in the distance. Something inaudible that made Kotler and Denzel glance at each other.

"It's them," Denzel said, his voice low.

"What do we do?" Kotler asked.

Denzel shook his head and managed to get to his feet in a painful, slow rise. "Move," he said, his teeth clenched.

Kotler straightened but immediately fell back against the tree. A sweat broke out all over his body, and he felt like he was going to vomit. He reined it in, held his gorge, and then clenched his own teeth as he made himself stand free of the tree and start moving again.

Their progress had slowed. Their bodies were betraying them. And the noises were getting closer.

Denzel stopped walking and turned to look back through the slatted light between pine trees. He glanced around, then stooped and gingerly lifted a fallen branch from the ground. He hefted it and began breaking off small limbs and twigs, dropping them to the ground.

Kotler nodded and looked around to find a suitable weapon of his own.

They would make their stand. Two severely injured men armed with clubs against a platoon of military-trained soldiers armed with the latest in automatic firepower.

"Roland," Kotler said, looking squarely at his friend.

Denzel shook his head. "Don't, Kotler," he said. "Let's just do this."

Kotler nodded, and the two of them took what shelter they could behind two of the larger pines, several feet away from each other. They pressed against the sap-oozing bark and peered around to see when their enemies would approach.

It didn't take long.

There were half a dozen men in military-style black uniforms, each moving at a slow and deliberate pace, sweeping the forest before them for any signs of their prey. Kotler and Denzel both ducked back behind their respective trees and glanced at each other, nodding.

When the six approached, both Denzel and Kotler spun from their cover, bringing their clubs down hard on the closest two figures. Kotler heard a muffled cry from under the balaclava of his man, who went down in a heap.

He didn't have time to check in on Roland's progress as two more men leapt at Kotler, raising their weapons and ordering him to stand down.

Kotler ignored them and managed to strike a second man

hard, hitting his exposed hands and causing him to fire wild into the woods.

Kotler was about to raise his club for another strike when the third man used the butt of his weapon to strike Kotler in the jaw.

It was too much.

Between his injuries and his exhaustion, the sudden slam to his jaw overpowered him and sent Kotler sprawling backward on to the ground. He tried to raise his head, to raise his hands in defense, to find the club and use it to fend off his attackers. Instead, he fell back, his vision going black, the pain finally subsiding as consciousness fled from him.

# CHAPTER THIRTEEN

THE INFLUENCER WAS NOT like the other Novensiles. And definitely not like the other Jani.

For a start, though it was common for the Jani to have members placed in the highest reaches of power and influence in the governments of the world, they hadn't yet embraced the reality of the *real* "new world power."

This was how the Influencer thought of the resources and tools he'd used to make himself too important for the Jani to ignore. Forget influencing laws and policies, taking power by creating more layers of government.

Real power, in the age of social media and worldwide connectedness, came from influence itself.

Directly or subtly, overtly or discreetly, it didn't matter. It really all came down to how you made people *feel*, and in that the Influencer might be the most powerful person on the planet. He'd made a lifelong practice of telling and showing and convincing people how they should feel. It had been his life. And more.

This version of "new world power" superseded governments. It was above the law. It was outside of the bubble of petty and worthless "rights" that people were always trying to preserve. The new world power was the ability to persuade the world to think as the Influencer thought, and to do as the Influencer would ask them to do.

Like. Subscribe. Click for notifications. Join my mailing list.

Buy what I ask you to buy. Because you love me. Because I entertain you. Because I inspire you.

Social media posts. YouTube videos. Podcasts. Sound bites and clips broadcast to billions of people worldwide, day and night, nonstop. These were the instruments that made the Influencer more powerful than heads of state or even dictators and despots. A gentle, subtle nudge from him and civil unrest begins, wars start, governments topple.

Or fighting ceases, peace gains a foothold, communities grow.

Secret and ancient Orders become visible, and their resources fall into his hands.

What was funny—what the Influencer really liked about how he'd come to be here, as a member of the Jani and then as one of the "seditious" Novensiles—was the fact that on the surface the Influencer had none of the traditional trappings of power. He wasn't a billionaire, though he did have money (multiple streams of income ... always necessary). He didn't have control of a world-dominating corporation, though he did have followers in the billions. He didn't have direct political influence, though he did have the ear of anyone in office.

The Influencer had no political appointments, no official titles, no teams of high-powered attorneys. He was just a guy who made funny videos and wrote funny posts and hung out with celebrities.

In the end, what the Influencer did have, the thing that

gave him power over the world itself, was simple: He had a strong brand. And that brand had a rabidly loyal following.

An expression on his face could tank sales for a particular soda. A label on his jacket could create a new fashion sensation. A FaceTime call with an A-Lister could get him into even the most exclusive venues on the planet, where he would start to learn about a secret Order that had its tendrils in everything, that secretly ran the world.

He'd started thinking of them as "the Hidden Persuaders."

It was sort of an in-joke—an old reference to the advertising industry. It came from the title of a book by Vance Packard, an expose into the world of advertising in the 1950s. The "Mad-men" era. It was a book that had changed the Influencer's life when he read it as a teenager. By extension, it was now changing the world.

The book was a warning, worded in the most dire terms possible, about how the advertising industry was using psychology and other tools of influence—including such fright-ening ideas as subliminal messaging and depth psychology—to motivate and manipulate consumers into buying anything they were selling.

Packard framed all of this as something of an indictment against media, but the Influencer had studied it like a how-to guide.

The Influencer had grown up in an era when social media and vlogging were beginning to create a new generation of media stars, completely self-empowered and self-motivated, and free from the gatekeepers of traditional media. He was born into an era where even people living in poverty could have global reach—way beyond their neighborhoods and villages—and could tell the world about their struggles and triumphs.

A boy in Africa could suffer through famine multiple times, could face death by starvation or disease or murder at the hands of criminals, and still end up on stage for a TED Talk about the windmill he made from bicycle parts. Or a 15-year-old girl could sing a song in her bedroom and have a hit record six months later. Or a woman in China could share a video of heinous acts by the Chinese government and instigate a revolution in the streets, taking over airports and bringing a whole country to a standstill.

It was a new world of individual empowerment.

Influence could rewrite history.

So this book, and the rise of social media, somehow intermingled in the Influencer's young mind and created within him a drive and passion for extending his own circle of influence and power. He studied, and he learned, and he discovered that he could be more significant than just himself. He could become immense, powerful, undeniable, as the one who could persuade a crowd. He could be much, much bigger than himself.

He could have power. Real power. Undeniable power.

He didn't need money or a position in government. All he had to do was use the right words, the right images, and the right sounds in the right combination at the right time. And people would follow him.

His YouTube channel had millions of followers. His social media networks were vast. He had employees—mostly virtual assistants—who took care of daily tasks for him, allowing him to create content at an unprecedented rate. And all of this expanded the Influencer, increased him, so that he *was* his network, and his power was total and complete.

But somehow, not enough.

What he needed now was a new challenge. He wanted his reach to go even further. He wanted to increase himself to the level of godhood.

That was when he had stumbled onto the rumors of an ancient Order with influence over everything.

Intrigued, he began to dig. And as he dug, as he asked his most powerful friends to get him into the most exclusive places, to meet the most elusive people.

Eventually the pieces started to come together. Whispered rumors were confirmed. New introductions were made. Tests—tests the Influencer hadn't even known he was taking—were passed.

The Jani were revealed.

He knew, instantly, that he had to become one of them.

Here was an ancient Order that used some of the same principles he'd used himself, extending itself into all of the centers of power, working by influence and persuasion to become vast and pervasive and inevitable. Hidden Persuaders ... the real power beneath and above and surrounding the perceived power. The real power, woven into the fabric of reality in such a way that no one even knew it was there.

It was like he was born to be one of them. He'd finally found his tribe.

Immediately the Influencer started putting things into motion. A comment in a particular conversation online, a joke in a YouTube video, a handful of Tweets, and an array of hashtags on Instagram. Before long, his secret message was encoded in all the right places, positioned to reach millions, even billions of people worldwide: *I am one of you, invite me into your Order.*

It had taken time. A lot of time. Weeks. More time than most things he had accomplished.

It was sort of sweet, really, to have to yearn for something for once, unsure if the message was really getting through.

But he knew—the message always got through.

The invitation came to him via the same sort of indirect

channels through which all things came to him. A comment on a social post, a response video with two-hundred-thousand likes, a thousand Facebook shares among a handful of closed groups.

It was code. It was nonverbal confirmation. It was his ticket in.

Eventually, someone reached out to him with an invite to an exclusive event, and it was there that he was recruited into the Order.

Things moved fast after that.

It was surprising how many Jani he already knew. People in positions of power in companies and government offices, people whom he'd had lunch with, coffee with, gone to parties with. He was surprised—though maybe he shouldn't have been—to learn that many of his closest friends in the inner circles of his digital media empire were Jani. The Order was everywhere he looked, but until now they'd been completely invisible.

And there was something else. The hint of something deeper.

Just as he'd sensed that the Order was out there, somehow hiding in plain sight, running things behind the scenes and between the seams, he began to sense there was something hidden among the hiding. A deeper layer, yet to be revealed.

Once again, the Influencer got to work. He shook hands. He took oaths. He swore allegiances. He met people who mattered. And he began to drop hints, to subtly redirect conversations and tease out what he was after.

And he found the thread. And then he followed it.

There was another faction buried within the Jani. A dissenting faction that had its own reach into the annals of power throughout the world. A group of members of the Order who thought there could be a better way, a better use for their power.

The Influencer knew the signs. He saw the signals, even though the rest of the Jani seemed oblivious.

The rabbit hole went deeper.

It hadn't taken long to position himself to become one of the Novensiles. In fact, it had been easier than becoming a Jani in the first place. All he'd had to do was signal that he thought things within the Order might benefit from some change, some improvements, some fresh perspective. The Influencer planted the seed that he thought the Jani could do more if they just shifted their use of resources, to start flexing some muscle rather than constantly remaining in the shadows.

Before even a full month had passed, the Influencer was recruited for a second time.

The Novensiles, he learned, were a growing subset of the Jani, staying just as hidden in plain sight, even more so, but desperate to cement more power. The Influencer had merely played to that desperation and had reaped the benefits of appearing almost god-like in his reach and his ability to not only assess the needs of the Novensiles but to meet and even exceed them.

He created ways to find more potential members, keeping recruitment on the down low and off of the radar of the Jani while bumping their numbers upward in profound leaps. He found ways to divert more resources into the hands of the Novensiles, to increase their power and might without raising suspicion. He slowly built networks within the network, unifying a group of barely organized dissenters into something with real teeth and formidable strength.

The Novensiles had been around for years. Decades. Maybe even a century. The Influencer couldn't be sure. But it wasn't until he joined their ranks that they really started to *grow*.

And now, the Influencer's plans for the Novensiles were starting to mature.

This current operation—the abduction of the congress-people—was a big step. It was a strategic move, and it had taken more effort than the Influencer had put into anything else in his life. But it was just the start. It was just a step along the path to godhood. Real godhood.

Manipulating the Novensiles, rising in power so that he was invited to be a part of the "dark council," and then pushing his agenda in all the subtle ways that it took to make it seem like it was everyone else's idea—that had taken time and effort. And resources. The cost had been high, as had the risk.

But now, here it was. The first in many steps toward a future in which the Novensiles rose to dominion and the Influencer led them there.

It came down to just ten congresspeople abducted, along with four of their aides. But that was only the surface view.

Ten votes influenced. A rising star in the Senate given the nudge the Influencer needed to make sure she came up with the right ideas at the right time. A slight tip in the balance of the US government that would yield enormous long-term benefits.

That was a better way to look at it.

There were multiple levels of play.

Recruiting, casting, orchestrating, planning. Crafting the right stories and placing them in the right ears. The Influencer had engaged the services of psychologists and mentalists, nego-tiators and conmen. For more than a year he had planted seeds and nurtured them, secretly whispering stories that would lead to these ten abducted congresspeople going the Influencer's way on one of the most crucial parts of his plan. Months and years of planning, preparation, and work, and it was all coming together.

Then there was the science.

Archaeologists. Mathematicians. Geneticists. Physicists. They spoke languages the Influencer didn't know, and didn't need to know. One of his tenets was "I do not need to know everything to use everything." And he was definitely set to use everything, and to rise to a level of power unseen on the Earth for thousands of years.

That was, if the Chairman didn't screw it all up.

The old man was becoming a problem. He obviously had his own agenda and his own resources. He had his own influence and power. He had his own reach, and it was extensive.

But his time was up.

The Influencer had been making his move against the Chairman for months now, and the timing was finally right. All it would take, to put things in motion, was a word here, a smile there, a well-placed Tweet and a seemingly unconnected YouTube video.

Within hours, things were going to go very wrong for the Chairman, and there would be no apparent connection between that outcome and the things the Influencer had put into motion, within the secret walls of the Novensiles or beyond, among the Jani.

It would appear, to anyone looking, as if things just happened all on their own. Just the way the Influencer liked it.

A career would be over, and a traitor to the Jani would face his fate. And then everything would turn up for the Influencer.

The Influencer was, after all, the most empowered Hidden Persuader of them all.

# CHAPTER FOURTEEN

THE FINGERPRINTS RESULTS WERE IN, but so far they weren't entirely helpful.

Two of the prints were from the same person—a woman who worked for a cleaning service and had likely been hired to make the apartment ready for a new tenant. Liz had to applaud her for her work. The apartment had been immaculate, to the point of being an anomaly.

Which made Liz believe that someone must have come in behind the cleaning service, and not just to give the job some extra "sparkle."

DB's contact, however, had known there would be something to find in that apartment. The fingerprints and DNA were the only things Liz had identified, and they were both in line with what she'd need her forensics kit to find. That made Liz believe that this was it. Something had to come out of this evidence.

The third print came back completely void of leads. There was nothing in the FBI database associated with it, which could mean a lot of things. But Liz suspected what it meant was that the second person was an illegal immigrant, working for the cleaning service.

The fingerprints were a bust.

She couldn't just assume, of course. She marked and filed the print all the same, and if it turned up at any other crime scene, there would be an alert. That was due diligence, but it didn't make Liz feel any better about all of this. She wasn't really interested in busting an undocumented worker who was just trying to make a living. But she couldn't just leave it out, either. If there was any chance that this person was tied to the abductions, it needed to be on file.

Without any immediate hits, though, the fingerprints were a dead end.

The DNA, however, revealed some surprises.

The first was that SUNY had already sent Liz some results that she could run through the FBI database. Maybe it was an urge to show the FBI that their facilities could be useful. Or maybe it was the heightened concern and anxiety following the abductions. It could even just be that SUNY wanted to impress her or, more likely, the famous Dr. Dan Kotler. Whatever the reason, they'd gotten the results back to her in just over 24 hours. That had to be a new record.

It had taken a few more hours to run those results against the database, however, and Liz was just returning from a quick sprint for lunch when she got a text alert. She was sipping broth from a to-go container of ramen as she stepped out of the elevators into the Historic Crimes bullpen, making her way to the forensics lab. She opened her text and read the message, then stopped in her tracks.

What she was reading ... just the hint of what she was reading ... it couldn't be true. It literally could not be true.

She quickly scanned her ID to open the secured doors of the forensics wing, and then raced down the glass-lined corridor to her office. She placed the ramen on the corner of her desk and bent to open her laptop, logging in and going straight to the DNA results.

The trouble, immediately, was that there was no direct result for the DNA. No one with that specific profile was currently listed in the national database—no one with a criminal past, no one with a medical history, no one with so much as an over-the-counter DNA ancestry test.

In the absence of a direct match, however, the system had returned the closest matches on file. These would tend to be relatives and descendants. Whether or not these relatives even knew the person from whom the DNA had been taken was often questionable, but the system was pretty good at getting to within a family group. And if someone in that group was a closer match than others, they'd turn up at the top of the results.

Right now, Liz had about a page of leads, but only two top-level results to consider—Dan Kotler and Jeffrey Kotler.

Brothers. And therefore closely linked in their genetic profiles. And, by extension, closely linked to the profile Liz had in her possession.

According to the results, the sample shared autosomal DNA with both Kotler brothers. This meant that whoever left the DNA was related to the Kotlers out to the second cousin level. In Dan Kotler's case, that would include his nephew Alex —unless Jeffrey had any dalliances outside of his marriage that no one knew about. Not impossible, but very unlikely given what Liz knew of the man's character.

The results could also indicate another sibling, a blood aunt or uncle, first cousins, even grandparents.

Or parents.

That last one was impossible, however. Kotler's parents had died when he was young. He didn't like to talk about it much, but Liz knew that their deaths had triggered within him the drive to become who he was now. Their deaths were a defining moment for Dan, though for Jeffrey it was something he'd been too young to truly remember.

Regardless, Liz could rule out a match with Kotler's parents. Which left only a few other options.

She sat and ran dozens of queries through the database. She quickly eliminated more potentials from the pool. Jeffrey had a profile thanks to a heritage test he'd taken. The same was true for Alex, Jeffrey's son. There were no known siblings beyond the two Kotler boys, though that couldn't be ruled out entirely either. Neither of Dan's parents had siblings, so there were no aunts and uncles, and thus no first cousins.

That narrowed the pool to only two potential options—a grandfather and a grandmother. And the likelihood would be for a paternal match since there was a hit on the Y chromosome. It didn't completely eliminate the possibility of a maternal match, but the odds favored a genetic line on the father's side.

When Liz had asked Dan about his grandparents, he'd told her that his mother's parents were long dead. He'd met his maternal grandmother when he was very young, but she had already been in an assisted living facility, and she had passed away before his own parents had died.

His paternal grandparents were more of a mystery.

Liz knew practically nothing about them. And that was because Dan himself knew practically nothing about them. He had looked into them, of course. He was infinitely curious. But she suspected he was less so about his own lineage. Something about the Kotler family history was deeply depressing for Dan. Or disturbing. Liz could never quite put together what was behind his reluctance.

And now, that lack of information was creating a mystery

that could somehow be tied to ... well, everything, if the contact she'd spoken with could be believed.

The origin and motivation behind the formation of Historic Crimes. The abduction of the congresspeople and their aides. Even, apparently, hidden aspects of Dan's past.

She needed to find a way to narrow down who this DNA sample belonged to.

It was time to call in some help.

# CHAPTER FIFTEEN

KOTLER AWOKE to a persistent and annoying beeping.

His head hurt. His side hurt. His body itself, from tip to tip, hurt. But he was alive.

And he was feeling oddly better, despite the pain.

He tried to raise his hand to touch his forehead, but found that it was held in place by a secured, padded cuff. As was his other hand.

He tilted his head forward, craning his neck to look around, and saw that he was in some kind of a hospital room, though there were no windows. Medical equipment protruded in clusters from the walls or stood in dedicated carts in every corner. The beeping he heard was a heart monitor, and Kotler could feel the leads adhered to his chest.

There was an IV drip bag filled with clear liquid hanging from a stand by his head. A tube dangled from this, terminating in a needle in his arm. He hoped it was saline, but judging by the fuzziness in his thinking he couldn't entirely rule out a sedative.

Kotler let his head fall back, and his eyes close. He was in trouble. But there was little to nothing he could do about it. He was hardly in any shape for either a fight or a daring escape. It was obvious that whoever his captors were—and he had some ideas on that—they were at least taking care of him, giving him medical attention. He might as well take advantage, rest, and let his body heal up enough that an escape or a fight might actually be possible. If he stood any chance at all, it would come after rest and healing.

He wondered about Denzel, but put all worry about his friend out of his mind, just as he had about his own predicament. Kotler couldn't control anything right now. Best to stay in the moment, keep his head clear, and get as much rest as possible. If an opportunity arose, he'd take it and figure out the rest as he went.

The door opened, and Kotler pretended to be asleep.

"We know you're awake, Dr. Kotler," a voice said.

A familiar voice.

A voice that should not be here.

Kotler opened his eyes and lifted his head again, and confirmed what could not be true. "Scope? How the hell ..."

Scope grinned at him. "Miss me? I know this is a surprise, but it really shouldn't be. You know the Novensiles have their own network of resources. Getting me out of prison wasn't much work."

Kotler knew this had to be true, but he'd been practicing a hopeful sort of denial about it.

Scope had been one of the few Novensiles to be captured during an all-out brawl in the Sonoma Mountains. Kotler and Denzel had found themselves caught between not only the Novensiles and the Jani, but local police as well. Kotler was being investigated for murder, at the time. A murder that Scope or one of his men had committed.

That fight had resulted in the discovery of a Jani treasure

vault—one that was quickly liberated of its treasures as the Jani swept it clean and made their exit. The site itself was currently under military guard, from what Kotler had heard. Though he knew there was precious little there to guard now, beyond the very impressive ancient architecture of the vault. Something he hoped to one day study, once the site was cleared as a potential threat.

"Where's Roland?" Kolter asked.

"He's fine," Scope replied, waving a hand. "But he's locked away. He's getting the same medical care you're getting, so don't worry."

"Why worry?" Kotler asked, raising his hands as high as the padded cuffs would allow. "We've only had our plane brought down and been abducted by a terrorist organization, separated and held in an unknown facility, God only knows where. It's like any other Tuesday."

Scope laughed a little at this. "For you, I could believe that. You certainly have a way of making trouble a habit."

The casualness of the remark irked Kotler. What did Scope know about him? Probably quite a lot. The Novensiles had access to the same network of resources and intelligence as the Jani, and it would be very little trouble to find out everything there was to know about Kotler. Not only was he a public figure, but he'd recently become a person of interest with the Jani. He couldn't have many secrets left, by this point.

"So why are we alive?" Kotler asked, letting some of his irritation seep into his words. "What is it the Novensiles think they can get from me?"

"Presumptuous, aren't you?" Scope chuckled.

"You're here, talking to me," Kotler shrugged. "Not to Agent Denzel. That tells me what you're after isn't something governmental or official."

"True," Scope said with a smirk.

"You've patched me up," Kotler continued. "You've got me on something for pain, but you made sure I would be lucid. You're after something only I can give you, which does narrow things down a little. Your people are obsessed with artifacts and power, so I'm guessing you want me to help you find something. Probably another vault."

Scope's smirk turned to an impressed expression, his chin wrinkled and his lips pursed as he nodded. "All that does sound plausible," Scope said.

"But what I don't understand," Kotler replied, "is why you'd shoot down our plane in the first place, if you ..."

He stopped.

Kotler felt a cold sensation spread through him. A chill of realization as the facts started to come together, as the possibilities were narrowed until only one was left.

"The drugs must be knocking some of the edge off of your intellect," Scope said, laughing lightly. "It took you long enough."

"You ... it wasn't you who shot us down," Kotler said. "If you needed me for something, you wouldn't risk killing me in a plane crash."

Scope smirked. "There you go," he said. "Though you're only about half right. I didn't shoot you down, but someone within the Novensiles did. A ... new faction."

Kotler's eyebrows shot up and he laughed. "You have to be kidding. *Another* fracture among the Jani? You guys need to work on your morale. Maybe go on some kind of team-building retreat."

Scope nodded. "It's a sticky problem. The Novensiles are finally coming into their own, and now this. There's someone new among the leadership. He's... causing trouble. And my direct line has put some things in motion to see if he can mitigate some of the damage. Oh, and survive."

"This is what happens when people don't communicate," Kotler said, shaking his head. "So I assume this is a 'cooperate or Roland dies' sort of situation?"

"Roland, you, maybe that attractive Forensics Specialist you're dating," Scope shrugged. "The possibilities are endless."

Kotler nodded to this, keeping his relaxed composure though the chill deepened inside. He had no doubt that Scope and his people had the sort of reach to do exactly as Scope implied. Kotler had been focused on his and Denzel's immediate danger and had not considered that Liz might be in trouble. And if Liz was, then others might be as well. His brother, Jeffrey, as well as Jeffrey's wife, Christina. And their son, Alex. Even Cristoff Vellar.

The only family Kotler had left.

If anything happened to them, because of him, he could never live with himself. If he managed to actually live through this.

"Relax, Dr. Kotler," Scope said. "Someone wants you taken care of. I mean, alive, of course. Someone with some influence in the Order."

Kotler blinked. "Who?" he asked. Then, thinking about it, the more important question. "Why?"

"You're needed for something," Scope shrugged, and then grinned. "Something that you are uniquely suited for. There's something you're going to want to see. But for now, rest up. We travel tomorrow morning."

And with that Scope left the room, and Kotler heard the decisive and foreboding sound of a lock turning into place from outside the door.

Kotler settled back into his pillow and stared at the ceiling. So many questions. So many new things to consider.

Who was his mysterious benefactor in the Order? He must be one of the Novensiles, if he was able to give orders to Scope.

Was it Scope's direct line? Scope had said his direct line was in trouble. Was he somehow using Kotler as a safety net?

What was it that they needed him to look at? Something he was "uniquely suited for." That implied something with historical significance. An artifact, most likely. Or an archaeological site—like those they had manipulated him into unlocking in the past. Sites like the one in Egypt, and the site in the Sonoma Mountains.

The Novensiles were on the hunt for Jani vaults, which contained treasures from millennia of pilfering and storing. Kotler knew that some ancient artifacts carried with them an immense potential for power, and power was something the Novensiles were desperately seeking.

There were more mysteries here than Kotler could think about, especially with pain killers circulating in his system. His head was swimming. He was still aching all over, and he was worried about Denzel, about Liz, about his family.

He closed his eyes and calmed himself, then let sleep flow over him. He would rest while he could. He would heal while he could.

And when they came for him, he'd try to think of a way out of all of this. Maybe even a way that he and Denzel and everyone else he cared about could survive.

# CHAPTER SIXTEEN

LIZ HAD NEVER BEEN to Jeffrey Kotler's home. She'd barely even met him—he'd more or less shunned his brother since the incident with Dan's former professor.

Jeffrey had been kidnapped and strapped to a bomb as part of a play to manipulate Dan into cracking a Cold War-era code. Dan's professor, Robert Wiley, had been siphoning off money from Dan for years and was working on a larger score.

Wiley was in prison now. The bad guys were all caught—or killed, in the case of Wiley's men-for-hire, Red Ryba and his younger brother, Cameron. Everything had turned out ok in the end. Except Jeffrey hadn't managed to forgive Dan for bringing this drama and chaos and danger into his life and the lives of his family. Jeffrey had forbidden Dan from calling or visiting. He had kept his son, Alex, from talking to his uncle, which Liz knew had hurt Dan far more than he was willing to let on. He and Alex were kindred souls, and had been very close.

The one and only time Liz had met Jeffrey was at Wiley's trial, where Jeffrey had testified. There had been a brief moment between Jeffrey and Dan outside the courtroom, and Dan had introduced Liz then. Jeffrey had been polite but cold. And afterward, he had left without so much as a goodbye.

So it was with a great deal of uncertainty that Liz knocked on the Kotler's front door and waited.

Moments later, the door opened, and Liz was greeted by a very pretty and petite woman, about two years younger than Liz. She was recognizable from pictures Dan had in his home.

Christina Kotler. Jeffrey's wife.

"Hi," Liz smiled, trying to appear warm and non-threatening. "I'm Liz Ludlum. Dan's ... friend. I called earlier."

To Liz's relief, Christina nodded and returned her smile. "Jeffrey is in his study. He's expecting you. Come on in!"

It was a good start. Liz had worried she'd be turned away, despite having managed to convince Jeffrey to let her swing by. He'd been guarded on the phone, and Liz hadn't gotten a solid read on how open he was to having her here. He'd only agreed to let her come when she said it was a matter of life or death.

Christina led Liz through the house, which was neatly kept and well organized. It was, in almost every way, the exact opposite of Dan's apartment. Both spaces shared the characteristic of being neat and orderly, but beyond that, they couldn't be more different. Where Dan's place was modern and featured an eclectic mix of ancient artifacts and replicas alongside advanced modern technology and furnishings—including the most complicated espresso machine Liz had ever seen in her life—Jeffrey's home was a study in warm tones and down-to-earth comforts. The furnishings were plush and comfortable, and oriented toward a stone fireplace. There was no sign of a television, in this main living space. But there were shelves on every wall, crammed with a variety of books on every possible subject.

Dan had told Liz that Christina had an active interest in

historic preservation and that Jeffrey himself was a history buff. Alex, their son, was something of a genius himself—a self-styled "boy detective" who took on cases from local children and shared his uncle's penchant for getting into and mostly out of trouble.

So there was no telling who was most responsible for the extensive library that adorned the walls of the Kotler home. Liz suspected that these volumes had been read and studied by all three J. Kotlers.

Christina led Liz down a hall to a closed door. She knocked lightly, and Liz heard a man's voice say to come in. Christina opened the door and gestured for Liz to enter, then closed the door behind her.

Jeffrey Kotler stood from a desk that was pushed up against one wall. It was organized but covered in documents. Liz couldn't quite make them out from her vantage point, but they looked like old census records. Local historical documents, maybe. Among these, as well, were the accouterments of study and research, including a magnifying glass with a light, mounted to a swing arm and attached to one side of Jeffrey's desk. There were also stacks of notebooks, a tin cup filled with pens in a variety of colors, folded maps ... everything one might expect from someone who studied history for a living.

Except Jeffrey Kotler, Liz knew, did this as a hobby. He was wealthy—having inherited a large sum of money from his parents, just as Dan had. And like Dan, Jeffrey had his investments. Despite his wealth, however, Jeffrey worked in construction. He had a knack for architecture and often sketched designs that he'd hand off to a certified architect, who would typically stamp them as approved without much modification. Jeffrey also tended to act as a general contractor, particularly on projects that Christina had taken on.

All this was something of a guise, meant to help Jeffery

blend in with everyone else in the neighborhood. The secret millionaire who was possibly more down to earth than the blue-collar contractors he hired.

He stepped toward Liz and held out a hand. "It's good to see you again."

Liz shook his hand and smiled. The greeting wasn't the warmest, but it wasn't exactly frigid. A good sign. Dan had said that Jeffrey was good at compartmentalizing. So maybe he had nothing against Liz, despite the fact she was dating his brother.

"Thanks for agreeing to help me out. It's ... well, I can't really tell you everything. But it's important."

"Is Dan in trouble?" Jeffrey asked.

Liz shook her head. "No. But he's not here right now. And I think ... well, I think you're more qualified to help with this than he is."

That brought the first light smile to Jeffrey's lips. "Is that right? Well, then, how can I help?"

"Dan says you've done a lot of genealogical research into your family."

Jeffrey nodded. "Is this about our great-great grandfather? The physicist who turned out to be a codebreaker?"

Liz shook her head. "No. At least, I don't see how it could be exactly. There could be a connection, I guess, but I'm looking for someone who may still be alive."

Jeffrey's eyebrows went up in surprise. "Alive?" He shook his head. "That's ... well, there isn't anyone. Dan and I are the last Kotlers. Or ... well, there's Alex. You don't mean him, though."

"No," Liz said, shaking her head and smiling. "It's just that ..." she paused, looked at Jeffrey's eyes, and sighed.

"It's a lot of secrets, isn't it?" Liz asked. "A lot of hesitation."

Jeffrey had been studying her as she talked, and Liz was struck by a sudden sense of recognition. For all their differences, Dan and Jeffrey shared a lot of qualities, particularly certain mannerisms. Jeffrey was looking at her now the same way Dan looked at someone he was "reading." Though Jeffrey didn't have Dan's refined and practiced skill with body language, Liz suspected there was a certain amount of natural talent there. Jeffrey was reading her, now, in his own way, to figure out what this was all about.

To figure out if he trusted her.

"Secrets are Dan's thing," Jeffrey said, with perhaps a twinge of bitterness to his tone. "I do have secrets of my own, of course. But they aren't my life, the way they are with my brother. I don't let secrets become my life. And I don't let them intrude on my family."

Liz understood the quiet statement that Jeffrey was making.

She nodded. "Ok. Then I need to tell you some things. Secrets. You'll have to agree to keep them. But if you think they're going to ... intrude on your family, like you say ... then all I ask is that you don't reveal anything I've said to anyone, after I leave."

"Will we be in any danger, if you share this with me?" Jeffrey asked.

Liz huffed. "I don't know. It's possible. But you may be in danger over this regardless, for all I know. One thing I do know for sure is that Dan is. Whatever all this adds up to, he's right at the heart of it. Powerful people are part of this. I'm trying to figure it out. To protect him."

Jeffrey glanced at the door of his study, which was still open. He walked to it, started to close it, then seemed to think better of it. "I have a little spy in my house," he said, looking at her with a slight smirk on his lips. "He's good at it, too. Better than he should be. I blame Dan for encouraging him. But maybe we'd better take a walk and talk about the rest of this?"

Liz nodded, and Jeffrey motioned her through the door, guiding her back to the front door.

"Go play in your clubhouse, Alex," Jeffrey said as they passed by a room with a slightly cracked door.

"Yessir," a young boy's voice replied, just from the other side.

Liz smiled and followed Jeffrey out to the street, then along the sidewalk until they came to the head of a walking trail.

They took the trail, moving along a tree-lined gravel path. Occasionally someone jogged by, going in the opposite direction. Beyond that, this seemed as private a place as Liz could have imagined. They eventually stopped at a clearing that overlooked a manmade lake. They found a bench under the shade of a willow and sat facing the water.

Fountains spewed upward at intervals in the middle of the lake, and ducks noisily paddled their way along the shore. It was a comforting level of white noise, masking their hushed conversation as Liz spilled everything she'd learned. She found herself confiding in Jeffrey, letting him in on everything from the research she and Dani were conducting to the help they'd gotten from DB, the mysterious phone call, even the fingerprints and DNA from the empty apartment.

More than she should have, perhaps. But talking to Jeffrey was, in a lot of ways, like talking to Dan. He was just as patient and attentive, taking in every detail, thinking it all through. Occasionally he'd interrupt with a question, but he kept this to a minimum. And in due course, Liz had unburdened herself of all of it.

She hadn't expected the feeling that would come with this. She'd been keeping all of this from Dan himself, confiding only in Dani. But Dani was an FBI agent, walking a fine line. There were things she couldn't know, to maintain plausible deniability. Just in case.

But with Jeffrey, Liz felt she could be open about all of it. She wasn't revealing state secrets or anything. But it felt good to have someone to talk to, and to bounce ideas and theories off of.

After about an hour she'd given him all the pertinent details and finally got to the big question.

"Is there any chance that maybe one of your grandparents is still alive? Or maybe you have an uncle or some other relative? Maybe someone you only thought was dead?"

Jeffrey considered this and shook his head. "I'm not going to say that I have FBI-level access to this kind of thing, but I've studied every publicly available document I can find on our family history. I can take you back multiple generations, though I don't think that would help. There just isn't anyone alive today, officially, besides me and Dan."

"What about unofficially? Anyone who maybe died under mysterious circumstances?"

Jeffrey watched her for a moment, inhaled deeply, and let it out in a slow breath. "Yes," he said. "Our parents."

Liz felt her pulse quicken.

She and Dan had talked about his parents, of course. But Dan had been unusually private about them. He'd told Liz about their deaths, on a high level. No real specifics. And he'd told her about being taken in by their father's research and business partner, Cristoff Vellar. It was Vellar, in fact, who had been a mentor and guide for Dan, inducting him into the life he now led.

"Can you tell me how they died?" Liz asked.

"I can show you," Jeffrey said. He stood from the bench and held out a hand. "Come with me."

# CHAPTER SEVENTEEN

THEY'D BEEN DRIVING for nearly two hours, and Liz had only just started to get used to the silence. Jeffrey had chatted from time to time, but he wouldn't give her much in the way of details about where they were going. "It will make more sense when you see it in person," he'd said.

In this way, Jeffrey was even more like his brother, Liz thought.

One of Dan's more irksome qualities was his tendency to withhold a reveal. Liz had at first assumed it was some sort of commitment to having all the facts or being self assured of his own hypothesis before letting people know what he was thinking. And that was true, Liz knew, as far as it went. But Dan also had a bit of a dramatic side. He could sometimes be something of a showman, using anticipation and curiosity to put an edge on an experience. He liked to make the reveal more impactful.

Liz suspected that Jeffrey had the same habit. Though Jeffrey was far more reserved than Dan, the two did share a sort of quiet mischief, just behind their eyes. A rebelliousness, Liz decided. Both men were strong willed and confident in their own perspectives. Dan was just more of a public showboat, while Jeffrey was more private and reserved.

They turned off of the highway and down a side street, then into a long drive that ended at a very large parking lot. A modern-looking building with a glass-arched roof could be seen beyond a stretch of trees and walking paths, as if a park rested between the parking lot and the main building. A well-lit sign told Liz where they were.

*Vellar-Kotler Genetic Research*

"WAIT ..." Liz started.

"The family business," Jeffrey nodded. "Dad was a geneticist. His pet project was researching the evolution of the human genome, using any viable samples that could be recovered from tombs and dig sites around the world. Mom was a Mathematician and a Physicist. She took on an advisory role with the company, aiding in some of the research. Especially the tangential stuff."

"Tangential?" Liz asked. She was feeling a little overwhelmed by all of this new information, and followed Jeffrey almost numbly as they stepped out of his car and walked through the parking lot, coming to stand at a sort of bus stop at the edge of the lot.

"Sideline research," Jeffrey said. "Related, but not always directly. I think she just wanted to do something that let her be close to our father. But I was pretty young. I barely remember either of them. I only have Cristoff's and Dan's stories to go by. And the journals."

"You have journals from your parents?" Liz asked.

"A couple," Jeffrey nodded. "I keep them here."

Liz looked toward the arch of glass in the distance. "Here? Why?"

"They contain some sensitive information, related to the company," Jeffery said. "Proprietary things that shouldn't be leaked to the public. It was safer to keep them here, as part of the exhibit."

Liz was going to ask what Jeffrey meant by "the exhibit" but stopped short as a black van with windows along each side pulled to the curb in front of them. The driver leapt out and opened the sliding door for them, and they climbed inside.

They rode to the front entrance of the Vellar-Kotler building in silence, and Liz marveled at how much she had already learned about Dan's history—things Dan had never even hinted at. Though now that she knew them, a lot of things clicked into place.

Dan and Jeffrey's parents were scientists. And not just scientists—they studied and practiced in fields that were similar if not an exact match to those Dan Kotler himself had ventured into. It said a lot about Dan's life choices. Liz already felt like she was seeing him in a new light.

The van deposited them in a half-circle drive in front of the Vellar-Kotler building, and they entered through a set of sliding glass doors. Jeffrey walked straight to the security gate, pausing long enough to chat with one of the guards on duty before depositing everything in his pockets into a bowl to pass through the X-ray machine, and then stepping through the metal detector.

Liz followed suit, and once she was on the other side of the metal detector she followed Jeffrey down a series of corridors until they came to a set of swinging doors. Jeffrey pushed through the one on the right, and held it for her as she passed through.

The space on the other side was breathtaking.

Stretching out to a distant artificial horizon, the entire space was filled with items of interest, stored in museum-level display cases and shelves. The items on display were not all that dissimilar to any modern-day museum exhibit, but Liz picked up on a fact right away ...

This was a museum dedicated to the Kotlers.

As she moved through the lanes of exhibits, with Jeffrey following slowly behind, watching her, she spotted photos and displays that featured the Kotlers and their two sons. She stopped in front of one and studied it.

Berrett and Alexandria Kotler, with a young Dan and Jeffrey.

It was easy to pick Dan out from among the two boys. Through all these years, he'd somehow managed to hold on to the impish smirk that his younger self wore. His eyes, though perhaps a bit wiser looking these days, nevertheless had the same sparkle of creativity and curiosity. His posture was still the same antsy, ready-for-movement pose he put on in meetings and anything that kept him nailed in place. This was the essence of Dan Kotler—a boy who now wore grownup clothes but still had adventures in dirt pits and caves and secret tunnels.

Of course, Dan was also a solid foot taller than his younger brother, making him that much easier to spot. And little Jeffrey was clinging to his mother's hip, a thumb in his mouth and his face barely visible from peeking out from behind his mother's skirt.

"I was shy, as a kid," the older, adult Jeffrey Kotler volunteered. "I mostly outgrew it."

Liz looked up to him and smiled lightly. "This is incredible," she said, waving to the rest of the exhibit.

"A memorial," Jeffrey said, nodding. "Kind of an ostentatious one, maybe."

Liz shook her head. "No, not at all. It feels tasteful. Just ... big."

Jeffrey nodded. "Cristoff insisted on this. It was only built about ten years ago. They've been dead for decades by this point, but Cristoff says they're still part of the DNA of this place. He even laughs when he says it. Irony, you know?"

"Irony," Liz nodded. She turned on her heels, taking in the vast space, wondering that two people could have had enough life to memorialize in a space this size, having died so young. "It's just amazing."

"The things you'll want to see are back that way," Jeffrey said, nodding in a direction. He walked away and Liz followed closely.

A few minutes later, after passing more than a few exhibits that Liz thought she'd like to investigate closer, they came to a room with freestanding walls, with glass windows darkened so they were impossible to see into. Something about it reminded Liz of Dan's apartment—polished glass and metal, a modern-looking structure standing like an obelisk among the softer, warmer artifacts of the past. A spot of cold, though still beautiful, in an otherwise warm space.

Jeffrey opened the door to the room, and Liz entered.

She shivered, though the temperature was fine. What had gotten to her was the feeling of this place. It felt dark and cold. It felt like something to dread.

In the middle of the room was a twisted wreck of torn and melted metal—what appeared to be a piece of an airplane's fuselage. Surrounding this were small exhibits, dotted throughout the space on pedestals and behind thick glass. There were also displays, video monitors looping digital footage again and again.

A plane crash site, from every conceivable angle.

News stories. Amateur video. Virtual recreations. The site was described and scrutinized and analyzed and inspected by hundreds of experts, reporters, law enforcement. It was as if someone had gone to the trouble of digging up every scrap of information about the crash, and put it all on display. Pieces to a puzzle that would never be put together to the unseen builder's satisfaction.

Liz watched some of the footage, but ultimately tore her eyes away from it all. From the news clips she recognized all the artifacts in this room. The twisted metal, the recovered items, the mounds of melted and burned objects.

This was wreckage recovered from the crash. The crash that had killed the Kotlers. The crash that had killed Dan and Jeffrey's parents.

It was horrifying.

"Why ..." she started, shaking her head. "Why would Cristoff put this on display?"

Jeffrey had stood beside her, and shook his head. "It wasn't Cristoff. This was Dan. He demanded it, making it part of the requirements. He compromised a little, allowing this small space to be built and making it a side exhibit, instead of forcing Cristoff to put this stuff out on the floor. But I think that was what he wanted all along."

"Wanted?" Liz asked. "You're telling me that Dan *wanted* this? Isn't this kind of ... I don't know. Morbid?"

Jeffrey shrugged. "To some people it would be. To Dan, and maybe to me, too, it's fine. It's ... comforting. In its way."

Liz shook her head, but didn't push it. She was thinking about all the conversations she'd ever had with Dan, about his family. About their deaths. Nothing like this had ever come up, and she wondered why. She also wondered what it was about it that bothered her most.

"Over here," Jeffrey said, waving her to where he'd taken up position by an item on display.

Liz moved closer, and saw that the item was a photo of the Kotlers seated on an aircraft. *This* aircraft? Liz hoped not. She prayed she wasn't looking at the last known photo of the two, seated in what would be their coffin.

Jeffrey raised a hand and pointed to the small placard next to the display.

Liz read.

It was a reproduction of a news story about the crash, cut from the local paper and made permanent through a laser-etching process that engraved the article into brass. It told the story of the crash, how the day had started off normal but had ended in such tragedy. It talked about the heat produced by the crashed engines, melting everything.

And then it took a turn.

AUTHORITIES HAVE YET *to confirm the cause of the crash, but a source with air traffic control claimed that the Kotlers may not have been on the plane when it went down. Black box recordings were damaged in the crash, and were only partially recovered. But in one segment the pilot states that he was incoming to retrieve passengers. The segment is badly damaged and difficult to decipher, leading investigators to dismiss it as part of the overall investigation.*

LIZ LOOKED UP TO JEFFREY, who was standing with his hands in his pockets, chin tilted to his chest. "They think your parents weren't on the plane?"

Jeffrey shrugged. "This paper did. This one, local paper. The only paper in the world to run this part of the story. Dan had it laser-etched for this placard. He has the original stored somewhere."

Liz shook her head. "He's never ... in all this time, he's never told me about this. Never even hinted at it. He seems so certain they're dead but ... does this mean they could be alive?"

"No," Jeffrey said. "Authorities found two corpses, burned beyond recognition. Teeth were wrecked. Fingerprints were gone. The only way to identify them was DNA. Vellar-Kotler ran the tests from samples they had here. They were exact matches. Our parents definitely died on that plane."

Liz turned to face him. "But Dan doesn't think so?"

Jeffrey sighed. "Dan ... has always had a hard time facing the death of our parents. Like I said, I was too young. I barely have any memory of them. But he was older. He knew them. He misses them."

"You don't?" Liz asked.

Jeffrey shrugged. "I miss the idea of them. But I had my brother. Mostly."

"What do you mean, mostly?" Liz asked.

"He was obsessed right from the start," Jeffrey said. "Determined to ... well, to get answers. Some kind of answers. Any kind."

"To the big questions," Liz said quietly. "Meaning of life. Meaning of human existence."

Jeffrey nodded. "Cristoff encouraged it. Got him into the best schools, got him the finest personal tutors. There was no shortage of money. We inherited everything from savings accounts to stock portfolios. Dan and I are fifty percent partners in Vellar-Kotler, between us. And the company makes a lot of money. So Cristoff indulged Dan in anything he needed. Dan was taught by some of the best teachers in every discipline, from all over the world."

"And he chose anthropology and quantum physics," Liz said, shaking her head.

"And psychology, survival training, hand-to-hand combat and weapons training. I know my brother can seem a little ... mild-mannered. There's a lot more going on with him than you'd think. His obsession with reading body language—that was something he started from early on. He wanted to be able to read people, to know what they were thinking. He studied with mentalists, psychologists, even marketing experts."

"He was learning everything there was to know about people," Liz said.

Jeffrey nodded. "And when he couldn't get whatever answers he was looking for in the present, he started digging into the past. I think his two PhDs were an homage to our parents. But anthropology and archaeology—I think he found something he was actually passionate about there. Something that ties in with his ... quest or whatever it is. But something that also makes him feel like his own person."

Liz was taking this all in. It explained a lot about Dan and the way he behaved. It opened windows into his personality that Liz hadn't even realized she'd been looking for. She wasn't sure how she could broach any of this with him, once he was back. She wasn't sure what, if anything, this changed about the way she saw him. But she was suddenly seeing him as far more complex than he appeared.

She looked back to Jeffrey, who was studying her with a sober expression. "You were right," Liz said. "This definitely qualifies as questionable circumstances." She thought for a moment. "Is there anything else here you think I should see?" She asked.

Jeffrey nodded and guided her out of the little room, leading her now to a door in the far wall of the facility. This one had a sign that read "Records, Restricted Access."

Jeffrey punched a code into a panel beside the door and it clicked open. He held it for her, allowing her to enter first, and then closed the door behind them.

Within this room were shelves and cabinets filled with documents, record books, and journals. "I come here sometimes, to comb through this stuff. My hobby ... sometimes it forces me to look."

Liz glanced up at him, and saw that Jeffrey was looking at one of the glass cabinets containing a set of journals and letters. His expression was neutral, but his eyes seemed unfocused, locked on something that perhaps wasn't even in this room. A memory, perhaps.

She followed his gaze to the case, looking at the organized stack. There were half a dozen journals with weathered covers and aged paper edges. They were held upright by bookends, and Liz could see labels on each spine, like those that would appear on library books.

She was about to turn away when she froze, then leaned in closer, studying.

"What is it?" Jeffrey asked.

Liz looked up at him. "Does anyone else ever have access to this vault?"

Jeffrey thought for a moment. "I can't be sure. Cristoff and I both have codes for the room. There would likely be more people here, of course. But these cases are locked with fingerprint scanners." He nodded to the small plate on the front of the cabinet. "Me, Dan, Cristoff ... as far as I know, we're the only ones with access."

Liz studied the case's contents again. "I think I need to talk to Cristoff," she said.

She looked up at Jeffrey, who nodded.

"I think that can be arranged."

# CHAPTER EIGHTEEN

AGENT DANI BROWN was tired of babysitting duty.

It was important, she knew. These were the families and close acquaintances of the abducted Congresspeople. They were in danger. They needed protection.

But it made Dani feel like a bandaid on a gunshot wound.

She needed to be out there, helping with the investigation, tracking down whoever was behind this and helping to bring the Congresspeople safely home. Instead she was stuck playing nursemaid to a group of uncomfortable, scared people who were becoming increasingly vocal about being unhappy.

It was petty of her to complain, she knew. Dani, of all people, was aware that duties such as these were every bit as important as storming the castle, gun leveled on the bad guys. And knowing that, she sucked it up. She smiled. She asked if her charges needed things—food, magazines, DVDs. She was sympathetic when they started to grouse and complain.

She was a good den mother, never losing patience because ultimately she knew that these people were victims. They were afraid and worried. Their loved ones were God knew where, suffering God knew what. And Dani would be damned if she'd add to their misery when any day now the news might come that the people they loved were dead.

Thankfully, at the end of the day, after her third day on duty, Dani was relieved by another agent. She left the safe house feeling weary and spent, and very much looking forward to sleeping in her own bed. Better yet, using her own shower.

She drove away from the safe house, taking a circuitous route before pulling into a parking garage more than twenty miles away—a precaution, to prevent anyone from being able to retrace her steps. Once parked, she walked from the garage to a shopping center nearby, and from there took a cab home. Another agent would retrieve the car later, driving it back to the pool. If her turn for watch duty came up again, she'd get a whole new route to take.

That was something to think about later, however. For now, it was home, shower, bed, with little else making even the top five of her concerns.

As the cab arrived on her block, Dani's apartment building took on the aura of the most inviting place she could think of. The cab deposited her on the sidewalk a couple of doors down from her own, and it was all she could do to keep from sprinting to her door.

She'd been away for days, sleeping in a spare room at the safe house, taking meals with the people she was guarding. Things had stayed more or less pleasant, but there was a rising tension, and it was taking its toll on her. These people wanted answers, and she had none to give.

She wanted answers herself.

Liz had been in sparse contact since the night they'd scoured that apartment for evidence. Part of that, Dani knew, was for Dani's protection. The less she knew about anything happening in a "grey area," the less she'd have to answer for.

But it was also possible—even likely—that Liz simply hadn't found anything.

Dani knew that things like this could take a bit to yield anything actionable. DB—whoever he was—had so far steered them to things they could use, so there was no reason to think he'd change his MO now. It was this mysterious voice on the other end of the phone that had Dani worried.

It felt suddenly as if she and Liz were being fed clues in some kind of scavenger hunt. The end result of which, Dani thought, might not be where the two of them intended to end up. The whole thing made her sweat.

And then there was the most disturbing revelation: Suddenly Historic Crimes, and even Kotler himself, were tied in with this abduction?

Liz hadn't made much of a deal about this, but it had been bugging Dani for days. What was the glue that made all this stick together? What did Historic Crimes have in common with whoever was behind the abductions? And whoever that turned out to be, what was the agenda? How did Historic Crimes play into it? How did Kotler, himself, figure into all of this?

Too many questions.

But right now she was too tired, and wanted a shower and then her bed too much to think about the implications of any of this. She'd have to trust that Liz was working all the right angles, and that when it was time she'd bring Dani in.

She unlocked her front door and flipped on the light in her apartment as she entered. The place looked the same as when she'd left it several days ago—a quick change of clothes still draped over the back of one of the chairs in front of her break-fast table, a dirty dish still on the table itself, a half-consumed glass of orange juice. She picked up the dishes and rinsed them in the sink, leaving them there to soak until later.

She turned then, intent on going straight to her shower, and froze.

Dani wasn't all that concerned about decor. She tended to keep things functional and utilitarian. Easily replaced, if needed. It made little sense to her to have more than a couple of chairs or one or two plates or bowls or sets of silverware when she rarely had visitors. And likewise, she would typically have eschewed owning a desk, considering she had a perfectly good breakfast table.

But the desk against the wall to her bedroom had been a gift. One of the few gifts she'd ever received from her estranged father. In fact, thinking back on it, she realized that in 38 years this was the *only* gift he'd ever given her. And though she wasn't fond of the man himself, the desk was very nice. Oak, with mahogany inlays. Not overly large, but enough room to spread out papers and a laptop. Lockable drawers. No hutch, and it was dressed and crafted on all sides, so it could sit against a wall or a window, or even out in the middle of the floor. It was the nicest piece of furniture Dani owned.

The thing was, though she did use it routinely, she never left anything on it. She made a point of clearing it, locking away anything she might be working on when she wasn't around. It was a habit left over from college and Quantico, and her early FBI days when she still needed a roommate to get by.

Putting everything away was an extra security precaution, in case someone broke in, or in case the landlord or a maintenance person stopped by. Too much of Dani's work was extremely sensitive, and she had to do all she could to keep it from prying eyes.

Which was why she was surprised to see an open and unlocked laptop on the desk's surface.

It was her laptop. That much she could verify. The little barcode sticker with the FBI seal was visible at the bottom-left of the screen. She knew the number sequence by heart. This was her FBI-issued computer. She had left it here, days ago, locked away in the desk. She was absolutely certain of that.

And even if she had somehow—unlikely but possible—forgotten to lock it away, in her rush to leave, there was no way it would still be unlocked. It was set to lock itself after only a couple of minutes of idle time. On that point there was no debate. Which meant only one thing.

Someone had been here.

Someone had not only unlocked her desk and found the laptop, they had also cracked the password. Someone had left it sitting there, screen active, waiting for her to find it.

She slowly pulled her weapon from its side holster. There was nowhere for someone to hide here in the living room, and she had already been in the kitchen, but she now entered the bedroom, weapon first, slowly sweeping the room. Eventually she ended up in the bathroom, pulling back the shower curtain, checking the linen closet.

Nothing.

Whoever had been here was long gone, it seemed.

She went back to the living room, holstered her weapon, and leaned with a hand on the desk, inspecting the laptop.

On the unlocked screen was an email with some photos attached.

In the *To* field was her official FBI email address. The *From* field, however, was a garbled string of characters that made no sense as an email address. The *Subject* line was straight forward and clear enough, though:

*I've found the missing Senators*

DANI SCANNED DOWN THE EMAIL, reading from what appeared to be an anonymous eyewitness tip, detailing the sighting of two black SUVs with darkened windows, driven by "military-looking people." The tipster went on to describe nearly turn by turn where the SUVs had taken their cargo, and then included haphazardly taken photos of hooded figures being hurried into a facility.

The email ended with a map—inserted from one of the online map services. A pin indicated what Dani assumed was the location from the photos.

Her new informant had given her everything, straight down to the physical coordinates and an address. And though it was impossible to know if the hooded figures were, in fact, the missing congresspeople, there was no denying that this tip would have to be followed up with an investigation.

Dani's phone buzzed, and she took it from her pocket to look at the text.

The number was blocked, but the message was clear.

*DB*

NOTHING ELSE WAS NEEDED. Dani knew exactly who this was from, and what they intended. She also knew that the information would turn out to be legit. And she would absolutely forward it to the people who mattered.

What she couldn't shake was the feeling that she was being manipulated, and that rankled her. She felt she had no choice but to play out the plan they'd forced on her.

But maybe she could take back a little control.

She looked up through her bedroom door, at the shower she

had hoped would be the end of her day. She could feel the longing for it in her bones, an ache deep inside, and an even deeper regret as she pulled on her blazer, checked that her weapon was secure and that her badge was in her pocket. She bent over her laptop to forward the email, just as she was meant to do, and made sure it arrived on her phone as well.

Then she locked the laptop away in the desk and left her apartment, on her way to her car.

If she was going to be forced into someone else's game, she intended to be a wildcard.

SOMETHING WAS HAPPENING.

Acosta noticed tensions rising in the room. She moved closer to the cluster of people who were whispering among themselves.

"It's too dangerous," one of the Senators said.

"So is just sitting here," someone replied.

Acosta peered around the group and saw that the person speaking was Cameron. He spotted her, and Acosta thought she saw something flicker over his expression. Something she couldn't quite recognize.

"I've seen through the door, when they opened it to bring in fresh supplies," Cameron said. "There are only two guards. One in the hall, the other bringing things in. We can overpower them."

"*Trained* guards," a Republican Senator said, scoffing. "Armed. Military types. You're going to get us all killed, son."

Cameron sneered at him. "We have no way of knowing what these people want, and it's pretty safe to assume they'll eventually kill us anyway. Or use us to hurt others. Remember 9/11? How many lives could have been saved, if everyone on the other planes knew they could fight back, the way the passengers did on Flight 93? We've been taught to just do what the terrorists say, to be compliant and not make trouble, and hope someone will rescue us. But that doesn't guarantee survival, and right now I'm thinking our chances go up if we fight back."

The group got quiet.

Acosta looked around the room, taking note of those who were clustered here around Cameron and those who were huddled against the wall. She looked back to Cameron, whose eyes flicked from the group to her in that brief instant. And suddenly, it was as if a light switched on in her brain.

Those who were against the wall, huddled in on themselves —they were the least effective Senators. They were those who were always on the fence, or always making excuses or trying to play both sides.

The Senators gathered around Cameron, as well as the members of her own team, were all known for taking action. Most of the Senators standing here disagreed with Acosta's Socialist plans, but they were also outspoken about what they did believe and what they wanted to achieve.

What they needed now was something to rally to.

Or someone.

"We should do it," she said from behind them.

The group all turned at once, looking at her with various expressions. Some seemed sour, disdainful, or skeptical. Some seemed curious. Cameron looked at her as if measuring her up, even as he took a small step backward.

"I haven't been in the Senate long," Acosta said, moving forward into the circle. "But I've learned one thing, since being here. The people who make the biggest and best changes are those who take risks and take action."

She looked at each of them. She remembered Cameron's

coaching, telling her that it pays, sometimes, to pause and be quiet, to look people in the eye, to let silence talk for her.

It was all about timing. If she waited too long, one of these people—probably one of the white, male Republicans—would speak up, would take control. They'd speak with authority, even if they didn't know what to do. She had to time this right.

Before anyone got to the point of breaking the silence, before they could assert their authority or take control of the conversation, Acosta asked, "If you knew for sure that these men were going to kill us all, that they were going to use us to manipulate the world and do real harm, wouldn't you act?"

*The person asking questions is in charge.*

Cameron had drilled it into her. They had practiced at length, again and again, in endless mock debates. She was getting better, but she usually tried to ask questions and flubbed it. After every failure, she'd be right back in the chair, going through another practice session, listening to feedback and starting again. And again. And again.

She'd started to wonder if she could ever get it right.

This time, she nailed it. She could feel it. She could see it in their faces.

In Cameron's face. He was watching her, from just outside of the circle, a small smile, tight and barely visible on his lips.

"We should fight back," Acosta continued, emboldened. "Fight to escape. If we die, we die on our own terms. But we have to do everything we can to keep these people from using us to cause harm out there," she waved toward a vague horizon. Everyone in the room followed her gesture ... which led them to look at the Senators who were huddled, afraid, on the floor.

It did exactly what Acosta hoped it would do.

It put steel in the backbones of these Senators standing in front of her. But it also gave them an example to look at. They saw what being afraid looked like. They saw what doing nothing looked like.

And as they looked back at Acosta—a young, Latino *girl* in most of their eyes—they saw what courage and bravery looked like. She held firm, kept her expression serious, kept her body rigid.

"Ok," one of the Republicans said. "I'm in."

The others, one by one, agreed. And a plan was made. Positions were taken. People readied themselves as best they could.

Cameron stepped in next to her, their eyes never meeting. "That was brilliant," he said.

"I had good teachers," Acosta replied.

"Well, let's hope this doesn't turn out to be a final exam," Cameron replied, and the two of them took up positions near the door, waiting for whatever came next.

# CHAPTER NINETEEN

KOTLER WAS RUDELY ROUSTED from his bed, woken from what was already a rough and troubled sleep, forced to his feet and then shoved ahead of a cluster of armed men. His hands were cuffed, and his head was covered in a hood that did not entirely block his vision, but did make it more challenging to see anywhere but straight down to his feet.

He was led from his room down a series of corridors until finally being pushed into the back seat of a vehicle. Armed guards climbed in on either side of him, and they all rode in silence for a long, indeterminate amount of time.

It was a rough way to start the day.

Though Kotler really had no idea of the time. Since opening his eyes in this place, he'd more or less been in a daze, pain killers dripping into his bloodstream. He'd slept, though he hadn't necessarily rested. Worry over Denzel, over Liz and his family, nagged at him. He dreamt of vile things.

The upside of being so abruptly yanked out of bed was that his adrenaline had kicked in, helping to burn away the lingering sedative in his bloodstream. He hoped it would be enough to clear the cobwebs and get him thinking at full tilt again. He was going to need every bit of his wits about him.

When the vehicle stopped, Kotler was pulled out of his seat and again roughly guided through a series of twists and turns and a number of doors, all barely perceived through the hood over his head. He limped along as best he could, sometimes assisted by his guards, who were less than gentle about it. His injuries were on the mend, but he was not yet anywhere near 100%, and as the sedative and pain killers were burned from his bloodstream, the aches and pains returned in force.

Eventually, he was led through a door and into a room, then pushed down into a hard-seated chair. The bag was ripped from his head, and a set of very bright lights snapped on. It may have been his imagination, but he thought he felt the light bounce from the inside of his skull, adding to the pressure of a growing headache that had started to take hold.

He blinked into the bright lights, which blinded him to everything else in the darkened room.

All of this felt a little too familiar.

He'd been in this situation before. More times than he cared to count. And though he'd so far managed to survive, these sessions were never fun. They invariably led to a lot of physical discomfort. Sometimes flat-out torture.

More adrenaline pumped into his bloodstream. He welcomed it but focused on staying calm and maintaining self-control. He needed the boost, but, even more, he needed to be clear-headed.

"Daniel Kotler," a familiar voice said.

Despite the familiarity, Kotler couldn't quite put a finger on who it might be. It wasn't Scope. This person sounded older.

A male figure stepped forward, silhouetted against the

array of lights, and Kotler brought his bound hands up to try to shade his eyes, to see who he was talking to. "Do I know you?"

"You do," the man said. "You did. But it's been a while, and I wouldn't expect you to remember me. For now, we'll forego introductions if you don't mind."

"If you insist," Kotler said. He was trying to appear unconcerned and unworried. But the bravado was half-hearted, and there was simply nothing at all behind it. Here, blinded by the lights, every inch of his body aching, his insides feeling like the results of a "will it blend" video, he wasn't feeling particularly brave.

"I've avoided bringing you into this," the man said. "You'll have some trouble believing that. But you ... well, you sort of insist on being in the middle of this kind of thing, don't you?"

"I'm sorry," Kotler said. "I don't remember getting an invitation to have my plane yanked out of the sky. I'm pretty sure I would have turned that down."

"That was a foolish plan," the man agreed. "The person responsible is new, and hasn't been appropriately ... vetted. I know you'll have a hard time believing this, but I was relieved to learn you survived."

Kotler shook his head. "Who the hell are you?" he asked.

Kotler couldn't see the man, but he could make out his shape in silhouette. Most of the signals Kotler would use to read someone were masked by that bright light, but he could see the man's posture, his hand positions, the tilt of his head. The man paused, just an instant, hesitant about how to answer the question.

He was hiding something.

Which, Kotler knew, was sort of a given, considering the circumstances. But this went beyond the cloak and dagger melodrama. There was something else this man was trying to keep to himself. A secret he didn't want anyone in the room—not just Kotler, but anyone else nearby—to know.

"Give me the room," the man said, turning his head from side to side. After a moment of silence, he spoke again, his voice hard. "Leave."

There was the sound of feet shuffling and stepping, a door opening and closing, and then silence.

The man walked away from the light, past Kotler. In a moment, the spotlights shut off and the overhead lights snapped on.

Kotler's eyes were already accustomed to a much brighter light source, and so the shift didn't cause him to blink. But it was almost a shock to his system to see the room emerge in full detail. He looked around, taking things in.

The room was bare except for the stand of lights. No windows, no furniture in sight, beyond the chair Kotler was seated in. It was just an empty, cinder-block space. The kind of room where someone could scream in agony for hours and never be heard.

The man walked back to his previous position, by the rack of lights. He stood in front of Kotler again.

Again Kotler felt a sense of familiarity. This time it hit him with a tiny shock of recognition. Kotler had a tingling sense that he knew this man, but couldn't place him.

The man was older, certainly. Maybe in his late eighties to mid-nineties, judging from his thinning hair, the wrinkles and the pallor of his skin. There were liver spots on his hands, and threads of blue veins in his neck and at his temples.

Despite his apparent age, however, the man seemed vibrant, almost youthful. His energy was full. His movements were unhindered. Kotler might have pegged him as being half his apparent age, based on the way his body moved.

"Daniel," the man said, his voice wry, almost gentle, but

still with that edge of warning. It had a hardness that told Kotler that familiarity would not soften his resolve.

And something else was obvious.

The tilt of the man's head, the set of his jaw, his hands in his pockets and his eyes slightly soft. The way his shoulders relaxed, and the way his eyes and his expression softened, just slightly.

This man knew Kotler. And more.

"I know you," Kotler said.

"You used to," the man replied, nodding. "Decades ago. Before."

"Before ..." Kotler started.

The word triggered something within him. It released whatever dam was holding back his memory, and the past flooded in on him in a deluge, washing over him and carrying him to places he had not visited, memories he had not wanted to think about for years. Decades.

"Before they died," Kotler said.

The man nodded.

"You're ... you're my grandfather."

The man inhaled, deeper than Kotler would have thought possible for someone his age. No wheezing. No coughing. No signs that he was as old as his appearance made him seem, or as old as Kotler knew he had to be.

His grandfather would have been 94 years old.

This was impossible.

The man nodded and glanced around. He spotted whatever he was after back in a corner of the room, and walked past Kotler again. There was a brief scraping sound, and the man reappeared holding a metal stool. He placed this on the floor in front of Kotler and leaned to sit on its edge, his hands coming out of his pockets and folding over each other in his lap. "It's been a long time, Daniel."

Kotler nodded. "Yes," he said. "Since, I don't know ... about a month before you died?"

The man chuckled. "Yes. About that ..." the man hesitated, whatever words he might have said lingered behind his lips. Secrets weren't something this man was used to revealing.

"Surprise?" Kotler interjected.

Again the man laughed lightly. "Something like that. I know you have a lot of questions. And you know that I'm not likely to answer any of them."

"Because you're a Knight of Jani," Kotler said. "And a Novensile."

"Maybe more Novensile than Jani, at this point."

"Funny," Kotler said, though nothing about his tone indicated that he found any of this to be funny.

"Daniel, I know you're feeling angry right now ..."

"No," Kotler said flatly.

The man paused, looking at him with surprise. "No?"

"No, I'm not feeling angry. I'm feeling contempt."

Another pause and the man nodded. "Alright then," he said. "Contempt is good. People who have contempt for someone tend to keep their minds focused. And that's what I need right now."

Kotler said nothing to this. He didn't need to. He knew exactly why he was here—if not the specifics then at least the gist of it. He was reeling from discovering that he had more living family than he'd expected, that his long-dead grandfather was somehow still alive and kicking. But he knew what was coming. If his grandfather was one of the Novensiles, then there was really only one thing he'd be after.

"So," Kotler said, "you're looking for another vault."

For once Kotler saw a flash of surprise register on the man's face, but it faded quickly, hidden by a practiced mask of composure. "Of course you'd know that," he said. "You've been through this before."

"First time at the hands of my dead grandfather, though," Kotler replied. He paused, thinking, pulling up details he never thought he'd have to recall. "Richard," he said. "Richard Kotler."

The man had a strange reaction to the sound of his name. He glanced at the door that stood just out of Kotler's field of view. Richard straightened and stiffened, just a bit, and his hands shifted just slightly, tightening, hiding.

"Around here they call me the Chairman," the man replied.

"Call signs and code names," Kotler said. "I wonder what they would have called me?"

"If you had already accepted their invitation?" Richard asked. "To join the Jani?"

"Was that your doing?" Kotler asked.

The man pursed his lips and shook his head. "No. That was someone else. And it was a move against me. Or maybe a move to flush me out."

Kotler thought about this. "You didn't know?"

Richard studied him for a moment, then shook his head.

"Manipulation," Kotler said, sighing. "I guess I shouldn't be surprised. Though I have to tell you, part of me really liked Granger. I'm a little sad to hear he's been using me all this time. There's something just a little flattering about being asked to join an ancient, secret order."

Richard chuckled again. "Well, if it makes you feel any better, Granger was likely just following orders from someone else. There are layers upon layers in this thing."

"So I'm gathering," Kotler said. He thought for a moment and held up his hands, which were still shackled. "No need for these," he said.

"No?" Richard asked.

"Grandfather," Kotler said, giving him a look. "What

exactly am I going to do? You have my friend. Your people have made it clear they have no problem with going after the people I care about. I don't know where I am, I have no weapons, and I'm still groggy from the drugs. Plus ... well, we are family, aren't we?"

Richard nodded, seemingly impressed by Kotler's self-aware perspective. He fished in his pocket and produced a key, then unlocked the cuffs.

Kotler rubbed his wrists as Richard sat back on the stool. "Ok," Kotler said. "That's a start. So tell me, does anyone here know who we are to each other?"

Richard shook his head. "No. And it would be best for you and for those you care about if you don't mention it."

"Is that a threat?" Kotler asked.

"Not from me," Richard replied. "But there are reasons to be cautious and concerned. There's been a split in the Novensiles. A new faction has emerged. Which means the number of enemies I have has effectively doubled. Someone within the Jani suspects that I am a Novensile, and so they invited you to join to give them leverage against me. Someone in the Novensiles wants to use the Order to further his rise to power, and he would gladly use my family—and anyone my family cares about—against me. You can see how dangerous this is."

"Yeah," Kotler replied, his tone bitter. "Thanks for that."

"Legacies always face the most terrific challenges, in this Order," Richard replied. His tone was bitter, even a touch ironic, and Kotler studied him closer, looking for any hint of what secrets were buried within the man.

It was a deep well. Though Richard's body language wasn't exactly an open book, Kotler could see that the man carried a great deal of grief, pain, and responsibility.

Secrets were heavy things. Their weight multiplied exponentially as their number increased.

"Ok," Kotler said, pushing against his knees and managing to stand, though a bit wobbly at first. He straightened, gained some control, felt his strength seeping back into his muscles.

Richard was watching him, almost wary but not quite. More curious.

"Let's go find this vault and get it over with," Kotler said. "Lead the way, Mr. Chairman."

# CHAPTER TWENTY

CRISTOFF VELLAR's office occupied nearly an entire floor of the Vellar-Kotler facility. Windows comprised walls on three out of four sides of the space, with the only solid wall providing a means of separating Vellar's workspace from the waiting area, where his secretary stood guard against anyone barging in unannounced.

To Liz's surprise, Vellar's office was only one floor up from the main level, with the rest of the facility's operations housed in the floors above him. She was sure that Dan would have some sort of observation about what the design and position of this space meant, psychologically. She wasn't certain, herself, but she thought it might be meant to show his employees that he didn't consider himself above them. That he thought of himself as being down in the trenches with them. And the wrap-around windows could be his way of keeping sight of the world, as well as the business he controlled. A way to see in all directions, psychologically speaking.

Or maybe he was just afraid of heights and liked the view. This wasn't really her field of expertise.

When they entered Vellar's office proper, off of the reception area, the man himself stood from behind a large, oaken desk, and immediately moved to Jeffrey. He opened his arms, and the two embraced in a wooden, stiff sort of greeting. Jeffrey seemed the most uncomfortable, though Vellar did seem guarded. Liz didn't know much about the man, beyond the fact that he'd taken in both Kotler boys when their parents died. But Dan had shared that the relationship between Vellar and Jeffrey had always been a bit strained, while Dan and Vellar had bonded.

"You never come up," Vellar said, smiling down, his hands on Jeffrey's shoulders. "I got the alert that you were here, but it's a pleasant surprise that you came up to see me."

Jeffrey nodded, and as the two of them stepped apart, he motioned to Liz. "This is Dr. Liz Ludlum," he introduced her. "She works with the FBI."

"The FBI," Vellar said, turning to her. His smile remained, and he reached out a hand.

Liz took it, returning the smile. "I'm here on unofficial business," she said.

Vellar nodded. "You work with Dan," he said.

She found she wasn't entirely sure how best to respond, and ultimately decided on the full truth. "I do, but we're also seeing each other," she said.

Vellar's face lit up at this. He moved his other hand to enclose hers. "Wonderful," he said. "I knew he'd met someone, but he hasn't really shared any details." He glanced at Jeffrey, then back to Liz. "Dan has had ... difficulties lately. In relationships."

She knew exactly how difficult things had been for Dan Kotler when it came to the women in his life. But she suddenly wondered how much Vellar knew. She decided it was best to keep everything surface level. Some of Kotler's life was more or less classified. Even she didn't know everything. It was better if conversations like this stuck to the basics.

"So," Vellar said, ushering them to a seating area ringed with a circular, plush white sofa. "Is there something I can do to help with your 'unofficial business,' Dr. Ludlum?"

"Please, call me Liz," she said, smiling. She took a seat, and Jeffrey sat next to her. Vellar sat across from the two of them. A large, round coffee table dotted the center of the seating area, and it was decorated with small succulents and artfully arranged magazines. The issues were current, but there was no sign they'd been read. Liz wondered if maybe they were meant simply to provide some ever-evolving color and texture to the seating area. Some warmth to contrast the stark white of the sofa, maybe.

"Liz," Vellar smiled, nodding and accepting her offer of informality.

"We were just in the memorial, downstairs," Liz said. "It's very nice."

Vellar nodded again. "Berrett and Alexandria were my closest friends. And my only family. I wanted to do something to commemorate not only how I felt about them but their contributions to this company, and to the world."

Liz took this in. It was such a grand thing to say. A larger than life sort of idea. And the purview of the very rich, of course. She couldn't imagine anyone from her family managing to pull together a museum-level memorial. Her grandfather— the doctor, and the patron of the family—had a bit of a shrine in the community center where Liz had grown up. And, of course, Liz carried his old, beaten up medical bag.

In a sense, she supposed, this was the equivalent of the Kotler memorial, in its small way.

The grandness and attention to detail, however, seemed appropriate when considering Vellar himself.

The decor of his office showed that he had a love for fine things. Art, furnishings, the books on his shelves and the adornments on his desktop—it all spoke to a love of quality and exquisite beauty. Vellar had invested a lot of money and attention to detail into the space in which he spent his time, that was clear.

Liz was also surprised at how *familiar* it all seemed.

It took a moment to realize why.

This place reminded her of Dan's apartment.

It was missing the artifacts and the hints of history, the notes of Dan's archaeological work, the well-thumbed reference materials and photos of Dan in exotic locations and ancient dig sites. It was also missing the immense espresso machine, of course.

But in other ways, Liz could see that there was a definite echo of this place in Dan's apartment. It was a sort of starkness coupled with extravagance. A stoic expression of modernist wealth, with just enough warmth to show that the occupant wasn't without a soul. It hinted at mental discipline.

It revealed a lot about Dan, in light of the other revelations Liz had already uncovered. Vellar, clearly, was a very strong third influence on who Dan was. His parents had gifted Dan with the same passion and love of history and science that they'd embraced. Vellar had gifted him with the discipline and drive to pursue those passions and turn them into a lifelong mission.

That line of thought brought her back to her own mission, and reason for being here.

"I was wondering," Liz said, "does anyone beyond you, Dan, and Jeffrey have access to the glass cases? The ones with the Kotlers' journals and papers?"

Vellar studied her. "No, not really. I suppose the security service might be able to access it, but I doubt it. When those

cases were put in place, and the security systems were acti-
vated, it was only the three of us who were allowed to have
access. It's controlled by biometric security."

"I saw that," Liz nodded, smiling. "So is there any other
collection of papers for the Kotlers?"

"Other collections?" Vellar asked.

"Journals," Liz shrugged. She paused, watching him, then
said, "Letters?"

Once again she wished she had Kotler's skill at reading
body language, but you didn't date Dan Kotler without picking
up a trick here and there.

Vellar hesitated, just a quick beat, before answering. "No,
everything that we kept from the Kotlers' estate is in that room.
That collection of documents is the total of everything we've
ever had. If there are other letters out there, I've never known
about them."

Liz nodded again, smiled again, shrugged again. "That's
what I figured. I've been looking into something recently, and
there was a bit of evidence that ... well, that led me here,
honestly."

"Evidence?" Vellar asked, surprised. "Is this something
criminal?"

Liz shook her head. "Not at all. At least, I don't *think* so."
She glanced around as if verifying they were alone and leaned
in slightly. "I'm looking into something tied to where I work."

Vellar took this in. "The FBI?" he asked.

She shook her head. "No. I mean, yes, but no. Not the FBI
itself. Just the division I'm working with. Historic Crimes."

She watched again. And again, there was that trace.

Vellar knew.

She looked at Jeffrey, who was watching both of them with
a sort of quiet curiosity. And when she looked back to Vellar,
she asked, "Why did you bring me here?"

Vellar studied her, and he too looked to Jeffrey before looking back at her. He sighed and chuckled. "What a relief."

"Relief?" Jeffrey asked. He looked slightly confused by all of this.

Liz said, "Vellar planted a piece of an envelope at a scene, where he knew I would find it. It has your father's DNA on it."

"My father?" Jeffrey asked. He looked at Vellar, perplexed. "Cristoff, what's going on?"

Vellar stood and moved to a cabinet beyond the seating area. He swung a rolling door up and open, revealing a well-stocked wet bar. He poured three drinks, without bothering to ask any of them what they wanted, and handed over the glasses before taking a seat across from them.

Liz immediately sipped from hers—a strong whiskey. She knew what kind of conversation this was going to be, then. The drinks would be necessary.

"I'm sorry, Jeffrey," Vellar said. "This was the only way."

"The only way to what?" Jeffrey asked.

"The only way to lure you and Liz here," he motioned, indicating his office. "To this place. To the only safe place. So we could talk openly."

Jeffrey shook his head and exchanged glances with Liz, who was watching him closely.

"Dan is in trouble," Vellar said. "But the forces at work here," he shook his head, took a long pull from his glass, and then topped it off again before placing the bottle back in the bar. "I needed to be sure."

"Sure of what?" Liz asked.

He looked at her. All of the joviality, the smiles, the relaxed nature he'd presented when they'd entered the room—it all faded. "I needed to be sure that you were who you seemed to be. That you really did have Dan's best interests at heart. There are enough people trying to use him, and I needed to know you were an ally and not an enemy."

"Cristoff," Jeffrey said, angry for the first time. He was always so stoic that it was a shock to see such open and raw emotion on his face. "What the hell is happening?"

"Dan is in trouble," Vellar said again, raising his glass. "There is a group—an organization that wants to use him to do something ... vile. Something so vile. They already have their claws into this place," he motioned to the ceiling, indicating the building, the company. Vellar-Kotler Genetic Research. "My every move is monitored. But I do have my means. And when I discovered that Liz was looking into the origins of Historic Crimes, it gave me a way to ... influence things."

"So it was you?" Liz asked. "You sent the messages? The phone? And DB? who is he?"

Vellar smiled, laughed lightly. "Actually, he's my butler. The initials, 'DB,' are a reference to DB Cooper."

Liz's eyes opened wide with surprise. "Your ... your butler is DB Cooper?"

Vellar laughed, shaking his head. "No. At least, I don't *think* so ..." he seemed to ponder this for a moment but laughed again. "No. He chose the name. He thought it would make him sound more mysterious."

"But he was working for you the whole time?" Liz asked.

Vellar nodded. "He was. He is. It was the only way I could manage this. I have a great deal of access to information, Dr. Ludlum. But I can't always put it to use without alerting certain factions." He looked at Jeffrey, sighed, and then said, "One of whom is your grandfather, Jeffrey."

"My ..." Jeffrey started, then shook his head. "My grandfather?"

"Richard Kotler," Vellar said. "He is alive. And well, actually. Very well, thanks to our work here."

"What does that mean?" Jeffrey asked.

Vellar shook his head. "He's been using a particular line of research here to treat himself, to keep himself vital, even at age 94."

"What kind of research?" Liz asked.

"The very illegal kind," Vellar replied, taking another drink. He let out a breath. "The kind that serves as the real, underlying purpose of this company, despite how it all started. Richard and his people have been manipulating things behind the scenes here since the day we started operations. Or, I should say, since the day I partnered with your father, Jeffrey."

Jeffrey sank back, and for the first time, he sipped from his own whiskey. "I feel like I'm getting too much information, and yet I still have no idea what's going on."

"I'm with Jeffrey," Liz said. She squared off with Vellar, her eyes hardened. "I think you'd better start from the beginning."

Vellar nodded, placed his drink on the table between them, then rose from the sofa. "Just know," he said, "once the box is open, neither of you will be able to put the evils of the world back in."

# CHAPTER TWENTY-ONE

KOTLER APPRECIATED that he was allowed to simply follow Richard—the Chairman, his *grandfather*—from the interrogation room to their destination. No cuffs. No hood. The guards were still there, lingering just behind them, ready to pounce if he tried anything.

He wouldn't be trying anything.

For one, despite feeling much better and much more alert, he was still limping along at what he figured to be around 80 percent of normal. He ached all over, he felt mildly dehydrated, and he could certainly tell that the pain meds were wearing off. He had refused the offer of anything more than Tylenol, however. He figured he would need his mind sharp. It was the last and only resource he had available to him.

He was still staggering from the revelation that his grandfather was alive.

And more—that he was one of the Jani. And a Novensile.

The hits just kept coming.

Kotler had only learned about the Order within the past

couple of years, but it had become an overwhelming influence on his life in that short time. And now he had some hint as to why: He was a legacy.

He wasn't clear on what that meant, in the grander scheme. But it explained a few question marks that had arisen since being contacted by Granger, back in that hotel in Denver, and the constant intrusion of the Jani and the Novensiles into his life ever since.

It was a lot of revelations and considerations for a brain still burning off sedatives. Kotler was just taking it all in stride, accepting the impossible as his new reality. Sort of the reverse of being in denial, though not quite full-on acceptance.

Richard led him to an elevator that took the two of them and their guards to a lower level. Kotler had no idea how far down they were. He had no idea what part of the world he was in, frankly. This facility could be literally anywhere on the planet, at this point. Maybe even off the planet, for all he knew.

Once he'd lost consciousness, all bets were off.

When the elevator doors opened, he was led out into a short corridor that terminated at an airlock.

"Decontamination," Richard said to him. "We'll go through one at a time."

One of the guards went first, followed by Richard. Kolter followed once he'd been given the all-clear. The remaining guard nudged him forward with force when he hesitated at the airlock door.

As the door *shooshed* closed behind him, the chamber Kotler stood in was filled with a clouded mist that made him cough and mildly irritated his eyes and nose. His skin felt tingly, even clean, as if he'd been swabbed with alcohol from head to toe. The set of clothes that the guards had given him, back in the makeshift hospital room, now clung to him as if the environment had gone humid.

Once on the other side of the airlock, however, the feeling of humidity quickly evaporated. Whatever the substance was, the climate control and low humidity of this interior space dried it fast, which immediately dropped the surface temperature of Kotler's skin, even under his clothes. It was like feeling a sudden chill—a little too close to the feeling one got when "someone just walked over your grave."

Kotler shivered.

When the second of the guards was through decontamination, they all proceeded deeper into the cleanroom, finally stopping before a long, metal table that rose to Kotler's waist.

Supported on the table, under the glare of examination lights hanging from an overhead array, was a stone sarcophagus. As he looked, Kotler saw that it was inscribed with hundreds of characters from languages Kotler recognized. And a few he didn't.

He glanced at Richard, who nodded his assent.

Kotler stepped forward to inspect the sarcophagus closer. He ran his fingers over the reliefs, inspecting them, gauging their age by any signs of tooling he could find.

"There must be a dozen ancient languages here," Kotler said.

"Forty," Richard agreed. "Our best count. The experts who would know for certain ... well, let's just say they're loyalists."

"Loyal to the Jani?" Kotler asked, looking back over his shoulder.

Richard nodded. "And as such, as you can imagine, they aren't willing to aid us in opening it."

Kotler straightened. "Open it? What's inside?"

"A treasure so vast that the Novensiles will never need to find another vault again," Richard said, the touch of a smile on his lips.

Kotler gave him a skeptical look. "All the wealth the Jani

have accumulated over the millennia ... you're saying that this one sarcophagus can outmatch that? I can't even imagine a treasure of that magnitude." He waved to the stone, moving his hand over it from end to end. "Not in such a small footprint, anyway."

Richard chuckled. "Not all treasures are measured equally, Dr. Kotler. You of all people know that."

It was true, of course. Kotler might have been limiting his thinking when it came to the term *treasure*. He did know, better than anyone, that even small and seemingly insignificant things could fetch value beyond imagining if the circumstances were right.

He had allowed himself to be lulled by his experience with the Novensiles to date.

So far, the Novensiles had sought what most might consider "blood antiquities." Material wealth that could fund them in their pursuit of power. It was similar to the method employed by some terrorist organizations, particularly in the Middle East, funding their operations by stealing and selling rare antiquities. The money from these sales was laundered in hundreds of directions, and funneled into the hands of despots and tyrants, allowing for the purchase of weaponry and supplies, and whatever other resources the cell might need.

It was a horrifically efficient system of raping and pillaging the annals of history to shift wealth into the hands of very evil people. The depraved had always sought the treasures of history, heedless of their real value to humanity. Those who dealt in blood antiquities twisted the wealth of history into something ugly and vile.

The Novensiles, from Kotler's knowledge of them, were no better than terrorists themselves. A fact that made him want to vomit each time he thought about his grandfather being one of them.

Beyond material wealth, the Novensiles also sought out objects with great cultural significance—the sort of thing that gave them more *psychological* power. Cultural influence could do a great deal to shift the balance of power in the world, as history had proven again and again.

Votes could be bought. Officials could be bribed. Reach and influence could be extended, with the right nudge, the right offer.

History had more power over the modern age than most people realized.

Kotler turned back to the sarcophagus. "Well, I see Sumerian, Greek, Sanskrit, Aramaic ... oh! That's interesting. This ..." he brushed at a section. "That's Mayan. And this section ... Chinese. Ancient dialect, not modern. I don't recognize these other markings, though. This thing is kind of a Rosetta stone," he said, looking up and smiling at his grandfather.

It was a reflex. A habit. Kotler was used to sharing the joy of discovery with whoever was present. His circumstances, being held captive, could be momentarily forgotten in the joy of uncovering something novel and interesting.

Richard, for his part, kept a neutral expression.

That was alright. Kotler knew they were both playing a dangerous game here. If the two Novensile guards discovered that Kotler was the Chairman's grandson, it could lead to trouble. For both Kotler and his grandfather.

But it was also a card that Kotler thought he might be able to play if it came to it. Some advantage, at least, that might come in handy eventually. He had so few cards left, he held tight to this one. He would protect his grandfather's secret for as long as he could.

He didn't believe for an instant that he could count on familial loyalty to protect *him*, however, if his grandfather decided that things were not going the right way.

Kotler knew practically nothing about this man—he had "died" when Kotler was a child. He remembered his grandfather only as a vague, grey figure who brought interesting birthday gifts and stayed only an hour or two at a time whenever he visited.

Their relationship might give Kotler an advantage in other ways. It might give him some leverage when he needed it. Right now, however, his best leverage seemed to come from solving whatever puzzle this box represented.

"We have translations of the various languages," Richard said, leaning in beside him. He, too, was studying the sarcophagus. His voice took on a familiar air of fascination. "They all say the same thing."

*That's my voice,* Kotler realized with a start. *I can hear myself when he speaks. Like a voice I have in my head, that I hear in moments when I'm my most curious, my most fascinated. His voice is my discovery voice.*

Kotler shook this off. He didn't want familiarity or any personal connection with this man, who had hidden from Kotler and Jeffrey his whole life. Where had he been, when their parents died? Why had he abandoned the Kotler brothers to be raised by their father's business partner? Why hadn't he made any effort, whatsoever, to be a part of their lives?

More importantly, did he have anything to do with their parents' deaths?

Kotler guessed that he did. That the deaths of Berrett and Alexandria Kotler had been one of the costs of his grandfather's continued existence. A cost of the man's mission, as a Novensile. Whatever that mission turned out to be.

Kotler straightened. "I can see that," he said, nodding. He translated.

"The souls of gods and kings rest, in honor and reverence, until the power above repels the power below."

Kotler rubbed the back of his neck with one hand, and moved slowly around the sarcophagus, verifying his own translation. It was rough, but from what he saw, it was accurate. And a glance at Richard revealed a slight nod, indicating that he agreed with Kotler's interpretation.

"The key here isn't their direct translations," Kotler said. "It's the message encoded within the repeated phrase."

Kotler continued to move around the sarcophagus, as much to distance himself from Richard as to study the artifact itself. "This thing is old," he said, then he stopped, looking Richard in the eye. "But not as old as it appears."

Richard gave him an odd expression. "How old would you say it is?"

Kotler shook his head and shrugged. "It's impossible to say for sure, but my best guess is that it's possibly two hundred years. Maybe as much as five hundred, but I doubt it." He pointed to a set of characters. "Mayan," he said. "And some Incan and Aztec symbols, though they're fairly basic. The Inca didn't have a written language, but they did use knot work patterns to communicate." Kotler pointed at a series of patterns. "These markings, in and of themselves, help to date this. Since the Americas were only discovered half a millennia ago, officially, there's no way these carvings predate that. And I know from what research I was able to do on the Jani that they didn't become heavily involved in the Americas until the formation of the United States. It's always possible they were here earlier, maybe even gathering treasure for one of their hidden vaults. But I think the odds favor a shorter runway."

Richard watched him as he spoke, and Kotler read something surprising in the man's features.

Pride.

Whatever path his grandfather had taken, all these years, it was clear he did still have some emotional ties to his past. They might be wispy and thinning with age, but they remained. Tiny tendrils connecting Richard to Dan, and maybe even Jeffrey and his family. Some vague tie, at least. Weak, but there.

Maybe that could give Kotler an advantage after all.

"The real question, Dr. Kotler, is can you open it?"

Kotler nodded. "Maybe. But why not just smash it open? If whatever is in there is as important as you say, is it worth it to try to preserve the sarcophagus?"

Richard chuckled. "Who said anything about preserving the sarcophagus?" He shook his head. "The contents within are valuable, and they're also fragile. This box was built by the Jani. It was constructed to preserve the contents perfectly, using ancient methods that have been lost for centuries. Long before hermetically sealed rooms and electronically regulated preservation systems, the Jani were using the ancient ways to protect their secrets. If we attempt to open that sarcophagus the wrong way, the contents will be destroyed. All their value will be lost."

Kotler listened, taking it in, and felt a thrill of excitement.

He had no doubt that Richard was telling the truth. He had seen, at some of the other Jani sites, the marvels of ancient technology the Order employed. They were obsessed with uncovering and collecting ancient technologies, lost to time. It was what made these vaults so valuable—and so dangerous.

Kotler glanced at the two Novensile guards. Both were fit, well-muscled, dangerous-looking men. He had no chance of overpowering them, especially in his current condition. His only option was to do what he was asked to do. His only shot at surviving this was to open the sarcophagus and give Richard—his grandfather—what he was after. Maybe that would earn him some sort of mercy or grace.

It was a card to play, though the hand Kotler held wasn't particularly strong. He'd play it to the best of his ability and pray it was enough.

"Ok," Kotler said, clapping his hands together. "Let's get to it."

# CHAPTER TWENTY-TWO

THEY HAD IMPROVISED a way to know the time.

Their watches, phones, and other personal effects had been taken when they were brought in. But one of the Senators had been in the military, and he'd learned how to build a clock of sorts using a plastic bag and water. They had rigged the device to drip at a regular rate and marked its levels with lines made from mascara. They took this directly from the smudged eyes of the women in the room.

It was clever, Acosta thought. And kind of confusing.

It was the first time she could remember ever looking at a situation where things looked so bleak, where it seemed like everyone had nothing, and realizing there were more resources than she would have ever imagined. The idea that people could make something, do something that empowered them, without outside help or the intervention from someone more powerful or more wealthy—it was a new and somehow troubling concept to her.

But it was useful.

The water clock dripped away the time as they sat, waiting.

And when the doors opened and closed, the guards entered and exited, the marks were made. Eventually, the captives had things mapped out. They knew the routine and the schedule. They had a way to measure the days as well as the hours, and that gave them what they needed to put a plan into action.

The bag was refilled, the day started anew, and everyone was set.

It was time to act.

As the water level dropped closer to the first mark, everyone tensed, waiting. Men and women moved into their predetermined positions. They each bore makeshift weapons— straps of torn shirt sleeves as garrotes, rolled up packaging from the rations as shivs, hardened by soaking the cardboard and letting it dry in its new shape, and dozens of variations on these themes. They even had a makeshift form of pepper spray made from water and a bit of spicy paste from one of the meals.

It was a ragtag, improvised sort of offensive, but they all agreed it was better than nothing. It gave them at least some small measure of power, some way to fight back. They would all rush at once, attacking whoever came through that door, attempting to blind and overpower their enemy. It gave them a chance.

The water level came closer to the line.

Closer.

Drip-by-drip, the level approached the mark, and the tension rose.

The door opened.

"Now!" Acosta shouted.

On her command, everyone rushed the door.

The two guards, taken by surprise, tried to recover and raise their weapons, but it was too late. The two largest men in the room slammed into each of them, and the rest of the captives piled on, grabbing at weapons, striking the guards' faces with fists, kicking them in the body and head.

Their weapons were seized, and the two men were dragged inside, tied with strips of cloth, gagged and secured.

They'd done it.

There was the start of a cheer, but Acosta and Cameron both waved them to silence. There was no way to know how many more armed men waited on the other end of the corridor. They had taken these two down only because of the element of surprise. Now they had to be more cautious. More strategic.

Some of the Senators were ex-military. Two of the men— one of the Republicans and Cameron, Acosta noted—took up the rifles liberated from the guards. They did things with the weapons that Acosta couldn't quite track, but they seemed competent with them. These two led the way then, as they all moved as a group, down the corridor, and toward the only exit.

Whatever lay on the other side of that door was their next challenge. They all knew that this could be the end for them. But there was a silent acknowledgment, Acosta felt, that this was alright. If they died, they died fighting back.

She felt as if her mind had suddenly been turned on. Adrenalin coursed through her, made her feel like her breath was running away with her. She felt her heart pounding. But above all, she felt something she hadn't felt since before becoming a Senator. Something she'd never felt in her entire life.

Power.

Power over her fate, but also something else. Power over this group. Over these people.

Even as an elected official, she'd never really felt as if she had any real power or influence. Now, with this mixed group of Congresspeople watching her, looking to her for leadership, she felt something shift within her. And she liked it.

This would change everything for her, she knew. Whoever she'd been when she was forced into this room, she would emerge as someone far different. She didn't yet know what this meant, or what she would do when she was free and back in the Senate. But she knew that this was the spark, and it was going to ignite a fire in the world.

She joined the captives gathered at the door. They paused, looked to each other, nodded to signal that they were all ready.

They raised weapons, they hardened their expressions, and they all took a breath as if they were one organism.

They pushed through the next door.

AGENT BROWN ARRIVED at the location and found a position where she could park and watch the facility. The area was rural Virginia, and that meant her black sedan would stand out for what it was. It was like parking a sign out front that read "FBI is here."

She tried to mitigate this by parking as far back as she was able and using a collection of trashcans and mailboxes for cover. The street had very few buildings, but what few were here looked bland and industrial, and mostly abandoned. If someone happened through, the sedan was going to be a signal. But it couldn't be helped. She climbed out, locked and checked her doors, checked the snap on her weapon and the comforting bulge of her bag in the inner pocket of her blazer, and started a slow walk forward, clinging to the deepening shadows of the evening.

The facility appeared to be an abandoned youth detention center. She used her phone to pull up as much information about it as possible, and uncovered a checkered history of abuse allegations and administrative corruption. The facility had been closed nearly three years earlier, and several employees were still under current investigation and scrutiny. The kids who had been held here were given psychological evaluations, and many of them were released into the custody of parents and guardians.

It was a sick sort of history for the place, but Dani didn't think it had anything to do with the Congresspeople. It was just a convenient, abandoned holding facility, she would guess. Perfect, really, for keeping a group of abductees off the radar. The facility and its grounds were quiet, isolated, and wedged firmly into the middle of nowhere.

Dani checked her phone again, this time to establish time tables and ETAs. She re-checked her weapon, re-checked her badge, and inhaled slowly. She exhaled as she stepped forward, keeping to the side of the street, taking cover behind the occasional tree or other objects, making sure she was obstructed from view as much as possible.

This was a terrible idea. A Kotler-sized mistake, she was sure.

Help was definitely on the way. She would have backup. Eventually. But she was moving a bit early, alone, because ...

She couldn't quite give a reason. Nothing that wasn't complete BS, at any rate. She was acting more on instinct than anything, which really wasn't like her. What was like her, though, was that she was mad.

Since all of this started—and she was mentally going all the way back to the formation of Historic Crimes—it had felt like she was being manipulated. If not directly, then indirectly through the manipulation of the entire department. She had felt, from the beginning, that something was off with Historic Crimes, with the constant drama that seemed to surround Dan Kotler, with all of it.

She'd been right.

Liz had shared everything she'd been given by DB and this

mysterious voice on the other end of a burner phone. She had also given Dani a rundown of where things stood so far. Dani knew that Liz was holding some things back, and she understood why: Plausible deniability.

Liz wanted Dani to be protected from any backlash that might come from some of her more "grey area" investigative methods. And Dani, for her part, was fine with that buffer. She had always intended to keep herself above reproach so that if and when it came time to make an arrest or take any official action, no one would be able to use her to botch the case.

That had been the plan from the start.

Dani appreciated it, but she was starting to get irritated with being out of the loop. It had started to feel like more manipulation. Especially now, with someone breaking into her home and leaving her a message meant to push her into action. The fuzzy lines were getting fuzzier, and Dani was starting to move past her look-the-other-way limit. She had decided it was time to be a little more proactive.

She had started taking a closer look at DB.

Dani had done what digging she could, on her own time. She had very little to go on, beyond a few surveillance photos and some scant physical evidence. It was clear that DB had some sort of protection.

Dani kept running into walls every time she looked into him. Every line on him came up as a dead end, and she found herself having to navigate an ocean of false trails and other BS.

But she kept digging, kept searching, trying to keep her queries low-level so they would go unnoticed. She couldn't push very hard—it might alert DB or whoever he was affiliated with, which could have unpredictable results.

This was the stuff Dani hated.

Her whole career path had been built around predictability and stability. She had worked her butt off in high school, studying and taking everything she thought she would need for a career in law enforcement—her lifelong dream. And she'd been blessed with some advantages. Her school offered a Criminal Justice track, with retired police Detectives as instructors, ride-alongs in police cars, tours of police stations and FBI offices. She ate it all up. She lived and breathed the whole idea, even when her mother came out against all of it.

Dani didn't care. This was her life. Her passion. She was fully committed.

When she'd graduated high school, she was immediately accepted into cadet training for the Police Academy. And in just a short time she was a beat cop, mostly putting parking tickets on windshields for the first couple of years of her career. But she never stopped studying.

She was enrolled in college night courses and filled her every day off of work by attending special lectures and seminars. At work, she took every advancement exam her department offered. She went to every optional training and development program in the district. She logged more career development hours than any other freshman on the Force, and it got noticed.

Her invitation to Quantico was like a gift from the heavens, and she couldn't accept it fast enough. Joining the FBI felt like a dream come true.

And it was. She couldn't deny that. She loved her work. She loved her role in protecting people, in making the world safer for everyone. Her mother hated all of it, but that was her baggage. This was Dani's life, and her dream.

She hadn't been prepared for the level of corruption she'd see, though.

For her, a lot of her disillusionment started with Director Crispen.

A few years earlier, Crispen had been implicated in not

only trying to frame Dan Kotler on charges of collusion and terrorism, but in the abduction of Dr. Evelyn Horelica, as well. Crispen, himself, had colluded not only with a rogue billionaire to steal the Coelho medallion, but had also collaborated with a terrorist cell that had nearly detonated a nuclear device under Cheyenne Mountain.

Crispen's plans had been uncovered and foiled by the efforts of Agent Roland Denzel, as well as by the work of Dr. Dan Kotler. Working together, they had brought the entire case to a head, rescued Horelica, brought down a billionaire, and stopped the terrorists. They had also brought down Crispen, landing the former FBI Director in a prison cell.

It had been a disgrace and a black eye to the Bureau. It had also shaken Dani's faith in the institution she'd dedicated her life to.

That had been the start of a shift. Or the birth of a new era in the FBI, depending on how you looked at it. Dani had watched all of it unfold, and had even benefited from the restructuring. She was promoted, which came with some nice benefits. But she was also recruited by Agent Denzel to join the new division he was heading. Historic Crimes, he told her, had a charter to look into the sorts of things that were going unsolved, even uninvestigated. Crimes that could have an impact on the nation, even the world.

He'd been right. And for a few years now Dani had been content enough with the work. She appreciated that they were catching bad guys who might have otherwise gone free, causing all sorts of chaos in the world. But she couldn't help noticing, after a time, that a bulk of their cases ended up revolving around one person in particular: Dr. Dan Kotler.

It nagged at her.

Why Kotler? What was it about the man that somehow magnetically attracted trouble on a global scale? And how was it that an entire division of the FBI had sprung up, practically overnight, centered almost entirely on the sort of work that Dan Kotler was best suited to deal with? It was as if someone, somewhere, with a great deal of influence and power, had custom-crafted a whole law enforcement department just for Kotler.

And with the founding of Historic Crimes, Dani noted, the need for Kotler escalated. The things the division dealt with became more pronounced and more prominent. To Dani, it was starting to look like the longer Historic Crimes existed, the more it needed to exist. And the more it relied on Dan Kotler to solve the mysteries, unravel the riddles, and make the world safe through the power of history and science.

That smacked of manipulation to Dani. It made her brain itch.

It led her to start looking into the whole thing, to see what was hidden behind the curtain. That, in turn, led her to recruit Liz Ludlum, whose personal relationship with Kotler was useful, but who also had a very sharp investigative mind of her own.

And now, the digging and searching had led Dani here, to an abandoned youth detention center in rural Virginia.

And alone, which was foolish.

That was what Kotler brought into the mix, somehow. Chaos. Disorder. Unpredictability. A definite deviation from protocol.

Dani sighed. She couldn't blame this on Kotler. Not directly. This was her choice. Her bad decision, she was sure. But it just felt necessary. She needed to *do something*. And she was tired of being manipulated.

Backup would be here within an hour, anyway. How much trouble could she possibly get into between now and then?

She moved forward again, determined to do a sweep of the perimeter of this place. She could provide intel, give the incoming team some details to work with. That would make her useful, and keep her out of trouble.

She stopped short when she heard the weapons fire.

*So much for keeping out of trouble,* Dani thought as she pulled her weapon from its holster and moved straight toward the sounds of combat.

# CHAPTER TWENTY-THREE

"The souls of gods and kings rest, in honor and reverence, until the power above repels the power below."

Kotler had repeated the translation under his breath like a mantra as he moved around the sarcophagus, running his fingers over the stone, his fingers rising and falling in the carvings and reliefs. He occasionally detected seams and gaps in the stone, points at which it might move or open, but had given these no more than token tugs and pushes and the occasional attempt to twist and turn something that seemed promising.

So far, nothing was happening.

Richard was shadowing him as he moved around, and the guards had split up, each taking a position on opposite sides of the room, weapons ready. Kotler was always on the verge of being gunned down, it seemed.

"Anything?" Richard asked. Kotler could sense his grandfather's impatience. Another sign that their familial bond would not necessarily save Kotler if things went wrong. *When* things went wrong.

But he had to admit, his grandfather was difficult to read.

Kotler shook his head. "Not so far. But maybe it would help to have some context. Where did you find this, originally?"

Richard smiled and even chuckled. "Actually, you found it."

Kotler blinked, shaking his head.

Richard continued, "It was part of the recovery from the Sonoma Mountain vault."

Kotler looked at him sharply. The events in Arizona were still painfully fresh in Kotler's mind. He still had scrapes and bruises from the whole event. And a lot of the most recent developments in his life were influenced by what went down there—including the invitation from Granger, asking Kotler to join the Jani.

The suggestion that this artifact came from that very same vault, hidden within a manmade complex buried in the Sonoma Mountains, stretched all credulity.

As he considered it, however, Kotler realized that it made sense.

The Novensiles had pressed hard to get into that vault, using Kotler's own research to uncover it. Once inside, the entire region became a battle zone. Kotler, along with Granger and his team, had pursued Scope and his men deep into the spiral of manmade caves, finally discovering the vault itself in an inverted replica of the mountains—the sky below, the peaks and valleys above.

It had been an incredible treasure trove, for certain. A lot of materials had been recovered, and it was certainly possible that the Novensiles had either gotten away with something from the site itself or pilfered it from the Jani after it was recovered. They may even have seized it from the military presence that took over the site once the conflict had ceased.

Kotler was thinking about the possibilities of this when he heard a sound coming from the airlock.

After a moment, the doors opened, and Denzel emerged, quickly grabbed by the guard closest to the door and moved roughly to one end of the room.

Denzel looked to be in rough shape. He'd obviously had some medical care, but was likely as drugged up as Kotler had been. He might still be, Kotler thought. He certainly looked less than his usual alert self. Though if he was still drugged, the Novensiles didn't think it would be enough. Kotler noted that Denzel's hands were cuffed in front of him.

There was another sound from the airlock and a third Novensile guard emerged, just as armed as his two predecessors, and just as clearly willing to shoot first and forget about questions altogether.

Kotler glanced at Richard.

"Some incentive," Richard said.

"You know I'm already helping you, right?" Kotler asked.

Richard shrugged. "We often don't fully realize the resources we can call upon until our options are narrowed."

Kotler blinked at the words and felt a little sick. They were familiar.

"My father used to say something like that," he said.

He tried to put some edge of warning into his voice. A message.

*I have some leverage, too*, he was saying.

"I'm aware," Richard replied, potentially as much to Kotler's unspoken message as to what he'd said aloud.

Kotler looked to Denzel. "Roland, are you ok?"

Denzel was a little unsteady on his feet, but nodded, holding up his cuffed hands. "Been better," he replied.

"Dr. Kotler," Richard said, waving a hand to the sarcophagus. "This would be a good time to get back to work."

Kotler glanced at his grandfather one more time, not bothering to mask his contempt. But he nodded, said nothing, and went back to studying the sarcophagus.

He was crouched at one corner, inspecting the patterns of symbols and characters. He had hoped he might uncover some hint, maybe in the arrangement of the languages. But so far they were all arranged as he would have expected. Nothing about them seemed unusual or hinted at an answer to the riddle of how to open this box.

*The souls of gods and kings rest, in honor and reverence, until the power above repels the power below.*

It was a poetic sort of instruction, but it was too vague to be of much use. Kotler had hoped that with a bit of context he might ...

He stopped, stood straight, and stepped back, his eyes wide. He spread his hands in front of him, framing the sarcophagus from end to end.

Context.

"Where?" Kotler asked.

"Excuse me?" Richard replied.

"Where in the vault did you find this? Do you know the exact location?"

Richard huffed. "I ... believe it was stashed on a platform near the ceiling of the main vault. It was disguised by faux stone. The team that recovered it found it almost by accident."

There was a lot of information in that statement that Kotler thought shed some light on how the sarcophagus came to be here. But the information that was most important, at the moment, was something subtle.

The sarcophagus had been on a platform, raising it to the top of the vault.

The vault itself, however, was an inverted landscape—an upside-down mountain above with an artificial starry sky in the floor below.

Or above, if you were oriented to the replica of the mountains.

"*Until the power above repels the power below*," Kotler said.

Richard shook his head. "I'm not following."

Kotler grinned and moved to the sarcophagus. He put his hands under one corner of it, lifting. It budged, but barely. It was too heavy for him to do alone.

"Help me!" he said to his grandfather.

"What are we doing?" Richard replied, moving to the opposite end of the sarcophagus. He mimicked Kotler's grip, sliding his hands under the edge of the stone.

"We're turning this over," Kotler said, grinning.

Richard caught on immediately. He looked to the guards. "Two of you help. You," he said to the guard nearest Denzel. "Move Agent Denzel over there," he nodded to a far corner of the room.

The guard grabbed Denzel by the arm and roughly dragged him over to the far end of the room. He stood apart from him, his hands gripping his weapon.

The other two guards took up positions on either side of the sarcophagus.

"On three," Kotler said, nodding to them. "One ... two ... THREE!"

They each picked up their side of the stone artifact, grunting with effort. Kotler was amazed that his grandfather, well into his nineties, would even have the strength to attempt this. But the old man was holding up well. Better than Kotler, at the moment.

They strained, and after a moment they had the sarcophagus turned on its side, then lifted and slid back before turning once more, flipping it the rest of the way until it once again rested on the metal table. This time, upside down.

There was a sound from the sarcophagus, as it came to a

rest. The sound of stone sliding against stone, and an audible click. Kotler was watching the flattened bottom of the artifact— a completely blank slate, with no markings. As he watched, however, the level surface rose upward, and a seam opened before them.

He nodded to the others, and they each wedged their fingers into the gap, lifting the stone slab up and away. They placed it on the floor, leaning against the metal table.

Kotler stood straight once again, huffing. He looked at his grandfather, who was also huffing and smiling. In that instant, for the first time, Kotler saw the features of his own father.

Different. Distorted by age and by being a generation removed. But there he was, in the twinkle of Richard's—his own father's—eyes, the set of his jaw, the crinkle of lines on his forehead.

It was an oddly disturbing image, Kotler felt. It stirred something up within him—a raw sort of pain and longing that he'd kept at bay for decades. And now, here it was. Exposed. A nerve sending tendrils of fire into Kotler's heart and soul.

Ironically, at that moment, any clinging sense of family was shed as Kotler saw Richard for what he truly was.

The enemy.

The adversary.

Richard's legacy within the Jani had taken Kotler's parents from him. The man himself might or might not be directly responsible, but there was no mistaking that their deaths were because of him. Him, and the Novensiles. Him, and the Jani.

"You did it," Richard said, a note of pride in the old man's features.

Kotler hesitated, got control of himself, and nodded. "Yes," he said. "But what did I just do?"

Richard stepped forward and leaned over the opening in the sarcophagus, bracing his hands on its side, looking into the maw of the stone. He reached in, and gingerly removed something.

A canister.

It was a cylinder of metal, and Kotler noted that it was fine craftsmanship. Steel, from the look of it, but with filaments of brass that had, at one point in their history, been polished to gleam. Now they were dulled by a patina of age, but still demonstrated the care and reverence with which they were crafted.

Richard glanced around and moved to a counter on the far side of the room. There was a rack on the countertop, and Richard placed the canister into it. He returned, lifting another, and repeating the action. By the time he was done, there were six metal canisters in the rack, and Richard knelt to remove a second rack from the cabinet below.

It went on like this for some time, until the entire countertop was covered in racks of these ornate steel canisters. And when Richard had exhausted the supply from the sarcophagus, he turned to Kotler and the others, gleaming.

"What are they?" Kotler asked, a sense of dread settling over him.

"The souls of gods and kings," Richard said, his voice sounding more youthful than ever.

Kotler shook his head. "I don't understand."

Richard laughed and moved forward. He stood before Kotler, placing his hands on Kotler's arms. "Your father," Richard said, "had a partner. The man who took you in, after your parents died."

Kotler nodded warily. "Cristoff Vellar," he said.

"Together they formed Vellar-Kotler Genetic Research," Richard continued. "An organization that has benefited the Jani for some time. The Jani, and the Novensiles."

Kotler took this in. "And you," he said, with sudden realization.

"And me," Richard nodded. "And now, their work will return life to some of the most powerful beings to have ever walked the Earth. Gods and kings, Daniel." He waved a hand to the collection of canisters on the counter, 36 in all.

He was practically glowing with excitement. Despite the age of his body, he vibrated with energy, like a man half his age. A third his age.

Kotler felt the sickness in his guts twist and grow, like some malignant creature devouring him from within.

Richard stepped away, turned his back to Kotler, and approached the canisters with the same quiet reverence, the same zeal, as a devout worshiper would give to his idol.

Without turning away, Richard whispered ...

"We will witness the resurrection of the gods."

# CHAPTER TWENTY-FOUR

LIZ AND JEFFREY STOOD CLOSE, leaving a gap between them and Vellar.

Liz thought it might be unintentional, on Jeffrey's part, but she found herself conscious of wanting a bit of distance between her and this man. She wasn't sure what she felt about him, except that she didn't trust him.

Whenever Dan spoke of him, it was with such respect and admiration that Liz had developed something of a rosy impression of the man. And even now, she had to admit, he really did seem kind. But there was a pall of darkness to him, considering the things she'd only recently learned. There was a shade of something sinister in his kindness.

The way in which Dan and Jeffrey's parents had died had been suspicious, to begin with, but with the revelation that their grandfather was still alive, things were suddenly cast in a bizarre light. Coupled with the revelation that DB was actually Vellar's butler, and that there was some secretive line of research happening within Vellar-Kotler—Liz was starting to think she'd better give Dani a call. This might be something the FBI should look into.

As the elevator continued to plunge downward, however, Liz found herself hesitating. She would see this part through, at least. She would see what Vellar was doing here. What he was hiding. And she would find out what Richard Kotler was doing with it.

She told herself she was doing this to protect Dan and Jeffrey. And maybe she was. But she was also suddenly questioning everything, unsure who to trust.

She needed more information.

After an excruciatingly silent descent, the elevator finally settled, the doors finally opened, and Vellar gestured for the two of them to follow.

Liz had seen thousands of labs in her career and a vast array of medical and research equipment. But the sight of this place made her dizzy all the same.

The space was open and immense, a warehouse-sized facility divided into pods that, from what she could tell, were dedicated to specific lines of research. She could see that the idea here was efficiency and modularity.

As if to confirm this, Vellar said, "Each of these pods can be reconfigured and moved to facilitate a new workflow. Our people can essentially build any type of lab they need, with full support from a network of resources."

"Impressive," Liz said, and she meant it. The approach meant that one space could be divided and used for multiple lines of research or streamlined for pouring more resources into a single task.

Among the rows of equipment, Liz spotted several DNA sequencing systems. Researchers were running samples at a dizzying rate, draped in sterilized lab gear and operating within makeshift spaces comprised of sheets of clear plastic.

*Clean rooms*, Liz realized. Just as reconfigurable as everything else here, almost infinitely expandable and versatile. She had worked within one similar to these alongside Dr. Emily Dawson—the Epidemiologist sent by the CDC to study the *Ahpuch* virus. That affair, in the jungle surrounding a lost Mayan city, had led to Liz joining Historic Crimes. It had been early days for her and Dan Kotler, as well. Flirting and near-death experiences had been their MO ever since.

"This way," Vellar said, motioning for them to follow him through the labyrinth of workstations.

Liz and Jeffrey followed without question. Liz glanced at Jeffrey to see how he was handling all of this and noted that he seemed stoic but interested. Maybe even fascinated, but it was hard to tell.

Here, Liz realized, was a key difference between Dan and his brother. Dan wore a lot of his emotions on his face, unless he was determined to hide them. In a way, this was Dan's "tell." As a master of reading body language, he knew exactly what mannerisms to suppress, to prevent anyone from knowing what he was thinking. But in doing so, he was shutting himself off in a noticeable way, to those who knew him. It was a signal even Liz could read. There were times where, if Dan wasn't lying, he was clearly hiding. Liz had seen it more often than she liked, but she tried to respect his right to keep any secrets he felt he needed to keep.

She was keeping a couple from him, after all. Fair was fair.

Jeffrey, on the other hand, was a study in emotional irony. From what Liz could tell, Jeffrey really had very few secrets. But he was imminently private, keeping his emotions in check, only occasionally slipping and letting something show.

Liz found it fascinating to see the contrasts of the two brothers. They could, in small ways, be so much alike. But in bigger ways, they couldn't be more different.

It actually helped her understand both men just a little better, to compare them to each other.

And then there was Vellar.

He was inscrutable, for the most part. His demeanor was pleasant, but he clearly kept secrets of his own. That might be expected, considering his work and his position. But Liz felt it went much deeper.

Vellar's secrets were not just business. He held onto family secrets as well. He had known about Richard Kotler being alive, and had never told either Kotler brother. Dan respected this man, considered him family, but Vellar had lied to him his whole life.

Liz knew Dan well enough to predict how he would take this news.

"Here," Vellar said, motioning them over to a large cube standing in one corner of the space. It was a room of solid walls, anchored to the floor, standing in stark contrast to the modular plastic workspaces that filled this level.

The cube was similar to the exhibit in the museum, where the plane wreckage was on display. Only this room was much bigger, occupying a considerable portion of the warehouse floor. It stood free from any other walls or pods, however. A cube of metal standing cold and isolated in its own corner of the space.

Liz watched as Vellar leaned slightly forward, allowing for facial recognition to unlock the door, which slid aside to give them access. He stood aside, holding a hand out to indicate that Liz and Jeffrey should enter. He followed behind them, and the door closed.

They were now perfectly isolated from the outside world, from what Liz could tell. A palpable silence fell over them, broken only by the whir of fans in a hidden environmental system.

The room was cold, and Liz rubbed her arms for warmth.

"Here," Vellar said, reaching to a set of hooks on the wall. He took down a pair of lab coats and handed them to both Liz and Jeffrey, then donned one of his own. "We keep the temperature and humidity much lower in this room. It helps with preservation."

"Preservation of what, exactly?" Liz asked.

Vellar sighed and stepped forward. "Of this," he said.

He was standing in front of an angled panel of controls and displays, which divided them from a series of large, cylindrical chambers standing in columns throughout the room. Liz counted ten columns in total.

Vellar tapped at one of the touch displays, and in a moment the columns began to rotate.

Liz watched as each began to reveal a green glow, emitted from shelves of glass. On each shelf were cylindrical containers, also made of glass, in which liquid gently sloshed. There were things suspended in the liquid of each self-contained beaker and dish.

Liz stepped around the control panel, moving closer to get a look at what was contained here. She leaned in close and was soon joined by Jeffrey, who did the same.

She studied the containers for a long moment, then shook her head, looking back to Vellar. "What is this?" she asked.

"Embryos, mostly," Vellar said. "Though some of those containers hold unfertilized eggs, genetic samples, and ..."

She'd been listening even as she turned back to the containers. She looked at Vellar again.

"Cloned biological material," Vellar said.

"Cloned?" Liz asked, looking back sharply.

It took her a moment, but something Vellar had said earlier came back to her. When Jeffery had asked what kind of research Richard Kotler was using to keep himself alive and vital, Vellar's answer had been chilling.

*The very illegal kind.*

"Human," Liz said, her voice quiet. "Human cloning."

Vellar nodded.

Jeffrey looked from him to Liz and back again. "Even I know that's illegal, Cristoff. What were you thinking?"

Vellar shook his head then. "You misunderstand, Jeffrey. I have no control over this. I have limited access, but I suspect that's largely so that Richard and the people he works with will have some leverage over me. But this," he waved to the array of genetic samples. "This isn't my doing. I have no say in this at all."

"Richard Kotler is using cloned cells to treat himself?" Liz asked.

"He has for years," Vellar nodded. "Decades. In fact, he used our research to cure himself of pancreatic cancer."

Liz inhaled sharply. "Cure?"

Vellar again nodded. "Among other diseases. The treatments he receives ... they've added decades to his life. But that's only a side effect. I am not privy to much about their plans, but the organization Richard works for intends to use this research for another purpose. They plan to use it to control the world."

"How?" Jeffrey asked.

"What haven't you show us?" Liz asked. She had turned to face the far corner of the space. She had noticed that one of the cylinders had not turned with the others. The green sheen of light that softly glowed in the room was reflected from the metal of the tenth cylinder.

She looked back to Vellar, who seemed hesitant.

"I have no control or say over this research," he said, as if reiterating the point.

"Show us," Liz said, her voice quiet but stern.

Vellar locked eyes with her for a moment, then nodded and turned back to the control panel. He made a series of motions, tapping a sequence into the display, and then hitting a set of controls.

Liz and Jeffery turned to watch as the tenth cylinder rotated, casting its own green glow outward, joining the rest in creating an eery haze into the room.

Liz inhaled sharply, and Jeffrey put a hand on her shoulder.

There, suspended in a semi-viscous solution and illuminated in the green glow, was a human figure.

With the face of Dan Kotler.

# CHAPTER TWENTY-FIVE

FROM WHAT DANI COULD TELL, she'd just entered a war zone.

Two men—one of whom she recognized as one of the abducted Senators—were firing automatic weapons as they took cover behind a couple of black SUVs.

Across the garage from them, Dani could see maybe half a dozen men dressed in black combat gear. They wore masks and were also using various objects in the room for cover, including more SUVs and a large rolling toolbox.

Dani had entered through a side door that was in line with the SUV that was clearly functioning as a beachhead for the Senator and the other man.

She dropped to the floor, staying hidden, with her gun extended in front of her, sweeping the area. From this vantage point, she could see that there were more people behind that SUV. Men and women. The other abductees, she assumed.

To Dani's left, across the room, the armed men who had abducted them, with military precision and competence, were acting ... strange.

They were fighting back, that was clear. Aggressively so, laying down fire and forcing the two men across the way from them to hunch for cover. But that was as far as these men took it. They made no move to cross the space and disarm their opponents, though from Dani's vantage point they easily could have.

Even more strange, they seemed to be terrible shots.

Round after round plunked into the SUV the Senators were using for cover. A few impacted the cinderblock wall, spraying a shower of debris onto the people below. But the shots never seemed to come anywhere near the two armed abductees. The Senator had left himself wide open several times, rising from cover and presenting himself as an easy target, and each time any shots fired in his direction missed by a wide margin.

From the standpoint of the senators, this had to be a terrifying firefight. It had to feel like they were in a hot zone. But from Dani's perspective, it wasn't clear that the bad guys were even trying.

Dani checked her weapon and began crawling forward, staying on her stomach. She was hidden from both sides of the fight by the vehicles and other objects in the room, and she needed to keep that advantage for as long as possible. After a moment, she found herself in a much better position—still within range of the exit, but angled so that she could see the bad guys clearly.

She made sure she had cover and a clear path for retreat, then rose, her weapon trained on the armed men.

"FBI! Lower your weapons! Down! Down! Down!"

The men reacted.

Dani had expected them to turn on her, to fire in her direction. She was prepared to draw that fire and had intended to create an opening for the Congresspeople to make their escape.

Her backup was on the way, and she figured she could hold these men off until help arrived. But her first priority was to get the abductees to safety.

To her surprise, however, none of her plans were necessary.

The armed men turned at her shout for surrender and took a few haphazard shots, causing Dani to duck. An instant later, however, they retreated.

Turning as one, like a herd of running deer, they sprinted from cover, darting through a door on the far end of the garage. Dani managed a headcount as they ran—five men in all. Each was armed, wore body armor, and had his face covered with a balaclava. Each was gone almost before the sound of gunfire faded.

Dani stepped from cover, almost in disbelief. She held her weapon with both hands, angling it toward the floor, ready to raise it if danger presented itself. Instead, she watched the door close behind the last man, then turned to see the two armed abductees standing out in the open, their weapons trained on her.

She raised both arms above her shoulders, her weapon held loosely in the fingers of her right hand, palms out. "Don't shoot, I'm with the FBI."

"Prove it," the Senator said.

Dani wiggled her gun. "I'm going to lower this to the ground, slowly, and then reach into the inner pocket of my coat for my badge."

The two men didn't budge, and Dani did exactly as she'd described, placing her weapon at her feet before slowly straightening and easing her hand into the inner pocket of her blazer.

When she showed her badge, both men visibly relaxed.

"Took you long enough," the Senator said.

"Believe me, I got here as fast as I could," Dani replied. She gestured to her gun on the floor. "May I?"

The Senator nodded.

"Back up is on the way," Dani said, stooping to retrieve her gun. She holstered it under her coat, hoping this would be the last time today that she'd have to draw it and fire. "But we need to get you out of here and to a safe place. Is anyone injured?"

"Nothing major," the younger man reported.

Dani nodded to the weapon in his hand. "You took that from one of these guys?"

The younger man nodded. "My name is Cameron Michaels," he said, lowering the weapon to his side.

He was stepping forward, his hand out, when a woman's voice broke in.

"He works for me," she said.

Dani and both men looked up to see Senator Arania Acosta —one of the abductees— stepping forward and moving toward them with determination.

Dani had seen the Senator on television and YouTube, hundreds of times. She was a Democrat, but also a Socialist. And a radical one, at that. But in all the footage Dani had seen of her, Senator Acosta had never looked quite this bold. She'd always seemed a bit naive. Girlish. Like a child playing grownup in a game that was just a little too real for her.

Now, however, she looked like she was ready for a fight.

"Senator Acosta," Dani said, extending her hand.

Acosta pushed past the two men who had been protecting her and the others, and shook Dani's hand. "Agent?"

"Agent Danielle Brown," Dani said. "I'm with the Historic Crimes Division of the FBI."

"Historic Crimes?" Acosta asked, frowning.

"It's ... a long story," Dani hedged.

She was about to start directing everyone out of the garage, to find someplace safe for them to be before things started happening here. Suddenly, however, she heard the sounds of sirens descending on the place.

Backup had arrived.

"This way, Senators," Dani said, motioning for them to follow her.

They emerged from the garage to the sight of hundreds of police and FBI vehicles arriving. Lights were strobing all around them, red and blue flashes. There was the sound of multiple helicopters, and officers shouting. Ambulances formed a second line, and beyond that, a swarm of civilian cars and news vans was arriving, prevented from getting too close by officers manning police lines.

Dani and the others were quickly ushered to a safe zone while a SWAT team infiltrated the detention center.

The questions started then—first from her compatriots and then, inevitably, from the contingent of media that were arriving in droves to the scene.

Dani begged off on most questions from the press, citing that she couldn't comment on an ongoing investigation. But she was happy to report that all of the abductees had been recovered safely.

Despite downplaying her role in the events, even claiming she had little to nothing to do with the rescue, Dani, all of a sudden, was a national hero. The savior of the day.

She caught only a few snatches of commentary from the press, with reporters doing standups against the backdrop of flashing police lights and armed SWAT members. Some of the Senators had been cleared to speak with the press, and there were interviews happening all over the scene. Many praised Dani for her bravery, crediting her with the rescue, alongside Cameron Michaels and Senator Nelson—the two armed abductees who had held the enemy at bay before Dani arrived.

All but two of the bad guys had gotten away. The two men the Congresspeople had subdued were brought out in cuffs, their faces covered. They were put into an armed transport, secured and guarded by Federal agents. They would be questioned. Answers would be sought.

The good guys had won.

It was a day for international celebration, it seemed. Even now, here on the scene, Dani could sense the sigh of relief from across the country, and around the world. She could feel the energy of celebration and victory. She felt like celebrating too. It was just ...

She just couldn't shake the feeling that this had been all too easy.

# CHAPTER TWENTY-SIX

KOTLER AND DENZEL were secondary concerns at the moment, but Kotler worried that this might change at any time. They were close to each other now, both handcuffed to a metal rack attached to one of the walls, but hadn't had the opportunity to speak.

The airlock was to their left. Before them, the guards were following Richard's instructions, building the cryogenic crates that would carry 36 canisters to wherever they were going next. The work of building was keeping the guards busy, but Kotler could feel seconds peeling away. Whatever came next wouldn't be good.

Richard left the men to their work and stepped up to Kotler and Denzel. He spoke in low tones.

"The next part of this is going to be difficult," he said.

"Which part?" Kotler asked. "Putting a bullet in our heads or leaving our bodies to rot in this facility?"

Richard smiled lightly and shook his head. "Do you really think I would let anyone harm you?"

Kotler laughed, louder than he had intended. The guards

glanced back, hands going involuntarily to the straps of the weapons slung over their shoulders.

Richard motioned that everything was fine, and they continued working.

"Daniel," Richard said, stepping a little closer. "Surely you understand that I must play all of this a certain way. If there is any hope for the two of us—" he glanced at Denzel, who seemed to have recovered enough to glare at Richard with unmasked anger. "The *three* of us," Richard amended, "to survive this, I must keep up appearances."

"Grandfather," Kotler said, his voice dripping with contempt. Denzel looked at him sharply at the sound of the word, glancing from Kotler to Richard and back again. Richard, for his part, shot a look over his shoulder, ensuring that the men present hadn't heard. "You'll have to forgive me if I think you're a lying sack of crap."

Richard studied Kotler for a moment, and in that instant, Kotler read genuine regret and even a bit of pain in his grandfather's features.

It took Kotler by surprise, but did nothing to change how he felt.

This man had known about the deaths of Kotler's parents. He had been alive all this time. He had hidden, leaving his own grandsons to be raised by Cristoff Vellar. And from what Kotler was learning, Cristoff had been in league with Richard from the beginning, which hurt Kotler worse than just about every revelation so far.

All of that, and then the ultimate betrayal: Richard Kotler was one of the Jani, and was, in fact, a Novensile, set to disrupt that ancient Order. There was every indication, from Kotler's perspective, that it was the Novensiles who had orchestrated the deaths of his parents.

There was not enough rage in the world for Kotler to feel toward this man, and toward everything he represented.

"There is ... a new influence among the Novensiles," Richard said, as if reading Kotler's mind. He suddenly looked pained and uncomfortable. "A man ... a young man, but very powerful. He is the one who orchestrated the abduction of the Congresspeople. At first, I believed we were making a tactical error, especially when the timetable was accelerated. The others on my council went along with this man—we call him Influencer—and I believed he was guiding us on foolish and hasty impulse. But now I realize that he intended for all of this to happen. He was counting on it. He intended to turn the Novensiles into his own personal Order, destroying centuries of meticulous planning and groundwork." Richard said this last with such regret that Kotler could read real and honest grief in his grandfather's features.

"Heartbreaking," Denzel said.

Richard glanced at him but turned back to Kotler before he spoke. "There's something else. Someone among the Jani knows about our relationship, and they invited you to become a part of the Order so they could draw me out. This places me in a great deal of danger, but it also threatens both you and Jeffrey."

"And you're concerned for us," Kotler said, contempt coloring his tone.

Richard ignored it. "Before I left my office, I collected a large amount of information. Digital files. Details about the Jani, and the Novensiles in particular. People in the Order who are in positions of power. People who are key to the Novensile's reach. Strategically useful information."

Kotler was watching him closely, unsure he could trust what he was hearing.

"Information is power, Daniel. You know this." His grandfather paused, glancing from Kotler to Denzel and back again.

"That's why I sent both of you a digital key. With it, you can unlock the data. It's stored in hundreds of places, on multiple devices you both have access to. It was the only way to safe-guard it. If someone in the Order uncovers one cache, they can disable it. There's nothing I could do about that. But my hope is that I've planted enough of these that you will be able to unlock one before it is found by the others."

"You're giving us all of this?" Denzel asked, skeptical. "Why?"

Richard nodded toward the three men who had finished assembling the cryogenic carrier and were now placing the 36 canisters inside. "The Jani protected those canisters for centuries. The Novensiles planned to use them to rule the world. We searched for them for decades. Now that I have them, I will use them to bring a new age to humanity. I will bring the gods back to this Earth, Daniel." His voice, though still quiet, was filled with an energy that belied his years. "I will be the father of gods. And all of this ... the betrayal, the deceit, the pain, even death itself ... it will all come to an end!"

Kotler recognized the signs of zealotry. The tones of madness.

"Grandfather," he said, quietly, his own tone sympathetic for the first time. "No."

Richard stepped forward and placed his hands on either side of Kotler's face. "It's already done. All of it. Now, you must survive." He glanced at Denzel. "And you. There's a reason I put the two of you together."

Kotler blinked, a shock running through him. "What did you say?"

"Historic crimes?" Richard said, smiling. "When you became involved in that affair with Anwar Adham, in Pueblo, foiling one of our plans, it was all I could do to keep the Order from having you assassinated. Both of you. Instead, I convinced them that you'd be much more useful to us if we used you to find the artifacts and vaults hidden by the Jani, all over the Earth. I arranged for some of our operatives to make a vote here, a nudge there. Budgets were reallocated. A new division of the FBI was formed. And now, here you are." He stepped back, leaving both of them to gape at the revelation.

"Sir," one of the armed men said from across the room.

Richard glanced back, noted that the cryogenic carrier was sealed and ready for transport. He nodded to the men, then turned back to Kotler and Denzel. "The key is in this room," Richard whispered.

Then, louder, he said, "We'll leave these two here." He turned back to his men. "I need all three of you to help me get this carrier out of here. We'll take it to the transport level." He turned to one of the men and stepped toward him. "Once we are all out of this chamber, I want you to detonate the failsafes from the outside. Seal this room so that there will be no escape."

"Yes, sir," the man said.

Richard turned back to Kotler and Denzel then. "You've served the Novensiles well, Dr. Kotler. And as a reward, I give you whatever hours remain. But this," he motioned to the space surrounding them. "This will be your tomb. Considering how often the two of you find yourself in one of these, I'm sure you'll feel right at home."

He turned back to the men and directed them to take the carrier through the airlock.

Once the room was cleared, Kotler turned to Denzel. They were still cuffed to the wall. Kotler was about to say something, to ask what Denzel thought they should do, when suddenly there was the sound of an explosion, only slightly muffled by the airlock door.

The entire place shook, and Kotler and Denzel both huddled against the wall as dust and debris fell from the ceiling above. Smoke began to fill the room, making its way through the compromised seals of the airlock.

Before Kotler or Denzel could utter a word, however, the room shook one final time, and the lights shut off, casting the two of them into complete darkness.

The tomb had been sealed.

# CHAPTER TWENTY-SEVEN

"I want an explanation, and I want it *right the hell now!*" Liz shouted, leaning in on Vellar.

The man was pressed against the outer wall of the lab, not quite cowering but certainly not comfortable with Liz's rage.

Jeffery had also squared off on him, and Liz noted that he had his fists at his side, clenched, ready for a fight.

"Things are not entirely as they appear," Vellar said in a calm but shaken tone, holding up his hands. "Please, allow me to explain. I know that looks like Daniel, but I promise it is not him."

"I *know* it's not him, Cristoff," Liz said, her jaw tight. "You're running a human cloning facility, in violation of more international laws and treaties than I can even start to count. What I want to know is, why are you cloning Dan?"

Vellar shook his head. "You misunderstand. That is not a clone of Daniel. It's not truly a clone at all—not in the sense you mean. It is a ... a host. A framework. And it is based on the genetic template of *Richard* Kotler."

"Our grandfather?" Jeffrey asked, incredulous.

"They bore a resemblance, when Richard was younger," Vellar nodded.

Liz backed off, letting the man step forward, but she remained on her guard.

"What the hell is happening here?" Liz asked.

Vellar sighed and moved forward. He motioned to the cylinder that held the humanoid form of someone who looked remarkably like Dan Kotler. Liz was having a very hard time shaking it.

"The form may look humanoid, but it's mostly a husk. Richard approached me decades ago, provided samples, and used significant influence to force me to dedicate resources to this program. The result has been some remarkable advances in the treatment of diseases—research I have ensured was freely shared as much as possible. Though I confess, we generated a great deal of false research to mask how we are getting our results. It was the only way."

"I somehow doubt that," Jeffrey said. "I've known you all my life, Cristoff. I know you well enough to know that the 'only way' is usually anything but. You may have been forced to do this in the beginning, but you've leveraged this research to make Vellar-Kotler successful."

Vellar studied him, then nodded. "Yes," he admitted. "I have. When it became clear that you boys were in danger, that you could be used as leverage, I embraced what we were doing here. I ignored the ethical ramifications, justifying my decision by telling myself that at least I was creating some good from the situation. The source material—it was Richard's. He was our donor and our test subject. He's benefited a great deal from what we've learned, what we've... harvested."

The word hung in the air between the three of them, and Liz looked at the suspended figure. The body was festooned with tubes and wires, monitors registered its every vital sign.

She looked to the displays in the panel before them and noted that there were stats for heart rate, blood pressure, oxygenation. But nothing for brain activity. Nothing to indicate that this was a being capable of thought.

It was a host, Vellar had said. It was grown for harvest.

Liz felt like vomiting.

She looked at Jeffrey. "We have to leave. Now."

Jeffrey nodded, and the two of them turned toward the door.

"Dr. Ludlum," Vellar said.

Liz paused, looking back at him.

"There's a reason I brought you into this. There's a reason you are here, now."

Liz turned back to the door, tried to open it, but nothing happened. She and Jeffrey both looked again at Vellar.

"This must end," Vellar said. "All of it."

"That's exactly what I was thinking," Liz replied.

"I brought you here so that you could do exactly as you plan," Vellar said. "I needed you to see this." He looked at Jeffrey. "I had intended to keep you out of it, Jeffrey. You and your family. Daniel ... he's the one who seems to have a penchant for getting into the middle of things. But I'm afraid that now there's no way to avoid any of this for either of you."

"Cristoff," Jeffrey said, his voice cold and stern. "Get to it. What do you need us to do?"

Vellar looked from Jeffrey to Liz. "Call your people, at the FBI. Get them here as quickly as possible. But do not tell them about this lab."

Liz actually laughed out loud. "Ridiculous," she said. "This lab is exactly why I would call them."

"The research, all our files, everything we've done and learned will be yours. Everything. But not this. I can't give you this. I don't have the power."

"What are you talking about?" Jeffrey asked.

Vellar looked mournful. "Once we entered that door, the people behind all of this were alerted. They will know we were here. If the contents of this lab are lost, Daniel will pay for it with his life. So will you." He paused, took a trembling breath, and said, "And so will your family."

The words shook Jeffrey, Liz could see. They made him angry, but they also made him afraid.

She was about to say something to him, to reassure him that the FBI would do everything it could to protect him. The words froze in her throat, however, as the sound of muffled explosions started in a progression all around them. They were coming from the outside—small detonations in a progression from near the door, moving around them in a circle.

The door opened then, and the acrid smell of metallic smoke wafted inside.

"Get out now," Vellar said. "Get out of the building. Get to your family, Jeffrey, and find somewhere safe." He looked at Liz. "Help him."

Liz wasn't sure what was happening, but she nodded. "I will," she said.

Liz and Jeffrey left the lab then, rushing through the door and dodging among the lines of makeshift labs and workstations, racing toward the elevator they'd used to come here.

Liz glanced back only once and saw Vellar standing in the doorway of the cube-shaped lab. The door closed as she watched, and the cube itself began to descend into the floor.

She had little time to consider what this meant as she and Jeffrey reached the elevator and tumbled inside. In seconds they were racing upward to the ground floor. When the elevator stopped, and the doors opened, they stepped out into a storm of chaos.

People were running for the exits, some carrying stacks of

documents and hefty-looking equipment. Liz and Jeffrey glanced at each other before threading their way into the flow of the exodus.

Once outside, Liz saw what had caused the commotion.

A number of military-grade helicopters and transport vehicles had arrived on the grounds, while the two of them had been downstairs. Armed men were pressing forward, knocking aside anyone in their way.

Liz and Jeffrey hesitated at the threshold of the elevator for a moment, peering through the chaotic crowd, searching for a path. Liz spotted something strange—four men, each manning a corner of a rectangular cube.

An older man accompanied them, with two armed guards on either side. It was the man who caught Liz's attention. Despite his apparent age he was spry and moved with the control and mobility of a much younger man. His features were somewhat masked by age, but Liz still felt a shock of recognition. She had never seen this man before—not specifically. She was sure of that. But she recognized his features.

This was Richard Kotler.

Dan and Jeffrey's grandfather.

The resemblance was strong, even with their differences in age.

"This way," Jeffrey said, grabbing Liz by the arm and dragging her to the side. "I know a place where we can take cover. Do you have your phone?"

Liz fumbled for it in her pocket and withdrew it. She immediately made the call, contacting the switchboard in the FBI offices. She relayed the situation, as much as she was able. She was told help was on the way, though Liz was told that they were shorthanded at the moment. Backup would be en route from another hot zone, from what Liz could determine.

"I need to speak with Agent Danielle Brown!" Liz shouted into the phone.

"Agent Brown is currently out of contact," the operator said. "She's still on site with the recovered Congresspeople."

"Wait," Liz said, "the abductees? They've been rescued?"

"Agent Brown found them earlier today, and a lot of our people are onsite."

Liz followed Jeffrey down a trail leading away from the Vellar-Kotler building. The two of them were racing along the gravel path as Liz talked.

She got as much information as she could, then hung up. She immediately dialed Dani's number, but the call went straight to voicemail.

Liz was about to type a text message when she realized she had an unread message from Dani herself.

*DB made contact. I've found the Senators. We need to talk about what this means.*

It had been sent while Liz and Jeffrey were in the laboratory below. The signal must have been blocked, and it came through as soon as Liz was topside again.

DB made contact.

Vellar's butler.

Vellar had given Dani a lead that had broken the abduction case open and allowed her to mount a rescue.

There were implications to this that Liz couldn't quite pull together at the moment. At the very least it meant that Vellar had known where the abducted Senators and their aides had been held. It might mean he'd been a part of the abduction. But Liz didn't think so.

She really couldn't be sure of his motives, but Vellar appeared to have risked everything to get Liz and Dani to start looking deeper into the origins of Historic Crimes. He knew it would lead them here. He knew it would inevitably uncover Richard Kotler's existence.

Liz wasn't sure how much she could trust Vellar, but something was telling her that he'd intended to do some good here.

Jeffrey suddenly grabbed her arm and pulled her into the woods, veering off the trail. They dropped to the ground, and Jeffrey held a finger to his lips.

Liz looked up and saw a squadron of four armed men jogging along the trail.

Were they looking for her and Jeffrey?

Anything was possible right now, and it seemed very likely that these men were hunting for them. All hell was breaking loose on the grounds, and it looked like things would escalate quickly. Her call for backup would bring help, but how long would that take? If everyone was preoccupied with the rescue of the Senators ...

Realization flashed through her brain with such abruptness that she almost made a sound.

The timing of this was not a coincidence. It was a given that any rescue of the abducted Congresspeople would result in a concentration of US law enforcement on that location, that event. Media, as well, would be drawn there. Finding and recovering those Senators and their aides would effectively create a blackout that someone could exploit.

And someone had.

Liz and Jeffrey would need to stay hidden until help finally got here. They'd need to survive.

She looked at Jeffrey—so much like his brother, at this moment. Grim determination, a calculation running through his head. He was looking through the underbrush, watching as the armed men passed. Liz knew he had only one thought: His family was in danger.

"We can't stay here," Liz said finally. It was the first time she'd fully realized it. "We have to go back to your place. We have to do what Vellar said."

Jeffrey looked at her, worry plain on his face.

"We have to get your family to safety," Liz said. "No matter what it takes."

# CHAPTER TWENTY-EIGHT

KOTLER COULD SMELL SMOKE, but that was as much information as he was able to gather from his senses. The darkness around them was total. Even sound had been tamped to mere phantom whispers in the aftermath of the detonations outside the airlock.

"Kotler?" Denzel asked from the darkness.

"I'm here, still alive," Kotler said. "For now."

"Weren't we just doing this a few days ago?" Denzel asked.

Kotler actually smiled and then laughed. "You're right. I think we're in a rut."

There was the sound of metal clinking metal. "I'm still cuffed," Denzel said. "You?"

In answer, Kotler clinked his own cuffs against the metal of the table he was cuffed to.

This was certainly a familiar predicament, he agreed. For the past three years or so Kotler had found himself in one dangerous scenario after another, odds stacked above his head, seemingly no way out.

But there was always a way out.

"*The key is in this room*," Kotler intoned.

"What?" Denzel replied.

"Richard said it before he and the others left and set off those charges. 'The key is in this room.' And then he made those references, remember? To this being a tomb? He made a joke about us ending up in tombs a lot."

"I remember," Denzel said, a familiar tone of impatience in his voice. "So what does it mean?"

Kotler was thinking. He pulled against the handcuff on his wrist once more. The clink of metal sounded pretty solid. But if his grandfather had really been giving them a clue—if he really was trying to give them a way out of here ...

Kotler felt his way around the cuff, prying at it with his fingers, trying to get an idea of it in the darkness.

As he moved a finger into the gap between the two curved plates of metal that formed the outer arc of the cuff, something moved.

The gap widened.

Kotler felt his pulse quicken as he pressed his fingers deeper, levering the gap wider until the cuff fell loose from his wrist.

"The cuffs are fake," Kotler said, grinning into the darkness. "They pull apart."

A moment later, there was another clinking sound, and Denzel replied, "I'm out."

Kotler laughed lightly. It was a far cry from being free of this room, but it was a start. And it meant, at the very least, that Richard really had been giving them some clue to an escape. That was hopeful news.

Kotler was far from trusting his grandfather. But he could at least believe him. This far, if no further.

"Now what?" Denzel said. He was standing closer now, and Kotler heard a faint strain in his voice.

*Claustrophobia,* Kotler realized, recognizing the familiar notes in Denzel's tone.

It didn't seem as though it was critical, just yet. But Kotler knew the longer they were in this room, the more stressful this would be for his friend. He'd gotten better at managing it, but he'd been through a lot lately. Physical injuries, drugs in his system, the strain of being trapped in this room—it would take a toll.

Kotler thought, then said, "The key is in this room. I think we can trust that. Richard means for us to escape. We just have to find it."

"How, Kotler?" Denzel said. "It's darker than Michael Bay's soul in here."

Kotler laughed. "Did you just make a Michael Bay joke in the middle of a dire situation?"

"You've had a negative impact on my sense of humor," Denzel replied.

Kotler laughed again and started feeling around, trying to find anything in the room that might help them with their current predicament. Sounds from the other side of the room indicated that Denzel had the same plan.

After several minutes of groping, Kotler found something.

A length of rubber hose. Kotler followed it with his fingers and found that it was connected to a jet in the wall. The other end was connected to a standard Bunsen burner.

"I may have something," he said. "Bunsen burner." He felt around some more and found a drawer under the countertop. Opening this, he sorted through the items inside until his fingers came upon something that made his heart thump.

A flint striker.

Kotler followed the line again, and when his fingers came once again to the jet in the wall, he found the valve handle. He took a breath, praying that the gas lines remained intact despite the earlier detonations. He turned the valve to the on position.

He immediately heard the hiss of gas from the burner.

Feeling it out, he used the striker, squeezing it a few times to generate sparks. By the light of these, he was able to align the striker with the burner, and on the next strike, there was a small burst, a tiny explosion as the gas ignited.

They had light.

"Good work, Kotler," Denzel said.

Kotler looked across the room and saw his friend in the flickering light. Relief was plain on his face and in the way he was standing. The light did wonders for pushing back Denzel's rising anxiety.

Kotler had to admit, it was a boost to his own morale as well.

"So, now what?" Denzel asked.

Kotler took a breath and huffed. "Richard said the key was here, so we can assume he meant that there's a way out. We just have to find it."

Denzel had moved and was inspecting the airlock. He tried the door, wedging his fingers between it and the frame it was mounted in. A gap had opened, after the detonation, but that was as much of an opening as they were likely to get.

Kotler didn't think the door was the key. Richard had been hinting. He'd given them a clue to work from. Maybe more than one.

He'd taunted them a bit, calling this place their tomb, pointing out that they found themselves in tombs often. Kotler had just been musing on this point himself, but maybe that was no coincidence. Maybe Richard had meant to force a mental connection in Kotler's mind. And Denzel's as well, apparently. He'd been the first to remark on how familiar this all was.

*The key is in this room.*

Richard had clearly followed Kotler's career. He, of all people, might have known more about Kotler's exploits than anyone. Maybe even more than Kotler himself, considering the nature of the Jani and the Novensiles, and their reach into the governments and centers of power in the world.

Thinking of the Jani reminded Kotler of the first time he'd met Granger, and consequently the first time he'd learned of the Jani. Granger had abducted him from a hotel room in Denver and driven him to Cheyenne Mountain. Kotler was being used to find and open the first of many Jani vaults. And since that moment, he'd helped them—willingly and unwillingly—to do the same, again and again.

Some sort of ploy, Kotler now realized. A move against Richard. A manipulation. A way to entangle Kotler in the affairs of the Jani, and use him as leverage against his grandfather.

But it was also a pattern.

This place, wherever they were, was controlled by the Novensiles. A secret base. An underground lab. It was likely something the Novensiles had coopted from the Jani, right under their nose.

Kotler had played with this band before. He knew the score.

This place was probably hidden in plain sight. For all Kotler knew, they could be in the basement of his apartment building. But it didn't matter where it was, or who controlled it. Kotler had been in this position before, and that familiarity gave him confidence.

There was a way out, and it was hidden in this room.

He began rummaging through cabinets again, opening drawers, pushing against walls, searching. Denzel, picking up on what Kotler was doing, did the same.

It was slow, tedious work, especially in low light. The

burner seemed to be on an infinite supply, at least. But Kotler did worry about potentially burning off their supply of oxygen.

It wouldn't matter.

If they couldn't find a way out, they'd die here anyway. Asphyxiation might be preferable to slowly starving to death.

After a thorough search, Kotler and Denzel stood in the center of the room, both clearly frustrated by the lack of progress.

"Nothing," Denzel said. "I think your grandpa was lying."

Kotler actually laughed at the word. It was wonderfully soft and informal, compared to how he thought of Richard. Kotler couldn't imagine having the sort of relationship with his grandfather that would lead to such a familiar name.

Richard had used him. Had used both of them. He might have granted them this last chance at survival, might even have been protecting his grandson. But his motives were clear. He wanted the contents of that sarcophagus. The souls of gods and kings.

Kotler paused.

He looked at the metal table, adorned with the stone sarcophagus, now upside down. The slab of stone that had been its bottom still leaning against the legs of the table.

It was an oddly appropriate thing to be at the center of this space, if one were to think of this as a tomb. Take away the stainless steel, the modern cabinetry, the hints of modern technology, and this was yet another locked room with a sarcophagus. Kotler had been in spaces just like this a thousand times, if he looked at it from that perspective. In the past two years alone, he'd been in the tombs of ancient gods from both the Mayan and Egyptian pantheons.

And both had hidden secrets that had been the key to his escape.

Kotler moved to the sarcophagus and the table, stooped,

inspected the floor.

It was too dark.

Denzel followed him as he moved back to the counter where the burner was providing their only source of light. "You've found something?"

"Maybe," Kotler said. He began rummaging again. He'd just seen it. It had to be here.

In one of the cabinets above the counter, Kotler found what he was looking for—a stack of rectangular boxes, filled with cotton swabs. He took one and tore it open, gathering the swabs in a bundle in his hand. Their long, wooden stems gave him something to hold onto.

He picked up a Scotch tape dispenser from the counter and gestured for Denzel to lend him a hand. Denzel nodded, pulling a length of tape from the dispenser and lashing the swabs together so Kotler could relax his grip a bit. He flipped over his makeshift torch, holding it from the taped end, and nodded his satisfaction. There was one thing left to do.

He zipped across the room and opened another cabinet, pulling a fair-sized jar from inside.

Petroleum jelly.

He dipped the end of his cotton swab torch into this, coating it liberally, then sprinted back to the burner. He held the torch directly in the flames, and it took only a second to ignite.

Kotler moved back to the table then, holding his torch, globs of molten petroleum jelly occasionally falling in flaming drips to the floor.

"Find something?" Denzel asked, following close behind.

Kotler stooped, examining the legs of the table where they were bolted to the floor.

The stone slab leaned against the two legs on this side of the table, and as Kotler examined the floor, he smiled.

The weight of the stone had opened a seam in the floor.

Kotler stood and put his free hand on the side of the sarcophagus. "Help me!" he shouted.

Denzel joined him, and together the two of them pushed the sarcophagus off of the table, letting it crash to the side. They then slid the stone slab away, dropping it to the floor. With that, they had cleared the table on all sides.

Kotler moved to one end of the table and nodded for Denzel to take the other end. "On three, we lift," he said.

Denzel nodded, and on the count of three, the two of them lifted the table upward.

It was heavy, and Kotler had to put his torch down briefly so he could use both hands. But in only a moment they had the table and about a six-inch block of floor lifted upward and tilted away. They hoisted it out and over, setting it down partially on top of the stone slab, and then the two of them stood aside, huffing as they looked at what their work had produced.

Before them was a gap in the floor, leading down into darkness.

Kotler picked up the torch, holding it over the opening and revealing a spiral of metal stairs descending into deeper darkness below.

He heard a noise behind him and looked to find Denzel gathering things from the cabinets. He was shoving another box of swabs into his pocket, along with the container of petroleum jelly. He removed the spool of tape from the dispenser and put this in his pocket as well. And after only a moment of searching, he found a set of sharp-pointed surgical scissors and a scalpel. He handed the scissors to Kotler, who nodded in acceptance. Any weapon would do, in a pinch.

"So," Denzel said. "Down?"

Kotler huffed and nodded. "Down," he said, and the two of them, torches and sharp objects in hand, started their descent.

# CHAPTER TWENTY-NINE

Liz followed Jeffrey through the woods, both of them trusting his experience with this place to guide them in the right direction. Once he had his bearings, he had a general sense of where the parking lot was. Their hope was that they might make it to his car and that there was a clear path of escape.

It seemed unlikely to both of them. But it was the hope they had, for the moment. They were a couple of hours from the Kotler home. There was no way to get there without a car.

Jeffrey's sense of direction paid off as the two of them emerged from the woods next to a clean white line of cement that marked the edge of the parking lot. They stayed low here, looking, trying to determine if anyone was watching.

It was broad daylight. That was working against them, making them visible at a distance. But the parking lot was brimming with vehicles, which Liz figured might help.

"Do you know how to find your car from here?" Liz asked.

Jeffrey raised his head up, looking around, getting his position. "I think so," he said. He nodded and pointed, "We're over there. In the priority spots."

Liz looked to where Jeffrey was pointing and felt a pang of dismay.

The "priority spots" might have been a perk for company executives and high-profile visitors, but they were a distinct disadvantage for two people trying to make their escape unnoticed. They were close to a pickup spot for the shuttle that made its way around the parking lot. And this was currently being used as a base of operations for a couple of armed guards.

This wasn't going to be easy.

"You think they'll spot us?" Jeffrey asked.

Liz looked at him. Once again, she couldn't help but see signs of Dan in his brother's features. Maybe it was the look of concern mingled with determination and self-contained panic that brought it out in Jeffrey, but at this moment the resemblance was very strong.

"I think they will," Liz said, her tone grim. "But I don't know what to do about it."

Jeffrey looked once again from the impromptu guard shack to the general area where his car was parked. He rose slightly, studying the parking lot in various directions. "I think we can get to the car without being seen, but from there it's going to be dangerous."

Liz agreed. But it was better than sitting here, waiting to be discovered by one of the patrols moving around the facility. And she knew that Jeffrey was currently very worried for his wife and his son. She also knew that Jeffrey Kotler was every bit as determined as his brother, and there would be no stopping him in this. Better to help him. Their odds went up when they worked together.

They whispered a few last-second thoughts and ideas about

their predicament, a strategy of sorts emerged, and with a nod of agreement, they both went to it.

Jeffrey was the first to leave the tree line, crouching and sprinting for cover behind the nearest car. Liz followed in the next instant, and they found themselves now hunched between two parked vehicles. They peered around the bumpers of each, making sure things were clear, and began moving from car to car. Jeffrey once again took the lead, picking out a path that they both hoped would eventually get them to his car.

Getting there unseen was one challenge, it was slow and tedious work. But it was also physically grueling. Liz felt a burning in her calves and thighs, and there was a tension in her neck. She was fit, but this was unusual activity, and it was taking its toll. She pushed through it.

They were a row out from Jeffrey's car when he stopped and motioned for her to come forward.

She waddled toward him, taking up a spot next to him and peering around the SUV before them, in the direction Jeffrey indicated.

His car was ahead of them, just across the gap in the rows. But Liz immediately saw the problem.

Through the space between Jeffrey's car and the one next to it, they could see the shuttle stop, occupied by the two guards.

Jeffrey and Liz both slid to the ground behind the SUV, leaning against its bumper. "There's no way we can get to the car without being spotted," Jeffrey said.

Liz agreed. She huffed and shook her head, thinking. "There's backup on the way," she said. "Maybe ..."

"No," Jeffrey said. His voice was hard, edged with determination.

Liz understood instantly what was going on in his mind.

It had been her idea to go back and retrieve his family, but in reality, she'd known that it would be Jeffrey's first plan. He would get to them, or die trying. Liz couldn't live with herself if something happened and she did nothing to help him. She knew that this was the only way. They couldn't simply stand by and wait for the FBI to arrive. Jeffrey had to do something.

And so did Liz.

She nodded. "Ok. Then we need a new plan."

Jeffrey was looking around the edge of the bumper, sizing up their options.

Liz leaned back, thinking through their circumstances, considering their options.

Suddenly she had a strange, vague sense of *deja vu*.

She'd had a thousand conversations with Dan about the things he'd been through, the ways in which he found himself in trouble and had to figure a way out. How many times had he faced imminent and certain death, only to come up with some clever solution at the last minute? How many times had he managed to survive despite all the odds being against him?

This seemed like exactly the sort of scenario Dr. Dan Kotler might have ended up in. Surviving was something he simply *did*.

What had he told her, about situations like this?

*It always comes down to figuring out what you know, determining what resources you have,* Dan had told her once. *You already know what you need to do. The trick is working out how to do it with what you have.*

It was the sort of wisdom that sounded simple until you started to put it into practice. Being in the middle of this, with armed men hunting them, crouched for cover among a forest of parked cars—what resources did they really have?

"I should have called Christina," Jeffrey said quietly. Then, with a voice filled with lament, he said, "I left my phone in the car."

Liz patted her pocket and removed her phone, handing it to him. "I'm sorry, it didn't even occur to me."

Jeffrey took the phone, nodded his gratitude, and dialed. After a moment he started talking to his wife in a hurried whisper, giving her instructions, telling her how much he loved her and Alex, reassuring her that he was going to be alright.

Liz tried not to eavesdrop on the call, but she couldn't help catching bits and pieces. And it stirred within her something she hadn't expected—she realized that despite the strength of their relationship, she and Dan did not yet have the sort of fluidity and unity that Jeffrey and Christina had. Their relationship was different. More restrained, in some way.

It could just be that they were new, as a couple. Dan had been through a lot, and they'd taken their time even getting to this stage with each other. But Liz thought there might be more to it than that.

She had learned a lot about Dan and Jeffrey, as a result of this experience. The exhibit, the conversations with Vellar, even the secret Vellar revealed in that hidden lab—it opened the weave on the tapestry of the Kotler's history. The deaths of Dan and Jeffrey's parents had impacted the two of them in different ways. Being raised by Cristoff Vellar had influenced them each differently as well. But she was getting a better sense of both men from all of this—especially Dan—and she felt something now that hadn't occurred to her before.

Dan was broken.

Not only broken but desperate to repair the damage that had been done in his life, to recover what had been lost. He had been young when his parents died, but old enough to make some connections, Liz believed. Old enough to feel abandoned and betrayed, if only subconsciously. Certainly, he had been old enough to come to a decision about his life, and the path he would take, even if he might not have been fully aware of the decision itself.

Dan's dogged pursuit of history and science, following in the footsteps of his parents, had been a child's way of coping with the feelings he was having. He'd poured himself into those pursuits, and mastered them on a level that would have made any parent proud.

But he'd gone further than that.

Dan had trained like a soldier. He took on skills that would give him something of a shield against the dangers of the world —as if he realized, on some level, that he was about to walk a very dangerous path, and so he had to be ready.

He'd learned as much as he could about survival, from bushcraft to resource conservation. He had qualified on a number of weapons and studied hand-to-hand combat. And he'd done all of this right alongside getting multiple PhDs in anthropology and quantum physics.

Liz had asked him once what it was he thought he was getting out of all of it—whether he thought working his tail off for a double Ph.D. had been worth it. Dan had replied that he only regretted that he hadn't yet gone for a Ph.D. in psychology. He had laughed when he said it, but Liz knew he was only half kidding.

And it was an ironic regret, in her opinion.

From what she knew of him, Dan Kotler probably knew more about human psychology than anyone else she'd ever met. The lack of a Ph.D. was a minor concern. It was just a credential. Dan already had the knowledge he craved. He'd already studied the field more than most experts. If there was anything he knew at least as well as he knew history, it was the workings of the human mind.

If anything, understanding how people thought and what

made them work was the heart of everything else he'd ever studied.

It was only now, though, that Liz understood a singular fact about Dan: His drive to learn was insatiable. But it also felt— frantic.

At least it felt that way now, as Liz crouched at the bumper of a car, trying to keep armed men from seeing and shooting her. Thinking of Dan was probably natural enough, she figured. Realizations about him were also natural, perhaps, as in the wake of adrenaline and fear and anxiety, she was suddenly having a sort of clarity. She saw everything from a different perspective, and it was revealing things she'd never considered.

Jeffrey handed her phone back, and Liz whispered, "They'll be ok."

He nodded. "I believe they will. I just wish I was with them."

From a distance, they heard sirens, and Liz thought for a moment that maybe back up was on its way.

And in a way, it might have been. But not the backup she'd called for. Someone here must have managed to call the police, and local officers were rushing to the scene. She prayed they were prepared for what they'd find.

There was a sound from one side of the SUV they were using for cover. She and Jeffrey glanced at each other, both with expressions of panic. In the next instant, one of the armed guards stepped from around the corner, his weapon trained on the two of them. "Stay down," he said calmly. "Hands out in the open. Do not move."

Liz and Jeffrey did as they were ordered, and the second guard came up behind them. He patted each of them down, taking Liz's phone. Then he forced the two of them to stand and put their hands on the hood of one of the cars.

The first guard used a radio and called in their find.

Liz felt her stomach clench. Dread and fear gripped her. And then ... something else. Something she hadn't been expecting, but welcomed.

Rage.

Good. Rage made her stubborn. Rage made her willing to do anything it took, make any personal sacrifice, to stop men like this. She knew, instantly, that she was going to die, and that took all the fear away. All that was left was the rage.

She felt her hands clench into fists, and muscles tighten. Her arms, her legs, her abdomen—she was a coil of springs, brought to full tension, ready to launch into the face of her enemy.

Suddenly there was an explosion of noise, erupting from above the woods nearby, and a helicopter roared above them, tilting, throwing them into the wash of its blades. The sirens they'd been hearing grew louder as well, and Liz turned her head to see three local police cruisers racing into the parking lot, followed by a black sedan.

A voice from the helicopter above was issuing commands, telling the men to drop their weapons, to stand down, to get to the ground.

The first guard cursed, and then the two of them spun, ducking to use the cars for cover, just as Liz and Jeffrey had. They were making a break for it, trying to get away.

Liz felt the tide of rage boil and rise until it was spilling over her, consuming her.

She pounced.

With a roar pouring from deep within her, she turned and launched herself toward the two guards. She barreled into the first man with all her weight, taking him to the ground in the lane between cars.

She started pounding and punching him, never letting him get his bearings, never letting his hands get near his weapon.

She had him on his back now, and her knees were pinning him at the shoulders. His helmet was askew, and she managed to grab it, tear the strap loose, and remove it. Then she started using it to bludgeon the man in the face.

She was so focused on this man, her rage taking over, that it caught her by surprise when the second man came tumbling to the ground beside her.

A shot was fired, going wild into the parking lot, and Liz prepared herself for another. She had a flash of a notion, that this was it, that she was about to die. The fight was over, and she'd lost.

But in that instant, she decided she was fine with it. She'd gotten in her lumps on one of the guards. She'd done more than wait for the bullet. She wasn't going quietly. She'd fought to the end.

She was ready.

But the second shot never came.

She glanced down at the man she had pinned to the ground. His face was a bloody mess, as was his helmet and her own hands. She worried for a second that he might be dead, that she might have killed him. But in the next instant, he groaned. He was alive but unconscious. And he was going to have a hell of a headache later.

Liz looked up then and saw that Jeffrey was on top of the other man. He had the man's rifle pinned against the guy's throat, and Liz saw some of the same rage in Jeffrey's eyes as she'd felt only a moment ago.

Jeffrey was protecting his family in that moment. That was what Liz saw there. Having felt powerless, he now took out his fear and frustration and worry on this man. She could practically see it, like a sign over his head. This was the only road open to him to actually *do* something, to protect his family. That was his fuel and his power.

So what had fueled her *own* rage?

She'd think about that later. Deal with it later. For now, she stood and kicked the first man's weapon away, then looked around to see what was happening around her.

The police had arrived like an invading army. The helicopter had moved off after Liz and Jeffrey had tackled their assailants, and it had landed on a pad next to the parking lot. Armed SWAT officers were moving into positions all around them, calling to each other, making plans.

Police were approaching Liz and Jeffrey with guns drawn. They were shouting, telling the two of them to show their hands, to stand aside, to get down on the ground.

Liz registered this and did what she was told. Jeffrey held on for a few seconds more until he finally realized what was happening. He tossed the rifle far away and then sank to the ground, hands on the back of his head.

Liz was about to say something to the officers, to identify herself, when she heard a familiar and very welcome voice.

"Dr. Ludlum," a woman's voice said. "Liz."

Liz turned her head, craning to look upward, and smiled.

Agent Danielle Brown had arrived.

Dani showed her FBI credentials to the officers and vouched for both Liz and Jeffrey. She then helped both to their feet, ushering them to the side as the officers took the bloodied and battered gunmen into custody.

"You made it," Liz said.

Dani nodded. "I got your message, and I picked up chatter from these guys as I got closer. It's ... been a busy day."

Liz slumped a little, letting her hands fall to her side. "Dani, there's something going on in that facility. Something big."

Dani studied Liz's face, looking from her to Jeffrey and back again. She motioned for both of them to follow her to the area where SWAT had set up a temporary base of operations. They were immediately led to a van where they were told to sit, given cups of water, and left to themselves.

"Give me all the details," Dani said, as they settled in. "Tell me what we're dealing with."

Liz and Jeffrey exchanged glances, and Liz inhaled and exhaled slowly. "This could take a while," she said.

"I've got time," Dani replied.

Liz shook her head. "No," she said. "You don't." And with that, she launched into everything she'd learned over the past 24 hours.

# CHAPTER THIRTY

As they moved deeper into the darkness, Kotler felt increasingly grateful for both the makeshift torch and the pair of surgical scissors. In a fight, they wouldn't be much of a weapon. But the mental security they provided was enough for now. It was something, at least.

The spiral of steel steps and railing terminated on a concrete floor about twenty feet below the lab. Kotler and Denzel had moved with caution, being as quiet as possible, and upon reaching the bottom, they turned in a circle to inspect their options from here. By Kotler's estimate, unless they wanted to go back up and take their chances in the lab, their options were narrowed to only two.

Here, with darkness pressing in from all around, they were standing in what appeared to be a maintenance tunnel that stretched into the distance in two directions. There was no way to know whether the tunnel ran north-south or east-west, and no way to know where either direction would lead.

"Well," Kotler said to Denzel. "Right or left?"

"Right," Denzel replied, with no hesitation.

Kotler blinked in surprise. "That was a quick decision. Do you know something I don't know?"

Denzel shrugged. "When in doubt, always take the right path."

Kotler was stunned for a moment, then laughed. "Ok, that is going into my mental catalog of survival advice. Clever."

"Let's see if it's clever enough to get us out of here without getting us killed," Denzel replied.

He started down the right path, with Kotler following close behind, sputtering torch in hand. The wooden shafts of the swabs were burning now, and Kotler worried that their only source of light might not last them much longer. They had the other set of swabs that Denzel had grabbed, but the rate at which these things burned meant they'd have to wait until the very last second to light the new batch. Once that one went out …

They'd figure something out when the time came. Kotler was already mentally cataloging their resources, trying to keep in mind anything they had that might be useful. For now, though, it was important that they keep moving, as quickly as possible.

"Where do you figure we are?" Denzel asked.

Kotler had caught up to him, and the two were walking side by side. He shook his head. "No idea. I'd guess this is a military base of some kind. The Jani have access to a few. They took me to one when I first met Granger."

"In Colorado," Denzel said.

"Cheyenne Mountain," Kotler replied, nodding. "There are a lot of secrets in that mountain."

"Do you think that's where we are now?"

Kotler thought for a moment. "I can't be sure, but maybe? We were literally flying blind to and from the facility holding Anwar Adham, and we definitely went down in the mountains.

I'm not much of an expert in identifying local geology, but our crash site resembled a lot of places I've been in the Rockies."

Denzel laughed.

Kotler, peering at him, asked, "What did I say?"

Denzel was shaking his head. "I'm just surprised to learn there's something you're not an expert at," he said.

Kotler chuckled. "Oh, there's more. Geology, meteorology, economics ... the social dynamics of romantic relationships."

Denzel again barked a laugh at this. "You're not alone on that one," he said. "Relationships are a complete mystery to me. Always have been."

"I've met some of the women you've dated," Kotler said. "They seem wonderful. Smart, attractive. I was never quite sure why you didn't have anything steady."

"I've dated plenty of amazing women," Denzel nodded. "I just haven't always been so amazing myself. I tend to put the work ahead of the relationship."

Kotler thought about this for a second. "Me too," he said.

Again Denzel laughed. "Yeah, I know Kotler. I've known you for three years now, and I realized a long time ago that for you, the work and the relationship are the same things. If it gets beyond galas and museum openings, that's when it's serious."

"Gee, Roland, don't hold back. Let me have it."

Denzel shook his head. "It's not a slam, Kotler. It's ... advice."

"Don't let work interfere with my personal relationships," Kotler nodded.

Denzel made another noise, a grunt of disgust maybe. "No, that's not it. Not really. The advice is, stick to the relationships with people who understand what you're doing and who you are. Stick with someone who knows you well enough to realize you aren't actually putting the work first. The work is a big part of who you are and how you relate to the world."

Kotler's eyebrows shot up, and he peered at his friend in the flicker of torchlight. "That's ... weirdly insightful," Kotler said.

"For a dumb FBI meathead with no PhDs, you mean," Denzel replied, smirking.

"I"ve never thought that, and never will," Kotler replied.

Denzel nodded at this, accepting it. "Liz is good for you," he said.

Kotler didn't say anything for a long while after that. Mostly because he knew his friend was right. Liz *was* good for him.

The problem was, Kotler wasn't so sure he was good for *her*.

Since the very beginning of their relationship, it was like the troubles in Kotler's life had a way of spilling over onto the people he was closest to. Denzel didn't quite count since it was more or less his job to deal with these sorts of troubles. But Evelyn Horelica. Eloi Coelho. Jeffrey and his family. Liz. They were all impacted by the things that happened in Kotler's life, sometimes in frightening, violent ways. Eloi's death still haunted Kotler—he still found ways to think of it as his fault. The same was true for Evelyn. Would she have been abducted and held all that time, if Kotler wasn't a part of her life?

And then there was Gail McCarthy.

A special case, for sure. She was the villain, after all. The head of the most powerful smuggling ring in history. Her death —well, it had literally been at his hands. But considering she'd been bent on world domination, and on empowering the highest bidder on the world stage with a tool that would make them all-powerful, maybe he shouldn't feel quite the same haunting regret over his role in her demise.

And yet, it did still haunt him. And he couldn't quite shake the guilt of it, nor the feeling that if not for him maybe she would have discovered a different path. Maybe she could have gotten past her boundless ambition, and put her incredible intelligence to work for something better in the world.

Or maybe she would have continued doing what she was doing, unchallenged, until she'd created something vastly evil in the world. He needed to keep things in perspective when it came to Gail.

But the question remained: Was it fair for Kotler to have relationships, to keep ties with anyone on that level when he might be bringing danger into their lives?

Kotler was still pondering this when Denzel put a hand on his chest, stopping him. He then nudged Kotler to the side of the tunnel.

"Hide the torch," Denzel said.

Kotler tilted the torch away from him and swung it behind his back, blocking it with his body. It wouldn't mask the light entirely, but he was reluctant to snuff it out. They had no way to restart it if he did.

They clung to the wall, and Kotler stared ahead, trying to see what Denzel had noticed.

As his eyes adjusted, he saw it.

Light.

Up ahead, distant enough that it was just a small glow from their vantage point, there was a light hanging from the ceiling. It cast a sphere of artificial illumination onto the walls, ceiling, and floor of the maintenance tunnel.

"Do you see anyone ahead?" Kotler asked.

"No," Denzel replied. "Looks clear." Despite the words, however, Denzel drew the scalpel, holding it out in front of him like a sword, ready for a duel.

Kotler did the same with the scissors, and then brought the torch itself forward.

Two warriors, woefully under-armed, hardly ready to face whatever lay ahead.

They glanced at each other and started to walk toward the light.

It was still quite a ways ahead, and at the pace they were moving it was taking a great deal of time to reach it. That was fine. If someone was there, it was best to approach as stealthily as possible. It might give them the only advantage they were going to get.

The maintenance tunnel was well-maintained, Kotler mused. That meant that people came here, and often. It might only be a matter of time before he and Denzel were discovered here, and the nature of the tunnel made it so that there was little they would be able to do to escape if things went wrong. They'd be at the mercy of anyone who happened along.

So walking toward the light was at once a hopeful and dreadful experience. Kotler was gripping the tiny surgical scissors so hard he could feel the metal rings of the handle digging into his palm. The torch, burning down towards its end, was pitiful, and more than once Kotler considered discarding it. But it was a resource, and one they couldn't get back, once it was gone. He carried on.

They moved cautiously, quietly, at a painful pace. As they inched closer to the light, certain details were revealed.

There was a door set into the wall on the lefthand side of the tunnel.

Upon reaching it, Kotler could see that there was a small window framed into it, a mesh of wire forming diamonds in the glass. He and Denzel both peered through it.

Beyond, there was another door. This time for an elevator.

Kotler and Denzel stepped back, looking at each other.

"What do you think?" Kotler asked.

Denzel shook his head. "That elevator is bound to lead somewhere that has people. Probably armed people."

Kotler peered down the corridor in the direction they'd

been walking, and then in the direction they'd been moving. He still held the torch in his hand, but it was starting to dim. If they were going to push on, they needed to make the second torch. Judging by the rate at which the first one burned, they'd have, at most, half an hour of light, once they left this place.

He looked then at the door with the window. On a whim, he reached out and tried the handle. It turned. The door pulled open slightly, with a light tug. It wasn't locked.

Kotler huffed and said, "Roland, I think we should risk it."

Denzel studied him. "Want to give me a reason why?"

"I don't have anything that's going to sound all that inviting. Honestly, it comes down to just facing this. I don't think we're going to avoid coming into contact with these people, whoever they turn out to be. I'd rather do it on our terms as much as possible, and maybe we can find a way out of all of this. Otherwise ..."

It hung for a moment, but Denzel picked it up, knowing exactly what Kotler was getting at. "We go down fighting," he said.

Kotler nodded.

Denzel took a breath and blew it out. "Ok," he said. "Let's do this."

Kotler tossed the makeshift torch on the floor, stepping on it to put it out. It brought to mind the apocryphal story of Captain Hernán Cortés, who upon his landing at Veracruz, on the path to conquest, ordered his men to burn their ships. They would have victory, or they would have death.

It was a noble sort of thought, but it did little to comfort Kotler as he gripped a tiny pair of surgical scissors with which he intended to face down an army of men with automatic weapons.

They pushed through the door, tiny weapons in hand, and then hit the button for the elevator. It opened immediately.

"Must be set to stay down here by default," Kotler said.

"Probably a safety measure, in case someone's down here, and something goes wrong."

"What about stairs?" Kotler asked.

Denzel shook his head. "I didn't see any. Maybe further down. But this could mean that we're about to take a very long ride."

He was right.

Once they were on the elevator, the doors closed and it shot upward at a sickening speed. Kotler and Denzel remained tense, pushing themselves to opposite sides of the elevator, ready to take cover at its front, when it stopped, and the doors started to open.

Kotler noted there was no control panel for the elevator. There was a single button, and above that, a keyhole that must have been similar to the controls firefighters would use to hold or call an elevator. Neither was marked. And the elevator had started moving upward once the doors were closed, indicating it must detect weight and activate automatically.

This elevator was meant for rapid transit between one floor and the maintenance shaft, and nothing else.

A few minutes went by as they ascended into the unknown, and then the elevator slowed until finally, it came to a rest with a slight bump. The door opened.

Kotler and Denzel were pressed against the front of the elevator, on either side of its door, waiting. As the door slid clear, they peered around and were immediately greeted by the sound of clacking military-grade rifles, and the sight of dozens of very armed, very serious soldiers gathered in front of the opening.

Kotler immediately spotted Air Force insignia, along with US flag patches on helmets and sleeves. And from behind, a balding man in Air Force blues stepped forward, four stars adorning his shoulders. "Who the hell are you?" he barked.

Denzel and Kotler stepped cautiously out into the open, each dropping their weapons, such as they were. They held their hands up and made no move to exit the elevator.

"General," Denzel said. "My name is Agent Roland Denzel, with the FBI. This is Doctor Daniel Kotler, a consultant with the Bureau. We've been held against our will for several days, and managed to find the maintenance tunnel that brought us here."

The General stepped forward, framed by armed Airmen in combat fatigues. "Not good enough, Agent," the General said. He nodded to his people, who stepped forward and took both Denzel and Kotler into custody.

They were hurried along within the facility, led through tunnels with concrete walls, until finally they were deposited in a windowless room, searched for anything they might be carrying.

One of the Airmen, a woman who had been patting Denzel down, took out the box of swabs, the Scotch tape, and the petroleum jelly. She held the items up, raising an eyebrow to Denzel.

Denzel blushed, which made Kotler smirk.

"It's for making a torch," he said to her.

She looked at him skeptically.

"I swear to God," Denzel replied.

The Airman shook her head and left the two of them alone, the door slamming shut with metallic permanence behind her.

"Well," Kotler said, smiling, "that went well."

"If you mean that we weren't shot, I agree," Denzel said.

"So, now what?" Kotler asked.

The answer, it turned out, was that the two of them waited. And waited.

And waited.


AT ONE POINT, a guard brought them trays of food, stood and watched them eat, and retrieved the trays before leaving. He wouldn't answer any of their questions, and only spoke to say that he had his orders, and they could eat, or he could take the food away.

They ate.

Kotler hadn't realized how hungry he'd actually been, but he was ravenous as he dug into the unidentifiable entree. Even Air Force rations were delicious—to a point.

After the meal, they resumed waiting, and Kotler genuinely thought he might lose his mind.

He and Denzel had exhausted every civil conversation they could have and had briefly bickered over some of the things that had obviously been on Denzel's chest, regarding Kotler's habits. His refusal to allow for an embedded tracking device, for one, was something that irritated Denzel. Especially considering how often Kotler was abducted or held prisoner.

The argument was short but bitter, and they'd decided it would be best if each of them got some sleep. They were both still recovering from their injuries, not to mention the tension and stress of the past few days. They each picked one of the bunks in the room, and were both asleep in minutes.

There was no way to tell the time in this place, but when the doors eventually opened, and both Kotler and Denzel were startled awake, it felt as if hours might have passed.

They were both ordered to follow the man who had burst into the room.

Kotler took it as a good sign that this man wasn't openly wielding a weapon, and that no other guards or soldiers were present. Groggily, Kotler fell in beside Denzel as they followed the man through the concrete corridors once more, until they finally came to a briefing room.

Kotler sighed in relief.

Sitting in chairs around a large, oblong table, alongside the General and a couple of other Air Force Blues, were men in suits that could only be higher-ups with the FBI. Kotler thought he recognized one of them, though he didn't know the man's name.

"Agent Denzel," one of the FBI men said, standing to shake Denzel's hand. he turned to Kotler and extended a hand to him as well. "Dr. Kotler," he said, smiling.

Kotler noted the smile was perfunctory. His body language was reserved, guarded.

Introductions were made, and Kotler and Denzel sat. They were given water, and a large tray of fruits and finger sandwiches was brought in. Everyone was invited to help themselves to whatever they liked, but it was clear this was meant for Kotler and Denzel, who dove in with no hesitation.

"Agent Denzel, Dr. Kotler," the General said, "I would like to formally apologize for the reception you received, upon your arrival. But you can understand our alarm when you stepped out of that elevator, into a secured facility."

"Yes, General," Denzel said around a bite of sandwich. He quickly swallowed. "No apologies necessary. We were ... in a challenging situation."

"I believe that, son," the General said, nodding. "Everyone here has been brought up to speed, based on the briefing you gave when you first arrived. Now we think you might want to hear about what's been happening since you've been gone."

"For a start," one of the FBI agents—Director Sharpton— said, "the Senators and their aides have been rescued."

Kotler raised his eyebrows. "They have! That's incredible! Were they safe? Was anyone hurt?"

Sharpton shook his head. "No, everyone came through without a scratch. Thanks in part to Agent Danielle Brown," he said, looking to Denzel.

"Danielle?" Denzel replied.

"She was instrumental in their rescue," Sharpton continued. "She received a tip via email. We're still running down the source, but it paid off. She showed real initiative, Agent Denzel. I've already initiated the process for a commendation."

Denzel smiled and nodded. "I'd like to add a letter to that commendation, sir. If you don't mind."

"Not at all," Sharpton said. "But there's more you should know. Agent Brown left the scene of the rescue upon receiving a message from the FBI switchboard. It seems Dr. Elizabeth Ludlum found herself in some danger, at a facility you may be familiar with, Dr. Kotler."

"Liz?" Kotler asked, suddenly on the edge of his seat. "Is she alright?"

"She's fine. And so is your brother," Sharpton said.

Kotler shook his head. "My .. brother? Jeffrey?"

"The two of them were present during an incursion at a Vellar-Kotler Genetics," the Director said. His tone had changed subtly. He was quieter. There was a harder edge to his voice. "One that is currently still in progress."

"Vellar-Kotler," Denzel said, looking Kotler's way.

"My family's business," Kotler replied absently. "An incursion? Is ... what happened there? Are Liz and Jeffrey ok? What about Crisoff Vellar? And the people working there? What happened?"

Sharpton had been watching Kotler as he spoke, his expression curious.

Absently, Kotler registered something in Sharpton's features.

Suspicion.

"Dr. Kotler, what can you tell us about what goes on at your family's business? What is it, exactly, that Vellar-Kotler Genetics does?"

Kotler shook his head and sighed. "Research, mostly. They use genetic research to test and vet treatments for diseases and illnesses, to try to break new ground on cures for things such as cancer and HIV. There are other lines of research—things my father and my mother were involved in before their deaths. But to be honest, Director, I don't keep up with what the company does. I have no knowledge of any of their ongoing projects, beyond what they share in shareholder reports. Cristoff runs the entire operation."

"I've gathered that," Sharpton replied. "What can you tell me about Cristoff Vellar?"

Kotler could see this was leading somewhere, but he wasn't sure where, and so he wasn't sure how to head off any potential danger.

Was Cristoff in trouble?

What Kotler really wanted to know was what was happening with Liz and Jeffrey. But this was a game. One he knew he'd have to play to the end, or he might lose by default. He had no idea of the stakes, but his sense was that they were high.

"Cristoff took Jeffrey and me in after our parents died," Kotler said. "He made sure we had the finest education, that we were taken care of in every way. He ... in many ways, he has always been family to me. If he's in any sort of trouble, I'd like to help."

"You are helping, Dr. Kotler," Sharpton said. "We're finding ourselves short on answers right now, so anything you tell us will be useful."

Kotler took this in and nodded. "Alright," he said. "I'll answer any questions you have, but I'd really like to know what's happened. Maybe that will give me some context, so we don't spin our wheels."

Sharpton looked to the other man, an aide who occasionally bent to whisper things to Sharpton, advising him. He did this now, and Sharpton nodded, apparently satisfied about which details he could share.

"The incursion," Sharpton started. "It was carried out by some sort of mercenary force. Well-armed, organized. Remarkably similar to the group that abducted the Senators and their aides. They arrived at the facility and took it over in minutes. Very efficient, as if they knew the layout well. They immediately fortified certain levels and had operatives patrolling the grounds. Our people have managed to reclaim all of the aboveground levels, but deep below the facility is a lab that we can't penetrate. They have it completely sewn up. Dr. Ludlum has given us a description of the place and told us some very disturbing things she witnessed there. Your brother, Jeffrey Kotler, corroborates her story."

The aide handed Sharpton a folder, and Sharpton opened it, studied something inside, and then dropped it in front of Kotler. "Do you recognize this man?"

Kotler looked and saw a fan of photos. The images were obviously pulled from security footage. He turned the folder and started sifting through each of the photos inside.

The man was Richard Kotler. His grandfather.

"He led a small group of people carrying that box," Sharpton said, reaching out to bring one photo in particular into view.

Kotler recognized the box but kept himself in check.

It was the cryogenic carrier.

The same that Richard had liberated from the lab before detonating the doors and sealing Kotler and Denzel inside. The carrier that contained "the souls of gods and kings." Cargo that Kotler, himself, had helped Richard obtain.

"He's known as the Chairman," Kotler said. He had decided to keep the rest of Richard's identity off the record for now. He didn't glance toward Denzel, but he hoped his friend recognized the importance of keeping this secret. If these men learned that Richard was Kotler's grandfather, Kotler himself would be out of the game. And he needed to stay in, for now. He needed some answers. He needed to help. For Liz and Jeffrey's sake, if no other reason.

But for Richard, as well. Because Kotler was now determined that he had to be there when his grandfather was brought down.

"The Chairman," Sharpton said, and his aide made a note. "Do you know his plans?"

Kotler huffed and looked around at the men in the room. When his gaze got back to Sharpton, he said, "He plans to raise the dead, Director."

The room became still, and silence hung over them all until finally, Kotler broke it. "And I may be the only one who can stop him."

# CHAPTER THIRTY-ONE

THEY ARRIVED at Vellar-Kotler by helicopter after a hasty flight from Colorado Springs to the local airport. Kotler had noted that they had, indeed, been within a section of Cheyenne Mountain.

The implications of this were astounding.

Three years earlier, Kotler and Denzel had worked together for the first time in an effort to bring down Anwar Adham, who was leading a small army of men on a mission to detonate a makeshift nuclear device under Cheyenne Mountain. Their goal was to strike a serious blow to US security and throw the entire nation into panic.

Kotler and Denzel had stopped him, as well as the billionaire who was financing him. And that had been the start of an astounding shift in Kotler's career.

It was less than a year ago that he'd been back to Cheyenne Mountain, this time helping to unlock a secret Jani vault—under duress, at first. It was then that he'd met Granger, the immense, enigmatic man who had begun slowly indoctrinating Kotler into the world of the Jani.

And now, after being abducted by the Novensiles—by his own grandfather, whom Kotler had thought was long dead— here he found himself once again within Cheyenne Mountain, once again facing life or death circumstances, once again finding himself to be a pawn in someone else's game.

This mountain was cursed, Kotler decided.

Or he was.

They had disembarked from the small plane and immediately boarded a waiting helicopter, and within half an hour, they were landing next to another set of helicopters on the Vellar-Kotler landing pad. It was getting a little crowded there, Kotler observed.

Kotler and Denzel were hurried along to a commandeered shuttle, and driven straight to the front entrance of the building. They made their way into the lobby, and from there were taken to the elevator that led to the lab below. Beside it a door stood open, propped open to reveal a set of stairs.

Kotler didn't like the looks of those stairs.

"We've shut the elevators down," one of the soldiers informed them. "We have people at every exit from that lab. We just can't get into the lab itself. There's a biometric lock, and everything is airtight. We think the panel itself is booby-trapped. If we do this wrong, our experts say we'll deadlock that thing. No way in."

Kotler nodded. "I was here when the security systems were installed. I'm listed as full clearance with every system in this building."

"Does that include this lab?" the man asked.

Kotler wasn't sure. He huffed. "Until today, I didn't even know that lab existed. So ... maybe? But from what I read in the briefing, Cristoff did have the lab itself on the books. The other thing, the room within the lab ..." Kotler could barely bring himself to think about Liz's recorded statement. Cloning? She'd given details about the embryos and the chambers. But Kotler couldn't help feeling she'd left something out. He knew Liz and knew how thorough she was. There were details that seemed a bit sketchy, considering who was giving them. There was something in that room she didn't want the military or FBI to know about.

"I never knew about the cloning work here. That room may be locked to me, if we can even reach it. Liz said that it sank into the floor as she and Jeffrey were leaving."

The man nodded. "We have a contingency plan for that. This way, sir." He led Kotler and Denzel to the stairs, and a long, painful, downward slog began.

Kotler still didn't have his phone, or a watch, but he could tell this was taking a very long time. Despite the assistance from gravity, going down was nearly as slow as going up might have been, if only because everyone was loaded to the hilt with ordnance and equipment.

Kotler was still recovering from his injuries as well, and was taking the stairs a bit more slowly and gingerly than he might have otherwise. So was Denzel, from what he could tell. And he suspected that the soldiers were setting their pace to the two of them.

Every muscle from his lower back to his toes was burning, and each jarring step sent flashes of pain through him. And the stairs continued on. And on. Deeper with each step, but seemingly never reaching the bottom.

Kotler was just on the verge of asking whether they might reactivate the elevator at least long enough to get them down to the bottom from this point, when they suddenly came to a halt. Before them was a large, steel door. Beside it was an array of biometric scanners.

And among the soldiers gathered around the door, ready and waiting, was Liz.

A wave of relief fell over Kotler, and he rushed toward her. She met him halfway, and they embraced for a moment before leaning back, smiling at each other. "I didn't expect you to be here!" Kotler said.

Liz shook her head. "They asked if I would be a part of the mission." She patted her body, indicating an armored vest with "FBI" emblazoned across it in large, yellow letters.

Kotler, wearing his own vest, did the same. "Where's Jeffrey?" he asked, concerned.

"With his family," Liz said. "They took them to a safe house. They figured I've been through training, so I'm not a civilian," she rolled her eyes. "What amazing luck."

Kotler smiled and nodded, then his expression turned serious. "And Cristoff ... he was part of this?"

"That part's tricky," Liz said cautiously. "But yes, he's known about this. He stayed behind. That cloning lab sunk into the floor like an elevator, just before the bad guys got here. I think he might be trying to keep it from them. I really don't know." She hesitated. "A ... a lot has happened, Dan. A lot."

There was something in her tone. Kotler knew her well enough to know she was hiding something, if not from him then from the men around them. Information she didn't feel she could share out in the open. Something she figured Kotler would care about.

Was she protecting him?

What did this mean?

Kotler wanted to ask, but knew this wasn't the time. There might never be a time, if he was honest. Any number of things could go wrong with this operation.

"Dr. Kotler," one of the soldiers said. "We need to get moving."

"Kotler," Denzel said, motioning to him from beside the biometric panel. "Can you open this?"

Kotler glanced back at Liz one last time and made his way to the panel. He stood in front of it, examining it.

This was the same as every other high-security panel in the facility. Kotler had consulted on the security for the building, calling on what he knew from some of the most well-guarded vaults in the world. Vaults that often held some of the world's ancient treasures. He had recommended a firm that had built security for some famous and infamous facilities around the world, including both the Vatican and Gibraltar. It had cost quite a fortune, but Cristoff had assured him it was necessary.

Now Kotler knew why.

He leaned forward, looking into the plate of darkened glass. A blue light pulsed, moving from top to bottom, scanning Kotler's face, reading both metric points in his features and the pattern of his retinas. He knew, as well, that sensors within the panel were calculating his height, and that cameras throughout the facility had already measured and recorded his gait. The system had verified his identity long before he'd reached the bottom of the stairs. This was just the final check.

In just seconds, there was a click from the steel door.

"Everyone stand back," the lead soldier said. He gave quiet orders to his men, who gathered on either side of the door, ready to press forward into whatever hell might lay on the other side.

They opened the door, and the next several moments were a rush of shouting, then smoke, then gunfire.

This was a hot zone, for certain.

Kotler, Liz, and Denzel took cover, with two armed guards standing between them and the door. Moments later, however, these two also moved forward and into the fray. As they went through, one of them motioned for Kotler and the others to follow.

They ducked through the door, immediately enveloped by

smoke from whatever crowd-suppression system the soldiers had used. Kotler covered his nose and mouth with his hand and ducked alongside Liz as they moved into the space.

"Kotler!" Denzel shouted. "This way!" He waved them forward, to a block of equipment that he and one of the soldiers were using for cover.

Kotler and Liz followed, staying low. The room was filled with the racket of combat, to the point of being deafening. The smoke made it impossible to see more than a meter ahead of them at any time. Shouts from the soldiers intermingled with the gunfire, sounding like chaos. But Kotler knew that this was a highly organized incursion. They'd gotten the layout from Liz and Richard, in as much detail as they could. The chaos was a diversion, keeping the enemy off balance as they penetrated to the spot where the cloning lab had sunk into the floor.

After a long moment, Kotler and Liz came to a stop just behind Denzel and a few of the soldiers. They were standing at the precipice of a large, square hole in the floor.

"This is it," Liz said. "The lab was here. Vellar did something and took it down below the floor."

"Look," Denzel said, pointing.

There were ropes tied off to some of the support beams of the lab, dangling down into the gap in the floor.

"They rappelled down," Denzel said.

"We'll have to do the same," one of the soldiers replied.

"We have no idea what might be waiting down there," Kotler replied.

"More guns, more fighting, more danger," the soldier shrugged. "But it's the only way down that we know about."

No one could argue that. And though he wouldn't say it aloud, Kotler was determined to get down there regardless. Cristoff and Kotler's grandfather were down there—two men who'd had more influence over Kotler's life than he'd realized.

Two men who had the answers he needed. Answers Kotler was determined to have.

The soldiers busied themselves with securing their own lines, sending down cameras, trying their best to assess the situation below before diving over the edge.

Kotler, Denzel, and Liz were given harnesses and gloves.

Soon the descent would begin.

# CHAPTER THIRTY-TWO

KOTLER HAD DONE these sorts of descents before, in conditions far more arduous and challenging than these. And yet this one might be the most difficult and dangerous of his life.

Difficult because he had injuries that made every move painful and laborious.

Dangerous because there was no way to know what was waiting for them once they reached the bottom.

Richard and his men were here, Kotler knew, along with a treasure they would protect with their lives. And, from what Kotler gathered from Liz's debriefing, the vault itself contained a treasure of its own.

Richard had been using the research started by Kotler's parents, to treat himself and keep himself vital and strong even into his 90s. It was profound in its implications. It meant that Cristoff had been sitting on something that could have saved millions of lives.

It also happened to violate both US and international law, which could explain Cristoff's hesitation in sharing.

Except Kotler didn't believe that.

He'd known Cristoff all of his life. The man had taken both Kotler brothers in after the death of their parents, raising and caring for them as his own, ensuring they had the very best of everything, including opportunities.

Jeffrey had his hangups with Cristoff, but Kotler had always loved the man like family. He'd always been grateful to him.

Somehow, in some way, all of this felt like a betrayal of what they had together.

And that was very difficult for Kotler to swallow. That, more than his physical injuries, made this controlled drop to the bottom of an immense elevator shaft more difficult with every bounce and zip.

It took several minutes to actually reach the bottom of the shaft. Kotler could hear the sound of boots making contact with metal, as one soldier after another landed and moved, taking up defensive positions. The sound was loud and distinct enough that there was no hiding it. It was like ringing a doorbell, again and again, letting the bad guys know they had arrived.

Stealth was out of the question.

Kotler, Liz, and Denzel touched down a moment later, taking position at the back of the squad.

"We're on top of the room," Liz said, looking down.

Kotler nodded. "Like being on top of an elevator car."

The soldiers were already working to resolve this problem.

There was a hatch in one corner of the square of steel beneath their feet. It was heavy and industrial, and sealed in place by a number of locking mechanisms. Next to the hatch was something familiar—another biometric panel.

The squad leader approached Kotler. "Sir?"

Kotler nodded, knelt by the scanner, and waited.

The blue light pulsed, moving from the top of his head to the tip of his chin, just as it had by the main lab door.

Nothing happened.

"I think we've hit my limit of access," Kotler replied, looking up at the squad leader. He wished he'd gotten the man's name when they'd met. Now didn't seem the right time to ask.

The man nodded. "We brought a contingency plan," he said. He pulled a velcro pocket open from his vest and took something out, then repeated the action on the other side.

He conferred with a couple of his men, who removed objects from their own vests.

Kotler managed a glimpse. C-4, along with blasting caps and a detonator.

The men busied themselves with placing small charges of C-4 at strategic points on the hatch. They used very little—the idea was to blow the hinges, not destroy the room beneath their feet. Kotler watched with admiration as the men expertly did their work.

They were all told to move against the far wall and to take cover. This largely meant hunching with their backs to the hatch, huddled in a group. The "civilians," including Denzel, were pressed against the wall, with the soldiers making an armored, human barrier between them and the hatch.

The squad leader counted down and squeezed the detonator.

The noise was deafening, despite Kotler having his fingers pressed tight into his ears. He had a slight ringing as he stood alongside the others, surveying the scene.

The locks and hasps that had held the hatch in place were reduced to twisted, jagged hunks of metal, and the hatch itself had been blown open and away, now leaning at an odd angle against one of the shaft walls.

Things moved quickly then.

The soldiers surrounded the hatch opening, weapons trained on the gap below. They quickly lowered a camera on a telescoping pole, letting it move smoothly in a circle, taking in the scene beneath them.

Once they knew the lay of the place, a collapsible ladder was unfurled, dropped into the hole and secured to the edge of the hatch. One by one soldiers dropped into the hole, though they were skipping the ladder. Each would grip the lip of the hatch, dangle his or her feet into the gap below, and drop to the floor. The drop couldn't have been more than ten feet.

Kotler, for his part, was grateful for the ladder. He consoled himself that if he'd been healed up, he could easily do as the soldiers had done. It was a slight comfort to his ego.

He took greater consolation in seeing Denzel use the ladder, after allowing Liz to follow Kotler down. Liz, Kotler knew, could have handled the jump. She'd done bigger drops while the two of them were rock climbing. She was helping him and Denzel save face, Kotler figured, and he was grateful for that.

Once in the lab, the soldiers busied themselves with checking and clearing the space. Kotler, Liz, and Denzel had been issued sidearms before this began, and they drew them now, ready for anything. Or as ready as they could be.

Kotler followed the lead of the squad as they cleared the space, but his attention was on his surroundings.

These were the chambers Liz had described, but they were powered down. Empty.

He looked up, about to make a comment, when he spotted Liz standing in front of one column. He went to her.

"It's gone," she whispered.

"Everything seems to have been moved out," Kotler agreed.

Liz turned back to him. She glanced past him, looking to the soldiers, who were finishing their sweep. She glanced then toward Denzel, who was trailing the soldiers, assisting.

She leaned in slightly. "There's something I left out of my debriefing," Liz whispered.

Kotler glanced back at the others himself now, and leaned forward. "I felt like that was the case. Can you tell me?"

She shook her head. "Not yet. Not now. Not ... here."

Kotler understood.

"But Dan," she said, "that man ... the older man."

Kotler felt his pulse quicken. He knew what was coming.

"He was your grandfather," she said. "Richard Kotler."

Kotler found himself startled to hear the name come from Liz's lips. "How did you know that?" he asked.

Liz made a strange, quizzical expression. "How did I? Did *you* know?"

Kotler nodded. "He was the man who held me and Roland captive, back at Cheyenne Mountain. He's..." Kotler hesitated, took a breath. "He's one of the Novensiles. His callsign is 'the Chairman.' He's been a part of their upper ranks, Liz. He's been a part of all of this since the beginning."

Liz looked as if she were about to say something else when the squad leader returned.

"Room's clear," he reported. "We've found the door out. It's open. Preliminary sweep shows a garage. Also empty."

"So they got away," Kotler said, the disappointment mingling with a strange sort of relief he hadn't been expecting.

He very much wanted to capture his grandfather. The man was a threat to everything—to Kotler, to Jeffrey, even to Liz and Roland. But to the world as well. He was dangerous, and everyone would be safer if he were thrown into a cell somewhere.

But Kotler wasn't as sure what he wanted to do about Cristoff. And that was where the sense of relief came in. There was still a part of Kotler that believed Cristoff had to have been manipulated in this. Kotler still believed, deep down, that Cristoff couldn't have willingly done this.

Too many questions. And no one to answer them.

"We'll secure this level," the squad leader told him. "It looks like we can get you back upstairs through this garage, so we'll go that route."

Denzel had returned to Kotler's side. "I'll need to get in touch with my people," he said. "Report back on where this landed."

"Yes sir," the squad leader responded, handing Denzel a radio.

Kotler and Liz slunk away, edging back toward the empty chamber Liz had been examining. "How much do we tell?" he asked.

And the meta-conversation went deeper. *How much do we hide?*

Liz seemed to register what he was really asking. "I think revealing that this was your grandfather is going to make it impossible for you to be a part of finding him," she said. She looked to Denzel. "Does he know?"

Kotler nodded. "Everything I know, at this point," he said.

She hesitated before speaking again. "Can we trust him?"

Kotler huffed. "Roland is an honorable man, and he serves his country. If he decides that this secret might present a preventable threat, he'll do the right thing."

"Which will effectively remove you from being a part of all of this," Liz said quietly.

Kotler looked her in the eye, then nodded. "It might even mean putting me in a cell somewhere until they can determine whether I was in on any of this. My fate is in Roland's hands. I'm ok with that, Liz. My fate has been in Roland's hands before."

"This time is different," she said, shaking her head.

"Every time is different," Kotler replied.

"Dan ..." she started, hesitated, looked beyond him to make sure they were out of earshot. "This chamber," she nodded to it. "There was someone in it."

"Someone?"

"A body," Liz replied. "Your ... grandfather's body. But ... younger. A clone. He looked just like you. Cristoff's people were harvesting materials from it, to treat Richard."

Kotler stared at her. The pieces clicked into place. His grandfather's unnatural vitality made more sense.

And so did the plan.

"Resurrecting gods and kings," Kotler whispered. "My God."

Liz shook her head. "What does that mean?"

Kotler looked at her. Her face was etched with concern, and that stabbed him deeply. It reminded him of the worry that was nagging at the back of his mind, at the bottom of his gut. If Richard Kotler wanted to control him or hurt him, he'd do it through Liz. Through Jeffrey, Christina, and Alex. Through Denzel. Through Kotler's real family.

"Richard ... my grandfather ... he has a plan. He has thirty-six containers of human DNA. All of it harvested from gods and kings, from throughout history."

Liz stared. "That's... he's going to use this technology to bring them back? Why?"

"Think of the influence he'd have," Kotler said. "Think of how many would follow him if they thought he was the father of the gods? This was a plan put in place by the Novensiles, or maybe even by the Jani themselves. But Richard was holding it as a contingency. And now he has what he needs. Everything he needs." Kotler looked once more to the men and women in the room, the soldiers clearing a path for them, ensuring none of the enemy remained behind. He looked to Denzel, who was communicating with the FBI.

"So will Denzel protect you?" Liz asked. "If he learns about this?"

Kotler didn't know how to answer, and before he could, Denzel and the others called for them, leading them out of the lab and into the garage.

They followed as the soldiers cleared the path ahead, guiding them bit by bit back to the surface world.

Kotler couldn't help thinking, however, that even as they rose toward daylight, things were getting darker, and he was getting in deeper.

He glanced at Denzel several times as they moved, the question still echoing in his head.

*Will Denzel protect you? If he learns about this?*

Kotler knew Denzel well. The man was like a brother to him. But this ...

He just couldn't be sure.

And more, he wasn't entirely sure what he *wanted* the answer to be.

They emerged from the lower levels through a large set of rolling steel doors, tucked into the landscape nearly two miles from the Vellar-Kotler Genetics building. Kotler blinked into the sunlight, grateful for it.

The questions would be answered eventually.

All of them.

# EPILOGUE

ACOSTA HAD SPENT days talking to the media, sitting through interviews, describing every facet of the abduction.

She had discussed how it felt to be held at gunpoint, and whether this firmed up her position on eliminating the Second Amendment. She had been asked about the conditions in the abandoned juvenile detention center, and how this impacted her position on the holding facilities at the US-Mexico border. She was asked about the eventual plan for escape, about her role in it, and whether this influenced her stance on the military. And she discussed her future but pulled up short of confirming any plans to run for certain higher offices. It was too soon. She was too young. But ... maybe. Who could say?

And then she was asked how she felt about all of it. How did she feel, being the victim of such a precision attack on the US? How did it feel to be put through all of this, for reasons that were still unknown?

Was she afraid? Did she worry it would happen again? Was she concerned about personal and official security? Did this change anything about how she lived her life?

She gave pat answers for everything.

Cameron and her team had prepared her. In fact, she and Cameron often appeared on television together—two heroes of the abduction and two leaders who helped with the escape. They were the darlings of media, building a platform together that, Cameron assured her, would give them a lot more influence and power going forward. It was remarkable, Acosta thought, how Cameron was able to parlay a situation like this into political advantage, almost automatically.

And there were other perks.

One benefit to come out of all of this was that their romantic relationship could now be public. In fact, Acosta's PR consultant had insisted on it.

"They'll see the two of you as being bound by your common experience," she'd said. "They'll believe that tragedy kindled the romance. You'll be America's power couple!"

She was right. When the media wasn't focusing on the abductions and the holding facility and the escape, or on how each of these influenced Acosta's political stance on various issues, they were pressing Acosta and Cameron for more details about their romance. They were giving knowing smiles, nods of approval, gestures of support. America, it seemed, was in love with the idea of two people falling in love in the midst of danger and intrigue. The fact that Acosta was also a Senator on the rise only added to the growing mythology surrounding her.

Cameron played to this more than Acosta did, but they both leveraged it to keep themselves in the spotlight. More so than any of the other abductees, Acosta and Cameron were the faces of the event. Every story that hit print, every feature in the media, every mention on social media, every YouTube thumbnail featured the faces of Acosta and Cameron. To the world at large, the abduction was *their* abduction. And to hear some talk, Acosta herself swept the bad guys aside like Wonder

Woman, deflecting bullets with her palms, carrying the GOP Senators out on her back.

She had to admit, she kind of liked the portrayal. So did Cameron and her team. At the very least, they did little to dissuade the media from pushing it. And if the Conservatives objected, they didn't dare say anything. Tides such as these could turn very quickly. Cancel culture loved Acosta right now, and would attack like rabid wolves if anyone dared attempt to tarnish her image.

Acosta had just arrived home, to her apartment in DC, and was glad of it. This had been a long day. She'd not only done another tour with the media, she'd also voted on some key issues, sat in with a committee, and sponsored a bill that she hoped would get through as free of GOP riders as possible. For the moment, given the sheen of her popularity, it was looking pretty good.

It had been a good day, but she was tired. She wanted a shower and a meal and bed. Cameron was at his place tonight, and she was glad of that too. Their public relationship was overshadowing their private one at the moment, and Acosta needed some alone time. Plus ...

Well, if she were honest, things were feeling a little rushed and overwhelming when it came to Cameron. She knew that the media was eating it up, every time they held each other's hand or smiled at each other or even just stood close. But Cameron was a nearly 24/7 part of her life all of a sudden. She'd gone from meeting with him in clandestine, secret moments, stolen here and there, to having him at her side day and night. She kind of needed a break. And she wasn't sure, exactly, what that meant for the long term.

She'd figure it out later. For now, she was happy to be home, alone, with the quiet and comfort of her own place, and not a soul there to intrude.

After showering, she made herself some tea. She'd have a light meal, a salad maybe. It was too late to really go heavy, and she didn't have the energy for an elaborate meal at any rate. She took a few things out of the fridge and was washing some lettuce and vegetables.

There was a knock at the door.

Acosta sighed.

The media wasn't supposed to have access to the building, but occasionally someone got through. It had been alarming at first—she'd been afraid of being abducted again. Or worse. But the media usually managed to bribe or con their way in, and it had happened often enough now that Acosta wasn't all that worried about it. Mostly, she was annoyed.

When they got this far, they usually peppered her with questions even as she was closing the door, telling them she'd be happy to chat in the morning. She tried not to be angry with them, but it was getting more difficult to keep her temper in check. It was just such an intrusion.

She toyed with refusing to answer her door, but the knock was repeated, loud and insistent.

She was in nightclothes, and though she felt a little self-conscious about that she went to the door anyway. She looked out of the peephole and saw a man standing in the hall.

A familiar-looking man. He was wearing jeans and a T-shirt but wore a sports coat over that. A casual, hip sort of look, but it somehow conveyed both wealth and power.

She couldn't quite place how she knew him. Maybe she'd seen him on television?

He was probably a news personality. Someone with enough pull and fame to convince security to let him in.

She sighed again and opened the door just a bit, not even removing the chain.

"I'm sorry," she said, "but it's late. I'm tired. I can do an interview tomorrow ..."

"Arania," the man said, smiling. "I'm not with the media. Not ... that media, anyway. I'm Kendell Young."

The name sounded familiar but took a moment to register. "The social media guy?" Acosta asked.

He nodded. "Can I come in?"

Acosta was still processing this but shook her head. "I'm turning in. It's been a long day."

Young nodded. "I know. I've been watching. You've been all over the place lately. Lots of screen time! YouTube is just overflowing with you. And you're trending on every social platform that exists. Very impressive approval ratings."

Acosta wanted to close the door, but something about the way Young spoke was almost hypnotic. He was looking at her as if he knew her intimately. He acted *familiar* with her, in a way she wasn't used to experiencing.

She'd followed his career. It was hard not to. He had millions of followers online and produced content at an exhausting pace. He appeared at A-list events and even hung out with heads of state.

Now that she recognized him, she had to admit she was feeling a little star-struck.

She closed the door enough to remove the chain, then stood back, gesturing for him to come inside. She closed the door behind him, and as he wandered into the room, hands in the pocket of his jeans, he turned and smiled at her again.

"Mr. Young ..." Acosta started.

"Call me Kendell," he smiled.

"Kendell," she smiled back, though she wasn't sure why. "Why are you here?"

Young nodded. "That's a fair question. But the answer is

long and complicated. So let's start by saying I'm part of an ... organization ... that could really use some fresh members. People with perspectives like yours."

"An organization?" Acosta asked.

"Think of it like a mastermind group," Young shrugged, smiling. "With a lot of influence. Maybe more influence than anything you've ever been a part of in your life."

Acosta listened. "And I'm guessing I've never heard of it?"

He smiled and laughed. "I'd be surprised if you had. But some of your friends have. Especially those in high positions in Government. And someone else. Cameron Michaels."

"Cameron?" Acosta asked, startled. "Did he send you?"

Young smiled again, and this time Acosta wasn't entirely sure what she saw in his eyes.

"Actually," he said, "I was the one who sent Cameron to you. I think you'll find that I've been here all along, Arania. Putting things in motion. Pulling strings. Making sure you were in the right place, at the right time. I'm something of a ... well, the people I'm here to represent call me the Influencer," he said. "And I've learned how to move the world with the right ideas, the right relationships. Influence is my currency. It's the currency of the whole world. I've been using that currency to make sure you got every possible opportunity. And now, I believe you're ready."

"Ready?" Acosta asked, feeling something stir inside of her. Excitement? Fear? Anticipation? They all felt the same, here and now. "Ready for what?"

Young smiled. He glanced around her apartment, then turned back to her. His eyes locked with hers, and she couldn't look away.

"Ready to begin," he said, his smile growing wider until it was all that Acosta could see.

.  .  .

KOTLER AND LIZ had been questioned separately and together, and then alongside Denzel, about everything leading up to the events at Vellar-Kotler. There were some uncomfortable conversations, but the three of them had agreed to tell the truth.

Most of it.

Certain facts were kept out of it, for the moment. The fact that the man known as the Chairman was Kotler's grandfather was chief among the details left unsaid.

They did reveal that the secret lab at Vellar-Kotler was being used for cloning experiments and that there had been at least one seemingly full-grown human clone. This caused a lot of follow-up questions that none of them could answer

Most of these questions were directed at Kotler.

The fact that his name was on the building did not bode well for either Kotler or his brother Jeffrey. In fact, Jeffrey had been grilled quite a bit himself. And he, too, had opted to keep the information about their grandfather secret. As far as anyone knew, Richard Kotler was dead. The Chairman was a member of a shadowy organization that Kotler could barely describe with enough detail to matter. And the cloning was something that neither Kotler brother had known about prior to these events.

The grilling and questioning were tiresome, but after several days their questioners seemed satisfied with most of their answers. The fact that neither Kotler nor Jeffrey could access that secret lab via biometric security had been key to alleviating some of the accusations they faced, bolstered by the fact that the building's security logs confirmed that neither Kotler brother had ever accessed that floor prior to the day of the invasion.

It helped. But none of this was over. It wouldn't be for a very long time.

It helped as well that several of the Novensiles had been captured in the raid of the lab. Many were subsequently identified as being part of various military branches, which prompted some introspection on the part of the armed services. Avoiding black eyes and public humiliation was occupying a lot of the higher-ups. Kotler worried briefly that he and Jeffrey might be made scapegoats, but to his surprise, they were both more or less exonerated. Or as close to exonerated as they were likely to get. There was always later.

Eventually, the Kotlers and Liz had been released, though they were all told not to travel for the moment. It was pretty clear, though, that this last edict was aimed primarily at Kotler himself. His history of moving freely in the world made him a flight risk. He agreed, in writing, that he would stick close to home until further notice. He intended to honor that, of course.

Kotler decided he needed a break. From everything. All of it.

With a travel ban, his options were somewhat limited. But this was Manhattan, after all. Being stuck here was a bit like punishing a child by sending him to his room in the age of iPhones and always-on internet.

Kotler decided that if he couldn't travel physically, he'd travel in spirit. He bought a ticket to a new exhibit on display in the American Museum of Natural History and was determined to spend the day reading every placard, studying every vignette, and eating only the overpriced food he could purchase from the museum's cafe.

He was partaking in a terrifically expensive hot dog and a cup of not-too-great coffee when Denzel appeared before him.

"Roland?" Kotler asked, surprised. "How did you find me here?"

"The Director ordered me to put a tail on you. Just in case you turned out to be a flight risk."

Kotler at first felt a flash of anger and annoyance at this, and was about to say something, but instead sighed and nodded. "Have a seat," he said, motioning to the chair opposite from him.

Denzel sat. "I have news," he said grimly.

"Are they arresting me?" Kotler asked. Surprisingly he didn't feel threatened by this. He was innocent of any crime, but he knew the optics of this situation were bad. He definitely did not want to go to prison, but he would figure it out if it happened. He'd manage, somehow.

To his relief, however, Denzel shook his head. "No. In fact, they're lifting the travel ban, starting tomorrow."

Kotler's eyes widened. "You're kidding! That didn't last long. I'm grateful for it, but what made them decide?"

"It came from higher up," Denzel said.

Kotler took this in and felt a sudden chill.

Richard had been a Novensile and a Jani. He'd played a role in the founding of the Historic Crimes division of the FBI, for which Kotler had consulted for the past three years. Richard Kotler clearly had tendrils that stretched into the upper echelons of the Bureau, and into the government as well. If orders were coming in from the top, it was almost a sure bet that it was the result of Jani influence. And that always came at a cost, Kotler was learning.

This knowledge, and this news, triggered something within Kotler. It clicked something into place, cementing some thoughts and ideas Kotler was kicking around. A plan that Kotler was considering, even though he'd only toyed with it in daydreams so far, suddenly became sharply focused.

He took a bite of his hot dog, chewed, and swallowed. "Ok," he said.

Denzel studied him. "Just ok?"

"What could we possibly do, if the Jani or the Novensiles

were manipulating all of this?" Kotler asked. "All we can really do is keep going, keep working. They may have plans for Historic Crimes, but we know we're doing some good with it. Let's just .... keep doing good." That was part of the plan, Kotler decided. Keep things going. Keep the resources flowing. Keep doing the work, and use it to further the other agenda. The new agenda.

Denzel sighed and shook his head. "I like the sentiment, Kotler, but that's not going to happen."

"What do you mean?" Again Kotler felt the dread well up within him.

"They're shutting us down," Denzel said. "Effective immediately, all personnel and resources are being reallocated. My entire team is being reassigned. Me included."

Kotler felt like vomiting. He put the remains of the hotdog down. He inhaled deeply, exhaling as he leaned forward. "Well, then," he said.

"Of course, this means you no longer have a consultant contract with the FBI," Denzel said.

"What about you?" Kotler said, ignoring Denzel's statement. "And Liz?"

"Liz will keep her department, actually," Denzel replied. "She'll just be reporting to someone else. Agent Danielle Brown."

Kotler's eyes shot wide again. "Dani?"

"She's been promoted," Denzel replied, nodding. "On my recommendation, but I think it may have been in spite of that for a minute there."

"And what about you?" Kotler asked.

Denzel shrugged. "Back to my regularly scheduled programming," he replied. "I'm a field agent again. Same pay grade, fewer duties. It's not bad."

Kotler studied his friend. There was more going on there

than Denzel was revealing. There was more that Denzel wasn't sharing. But for now, Kotler was going to let it drop. If Denzel felt it necessary to play something close to his vest, Kotler more than respected that.

He was just worried about his friend.

Kotler leaned back and sighed. "The end of an era," he said. "It feels like everything just reset to three years ago."

Denzel nodded. "It does seem that way."

Kotler also nodded. "Ok, then," he said. "If I'm no longer under a travel ban, I think maybe I'll arrange a little trip."

"Where to?" Denzel asked.

Kotler shrugged and shook his head. "I'm not sure yet. But there are plenty of sites out there to explore. Plenty of digs that could use a hand. Plenty of papers to write and talks to give."

Denzel took this in. "What about ..." he hesitated. "What about Liz?"

Kotler also hesitated. "We decided it might be best to take a break," Kotler said.

"We," Denzel said, "or you?"

Kotler watched Denzel, who was watching right back.

"I brought a lot of hell down on everyone I care about, Roland," he said quietly. "They deserve some space. Some time."

"None of us are asking for it," Denzel said. "In fact, we all want to be here for you."

"I appreciate that," Kotler said. "But ... I guess I need some time, too."

"How does Liz feel about this?" Denzel asked.

"She's not thrilled, but she understands," Kotler replied. "Or she says she does." He huffed and moved the hotdog and the coffee cup around a bit on the table in front of him. "Anyway, I think this is best. I'll start making plans tomorrow."

"And ..." Denzel started, then hesitated. He shook his head and continued. "What about money?" he asked. "Vellar-Kotler is shut down, all their assets seized. Are you going to be ok?"

Kotler laughed then. "Well, yes, actually. I'll admit, Vellar-Kotler was a large source of income for me. But I was a shareholder, not an owner. Not ... specifically. Cristoff had set things up so that Jeffrey and I would benefit from the revenue without being liable for anything the company did. We're protected. And I've told you before, I have investments. I'm at least a partial owner in several businesses. I'm pretty well diversified. I'll be fine."

Denzel nodded. "Ok, then."

Kotler looked around, took in the cafe and the people in it, then rose from his seat. He stood over Denzel, who looked up at him, expectant, waiting.

"Will we see each other again?" Kotler asked.

Denzel paused but nodded again. "I think so, yeah," he said. "I'll make the effort if you will."

He also stood then, squared off with Kotler, and put out a hand. "I'm always here for you," he said.

Kotler took his friend's hand, gave it a squeeze, nodded, and then left.

Once he was out of the museum, he paused, considering whether he should get an Uber. Instead, he decided it was a nice enough day for a walk, and that he could use the fresh air and exercise. And the time to think.

He hadn't lied when he told Denzel he was going to plan a trip. But getting away was not quite his motivation.

The Novensiles—really, the Jani themselves—had been a bigger influence in his life than he'd ever realized. They'd orchestrated things from behind the scenes, altering his course since before he'd even been born. They had cost him his parents, cost him relationships, and created pain in the lives of the people Kotler cared most about.

It was time someone did something about that.

# A NOTE AT THE END

In a lot of ways, Kotler's life and adventures parallel my own.

Ok, sure ... I'm not exactly tackling terrorists, dodging bullets, clinging to rock faces, or helping the FBI bring down vast international smuggling rings. Yet. But if Brad Thor can be a part of Homeland Security's Red Cell, I don't see why I couldn't be a part of some FBI-led think tank.

I digress ...

Where Kotler and I are somewhat parallel is in the way we move about in the world, and what we do while we're out there. We're both public speakers, attending conferences and giving presentations. We both study history and other cultures, and write and speak about those. We both travel extensively. We both have a passion for learning that drives everything we do. Heck, we both have friends named Roland Denzel ... no relation (and purely a happy coincidence, I assure you).

There are enough parallels in our lives that it makes it that much easier to write this character. It's barely what one might call autobiographical, but maybe something similar? *Autoexpe-*

*riential?* I just made that word up, and now I'm quite proud of it.

This book draws heavily on those *autoexperiential* parallels in order for me to explore a few things that have been on my mind, and have been building to a boil throughout the past several books in this series.

I try not to be overly or overtly political in these books, but I'll freely admit that my conservative views do often bleed through. Certain characters hold a perspective that reflects my own, even if just a little. And certain other characters hold views that are completely opposite of mine.

Ultimately, that's where I think I get to learn the most about myself.

Right now, our culture is dealing with a lot of toxicity. Both "sides" (I'm not certain I believe there are only two sides) seem to agree on this point, though they vehemently disagree on its cause. The problem, as I see it, as that everyone wants to blame "the other," and no one seems to want to take responsibility for their own role in it all.

I believe that there's a reason for this. And that reason is, primarily, that there are people in power who benefit from all of this divisiveness and vitriol.

I'm not going to name names, because honestly, I'm not sure I could. I can conjecture, but I can't *know*. I can assume, but we all know where that leads.

But let's just consider the media. They certainly benefit from all of this "cancel culture" and "outrage culture" back and forth. In fact, they've been empowered by all of this to the point that they can literally say and print anything they want, with or without vetted or verifiable sources, with perhaps no sources at all, and they get away with it. No apologies. No retractions. Just lies presented as truth, and then referenced later to support even more lies.

My advice: Stop paying attention to mainstream media altogether, particularly when it's discussing something that isn't a black or white, on or off, one or zero fact. Today's media lives in the grey area between fact and fiction, and it thrives there.

But honestly, this isn't new.

The title of this book, *The Hidden Persuaders*, is an homage to the actual book that the Influencer references in one of the early chapters. It's a real book, written by Vance Packard and Mark Crispin Miller, and it takes a look at the "hidden world of 'motivation research'" employed by the advertising industry. Written and published in 1957, it was specifically referencing the "Mad Men" era of advertising, but its implications and repercussions extend right up to today. We are, daily, manipulated by media. Some of us have been for literally all our lives.

Reading back over that last sentence, my first impulse is to delete it for being too "conspiracy theory." But I'm going to roll with it because this isn't a conspiracy "theory," it's demonstrable by fact. There was, at a specific point in history, a decision, made by advertising executives, to employ psychologists for the specific purpose of learning how to influence and even manipulate the human mind. And it's worked for decades.

We all know, and we've all seen the evidence, that the media uses psychology to influence and motivate us. We sort of agreed to it, really. We all clicked the box on the terms and conditions. We all chuckled when the manipulation was made obvious, as a sort of ironic gag. We got it, and we were willing to play along because honestly, it feels good. We're being manipulated to feel good. How wrong could it be?

Where I diverge from the path through the conspiracy woods is with the belief that all of this is inherently evil. It isn't. In fact, more often than not, influence is used for the good of everyone.

MADD—Mothers Against Drunk Drivers—has used this

sort of thing for the past few decades to help deter people from drinking and driving. Television programming such as *Mister Rogers' Neighborhood* used subtle influence to encourage children to be tolerant, kind, helpful, and beneficial members of society. Ad campaigns such as those featuring Smoky the Bear encourage people to be cautious and aware while camping or doing other outdoor activities, to help prevent forest fires—they even personalize the messaging by saying "Only *you* can prevent forest fires," making it something easy for you to identify with.

Do some programs such as these push another, hidden, more sinister agenda? Probably. In fact, we know that some do. But having an ulterior motive is another rabbit hole to dive into, at another time.

Suffice to say, not all intentions are bad intentions, and not all emotional manipulation is bad either.

Heck, as a copywriter for most of my career, and now as a novelist, I've used influence and emotional manipulation on a near-daily basis, with my only intention being to "inform and inspire, educate and entertain." Those four tenets prop up everything I do, and psychological influence is one tool with which I deploy them.

Where I worry that this sort of manipulation is put to nefarious and dreadful use, aside from the media, is in government.

I have a B story running throughout this book that involves a freshman Senator with leanings toward Socialism and some extreme views on how government should work. I'm not going to specifically name the real-world counterpart for this character, though I figure it's pretty obvious.

Believe it or not, I mean no disrespect to this person, with the homage I've written to her. I don't agree with, well, *anything* this woman says or does. I particularly don't agree with her push for socialism, especially since it's obvious she has no concept of what socialism actually is or what it means for a free and thriving democratic republic. But I came to a realization about this Senator, and that is I believe she actually means well.

I believe we should always consider the motives and intentions of a person if we can know them. We should always put things in as much context as we are able. We must always attempt to empathize with someone, so we can learn from them and grow and maybe make the world a better place for our understanding and consideration.

She doesn't seem to share these beliefs just yet, but I'm giving her time.

The character, Arania Acosta, was a sort of parody of this Senator, and she certainly holds views that I do not share. And that was exactly why I felt she was such a great character. She's naive, but she's not stupid. She's going with the flow only because she lacks the experience that would tell her how to take up her own oar and guide her vessel where she really wants to go. Her lack of experience is being weaponized against her, and her ego is finishing the job, making her vulnerable to manipulation, making her the perfect pawn in a game of power and influence.

We'll be seeing her again. She's still a character in progress.

But what I wanted to say was that having Acosta as a character in this universe has prompted me to consider the views of her real-life counterpart. I don't agree with her, which makes me stretch in order to write her as a plausible, living character. And that, profoundly, forces me to reanalyze some of my own biases and beliefs.

That's a good thing.

Because of that reconsideration, I'm learning and growing past my own limitations. And my hope is that translates onto the page.

I'm probably never going to agree with the person on whom Acosta is based. Her perspective is too naive, and her positions are too radical, even for her own political party. But studying her and empathizing with her and attempting to see things from her perspective does help me find some of my own rough edges. I'm not exempt from mistakes in judgment. There's much for me to learn.

This book is meant to tie up some previous loose ends, and I believe it does that, but it also introduces all-new but connected threads for Kotler and the other characters to explore. It creates new complications and obstacles to overcome. It puts Kotler on a new path. And by doing so, it puts me (and you, too) on a new path as well. And that's pretty exciting.

Changes are coming.

Kotler will still be the same guy, with the same drives. He has an additional new motive, however, and that's going to temper him in new ways. I'm really looking forward to seeing how he evolves in future books.

How will the dissolving of Historic Crimes impact Kotler's life? What will this mean for Denzel? Will Liz and Kotler come back around? What will she do, now that she works for Dani?

And what about Kotler's grandfather? And the Influencer? What are they planning, and how will that shape up?

See, I don't know the answers to these either, so don't feel left out. We're going to discover this together. And that's where all the fun happens.

This is the ninth full-length book in this series, and through all of them, I've learned and grown as a writer. Or I believe I have, at any rate. I'm getting better at this, and I hope it shows. I do it for you, as much as for me.

Thank you for being part of this. Thank you for the kind emails and social media posts, for the glowing reviews, and for sharing with me the excitement of these books and Kotler's adventures. As far as I'm concerned, the ride is only just starting.

And I can't wait to see where we go next.

Kevin Tumlinson
Sugar Land, TX
September 19, 2019

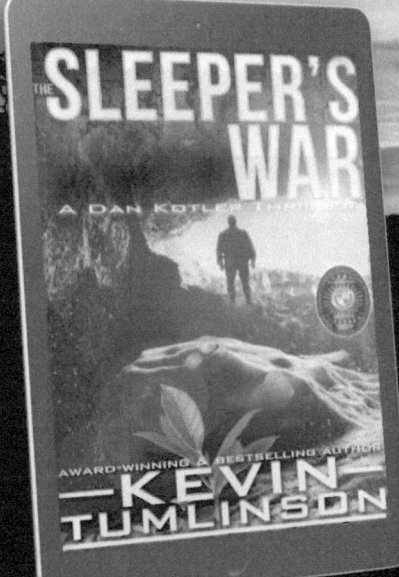

# ALSO BY J. KEVIN TUMLINSON

## Dan Kotler

The Coelho Medallion

The Atlantis Riddle

The Devil's Interval

The Girl in the Mayan Tomb

The Antarctic Forgery

The Stepping Maze

The God Extinction

The Spanish Papers

The Hidden Persuaders

The Sleeper's War

The God Resurrection

The Demon Core

## Dan Kotler Short Fiction

The Brass Hall - A Dan Kotler Story

The Jani Sigil - FREE short story from BookHip.com/DBXDHP

## Dan Kotler Box Sets

The Book of Lost Things: Dan Kotler, Books 1-3

The Book of Betrayals: Dan Kotler, Books 4-6

## Quake Runner: Alex Kayne

Shaken

Triggered

Compromised

Aftershock

## Historic Crimes Crossovers

The Man Below

The Outsiders Gambit

## Evergreen

Evergreen: Book 1

Evergreen: Trace Contact

## Citadel

Citadel: First Colony

Citadel: Paths in Darkness

Citadel: Children of Light

Citadel: The Value of War

Colony Girl: A Citadel Universe Story

## Sawyer Jackson

Sawyer Jackson and the Long Land

Sawyer Jackson and the Shadow Strait

Sawyer Jackson and the White Room


## Think Tank

Karner Blue

Zero Tolerance

Nomad


## The Lucid — Co-authored with Nick Thacker

Episode 1

Episode 2

Episode 3


## Shorts & Novellas

Getting Gone

Teresa's Monster

The Three Reasons to Avoid Being Punched in the Face

Tin Man

Two Blocks East

Edge

Zero

God Mode

## Collections & Anthologies

Citadel: Omnibus

Uncanny Divide — With Nick Thacker & Will Flora

Light Years — The Complete Science Fiction Library

Dead of Winter: A Christmas Anthology — With Nick Thacker, Jim Heskett, David Berens, M.P. MacDougall, R.A. McGee, Dusty Sharp & Steven Moore

## YA & Middle Grade

Secret of the Diamond Sword — An Alex Kotler Mystery

## Wordslinger (Non-Fiction)

30-Day Author: Develop a Daily Writing Habit and Write Your Book In 30 Days (Or Less)

Watch for more at kevintumlinson.com/books

# HERE'S HOW TO HELP ME REACH MORE READERS

If you loved this book, you can help me reach more readers with just a few easy acts of kindness.

## (1) REVIEW THIS BOOK

Leaving a review for this book is a great way to help other readers find it. Just go to the site where you bought the book, search for the title, and leave a review. It really helps, and I really appreciate it.

## (2) SUBSCRIBE TO MY EMAIL LIST

I regularly write a special email to the people on my list, just keeping everyone up to date on what I'm working on. When I announce new book releases, giveaways, or anything else, the people on my list hear about it first. Sometimes, there are special deals I'll *only* give to my list, so it's worth being a part of the crowd.

Join the conversation and get a free ebook, just for signing up! Visit https://www.kevintumlinson.com/joinme.

## (3) TELL YOUR FRIENDS

Word of mouth is still the best marketing there is, so I would greatly appreciate it if you'd tell your friends and family about this book, and the others I've written.

You can find a comprehensive list of all of my books at http://kevintumlinson.com/books.

Thanks so much for your help. And thanks for reading.

# ABOUT THE AUTHOR

Kevin Tumlinson is an award-winning and bestselling novelist, living in Texas and working in random coffee shops, cafés, and hotel lobbies worldwide. His debut thriller, *The Coelho Medallion*, was a 2016 Shelf Notable Indie award winner.

Kevin grew up in Wild Peach, Texas, where he was raised by his grandparents and given a healthy respect for story telling. He often found himself in trouble in school for writing stories instead of doing his actual assignments.

Kevin's love for history, archaeology, and science has been a tremendous source of material for his writing, feeding his fiction and giving him just the excuse he needs to read the next article, biography, or research paper.

*Connect with Kevin:*
kevintumlinson.com
kevin@tumlinson.net

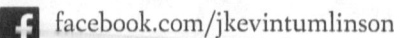

facebook.com/jkevintumlinson

x.com/kevintumlinson

instagram.com/kevintumlinson

bookbub.com/authors/kevin-tumlinson

amazon.com/Kevin-Tumlinson/e/B007POXGEG

# KEEP THE ADVENTURE GOING!

## GET MORE THRILLS FROM AWARD-WINNING AND BESTSELLING AUTHOR, KEVIN TUMLINSON!

★★★★★ "Half way through I was waiting for Harrison Ford to leap out of the pages!"
—Deanne, Review for *The Coelho Medallion*

★★★★★ "Kevin has crashed onto the action-thriller scene

as only an action-thriller author can: with provocative plot lines, unforgettable characters, and enough adrenaline to keep you awake all night."
—Nick Thacker, author of *Mark for Blood*

★★★★★ "Move over Daniel Silva, James Patterson, and Dan Brown."
—Chip Polk, Review for *The Atlantis Riddle*

★★★★★ "Move Over Indiana Jones, there is a New Dr. in Town!"
—Cycletrash, Review for *The Coelho Medallion*

★★★★★ "[Kevin Tumlinson] is what every writer should be—entertaining and thought-provoking."
— Shana Tehan, Press Secretary, U.S. House of Representatives

★★★★★ "I discovered Kevin Tumlinson from The Creative Penn podcast and immediately got his novel, Evergreen. I read it in like 3 seconds. It's the most fast-paced story I've encountered."
—R.D. Holland, Independent Reviewer

★★★★★ "Comparison to Clive Cussler is a natural, though Tumlinson's 'Dan ' is more like Dan Brown's Robert Langdon than Dirk Pitt."
—Amazon Review for *The Coelho Medallion*

**FIND YOUR NEXT FAVORITE BOOK AT**
**KevinTumlinson.com/books**